IRIS VALLEY

CHAD W RICHARDSON

Chad W. Richardson
10/19

SHADOW DREAMWORKS LLC

SHADOW DREAMWORKS LLC

Visit the author website:

chadwrichardson.com

Or email; chadwrichardson@yahoo.com

Iris Valley
Is a work of fiction. Names, characters, places and incidents either are the product of the author's imagination or are used fictitiously, and any resemblance to persons, living or dead, business establishments, events, or locales is entirely coincidental.

Publisher:
Shadow Dreamworks LLC
The Publisher is not responsible for websites (or their content) that are not owned by the publisher.

Cover Design by:
SQUIDPIXELS.COM

❀ Created with Vellum

FOREWORD

To my wife Anna;
  Through it all, we keep climbing the mountain, and finding each other's hand.

And to our six wonderful children; Jacob, Maia, Ellen, Fiona, Finnegan and George;
  May courage and fear be your best friends whilst conquering the world

CHAPTER 1

$\mathcal{T}$HE TOWN OF IRIS VALLEY is located northeast of Atlanta near the foothills of the Blue Ridge Mountains. It's a small town sandwiched between other small towns and vast fields of farm and forest. Since birth, the town has had a history of interesting events that have shaped its growth and culture.

Even the town's name was a source of much debate and furor. The original name of the town was Hillfield. But they changed the name in 1897 when the town's mayor, Frederick Earl II, ran a heated campaign to change the name in honor of his mother and father. No small feat considering the illegitimacy of his birth and the older townsfolk holding the general opinion his mother was nothing more than a slave's whore.

From an early age, Iris Stanfield was exposed to books, rich in text, deep in meaning. The words of the world matched her depth of joy for discovery. She dreamed of traveling the world, soaking in the fabric and textures of life. Not that she wasn't happy with her upbringing or felt deprived or ignored—it was more a feeling something held her back, an invisible tether or harness.

It was when she felt the first blooms of womanhood when her father felt it was time she learned the meaning of hard work. The kind of work her father learned as a kid that taught him the proper respect for his parents. She wanted to be free, to run the wild. She loved her father but when he pulled on the reins; she fought for freedom. And as she grew, her bucking grew stronger and his leash more weathered and frail. And this wasn't acceptable.

The family position could be viewed as belonging to the upper crust of society and her father would not tolerate the slightest violation of social etiquette or proper decorum. Unfortunately, he sired a daughter who had a mind of her own and a limitless enthusiasm for life. In today's world, she could have run her own global company but for the times, she was an imprudent and impetuous child. It was after one of her more public displays of imprudence that her father realized he needed a stronger leash. It wasn't hard to find. His back still bore the scars from the countless beatings he received at the hands of his own, merciless father. It straightened him out; she deserved no less.

As such, her father declared, with the hand of the tyrant, that Iris shall be sent to his father's farm. And beginning on her thirteenth year of life, from July to November each year, they sent Iris to work on her grandparents farm several miles north in the hills of the Blue Ridge Mountains. Under normal circumstances, one would think the experience of spending your fall days within the colors and beauty of the mountains and enjoying the biased affections of your loving grandparents would cause splendorous memories of youth. However, the cruel and unforgiving hand of her grandfather gave rise to sympathy and understanding for her own father's inner wounds.

Iris was not assigned a simple chore such as a caretaker of the house or mild duties of animal husbandry. Each year, she arrived in the wagon and her grandfather would be waiting with crossed arms and ferine temperament. She knew better than to approach him. She exited the wagon, curtsied and scuttled to her quarters. There was no warm and loving welcome. He followed her inside and stood outside of her quarters. He gave her a couple of minutes to change. It was her second year when she learned a valuable lesson. She felt rebellious and instead of changing, sat on the small bed. He charged in and threw her against the wall. As she bounced off the wall, he slapped her so hard across the face, the ring on his finger cracked a tooth. That was the one and only time he struck her. She learned to avoid him and his temper.

Each year, the routine never changed; she changed and one of the slaves led her down the path to the apple orchards. Along the way, over the hill and out of sight, her grandmother would hide in the bushes with a fresh basket of food. Sometimes, she would stick her hand through the bush so all Iris would see is an arm holding a basket. As she approached, her grandmother would start giggling and Iris would laugh with her. Her grandmother created balance; evil will not prevail. Iris took her bounty and continued to the fields where she would work until sunset that day. Her grandfather insisted Iris be treated no better than a common slave. As such, back at the farmhouse, Iris received no more than a cold meal, lying on a tin plate, outside her small room; a room no larger than a modest prison cell. Often, the mice of the house would have their fill before her arrival. At sunrise, it was back in the field. Her main job simple yet tedious, as Iris spent most of her time on a ladder, separating and picking the ripest apples from the trees.

It is interesting how the treatment of a human being can affect their spirit and wherewithal for life. Iris was born a fighter and with a great passion for life. The idea, a remorseless decision to "teach her a lesson" would crush her spirit and provide the necessary impetus for conformity was quite simply, an exhaustive exercise in tomfoolery. Had her father taken the time to develop a meaningful relationship with his daughter, he could have seen the futility of his decision. Perhaps, he could have grown to love the passion in which she viewed life. But, it was not to be. His own father had successfully passed on the legacy of cruelty.

Iris learned to never expect love from her father, but she wasn't without the capacity for love. Quite the opposite. She viewed the world around her as an eternal gift. She felt lucky to be a part of something so special. Wherever and whatever she was doing. It was this passion that ignited something that changed everything.

IT WAS HER SECOND year on the farm, not long after her beating, when she found herself on a rickety wooden ladder, struggling to pick the fruit as her head rung with pain. She felt a small tap vibrate the base of the ladder. She looked down and viewed a hand extended toward her. She doesn't know why, but she reached down and grabbed it. He led her down the ladder and under the shade of the tree. He returned to the ladder and continued her job. She watched him. He was around her age. He didn't move very well, movements slow and measured. Several times she tried to resume her duties and each time he shushed her away. At some point, she fell asleep against the base of the tree. When she woke, baskets of fresh-picked apples surrounded her. He was nowhere to be found.

One day, she confessed to her grandmother who picked the apples that long, suffering day. Her grandmother looked surprised. She found it hard to believe. She said the same boy had been beaten badly by her grandfather that very same day. He had been left in a ravine with orders that no one shall approach or help him. Her grandmother suggested they keep the story of the boy's help a secret.

Iris kept it a secret, but it wasn't long before curiosity drove her to seek out the young man. She soon used her limited freedom to find trees, ripe for picking, at or near the vicinity of the tree the young man tended. It was because of this, she didn't mind the hard labor, the hours spent standing on a crooked ladder. She faced the grimacing aftermath of stretching and bending over to pick the most succulent fruit with quiet vigor. In fact, she secretly enjoyed the prospect of apple picking on the farm. And... she found a way to do it, year after year.

EACH JUNE, DURING HER formative years of womanhood, her father announced whether she would be going to the farm. His decision had nothing to do with love, devotion or kindness. The memories of his own childhood held none of those things. His childhood was one of silent pain and suffering. He felt he had given his daughter, Iris, so much more. But she returned his graciousness with nothing more than acts of impropriety and disappointment.

Iris dearly wished her father would love her but there was an overpowering need to disobey him and continue her punishment in the apple fields of the Blue Ridge mountains. She did everything in her power to make sure that happened. It did not take much. A simple, finely constructed rebuttal to a command, given by her father. A momentary, public display of immaturity or distasteful exhibition of social etiquette. Her father would turn ostentatious shades of crimson and she would spend many an evening sequestered to her bedroom. It was no surprise, each year, when her "punishment" was handed down with her father's iron hand.

Please understand the inner workings of a young, innocent woman. Her actions were not designed to cause unnecessary suffering or pain. She had a strong desire to see her father in a good light and vice versa. But, in the deepest parts of her soul,

Iris felt hopelessly in love. She no longer desired to travel the world, her dreamy wanderings exposed for what they were; a yearning for love. Passionate, beautiful, everlasting love.

He was young, strong and since the day of their acquaintance, the kindest soul she had ever met. It was nary a season before they rarely found the two outside of the same tree; picking and laughing, the leaves hiding stolen kisses and moments of tenderness. For them, their future was bright and limitless. But to the outside world, there was a problem. A problem rooted in cruelty, ignorance and immorality. For this young boy turning into a full-blooded male was named Frederick Earl.

And young Frederick was not the same color as Iris.

Nor did he enjoy the freedom of leaving his confined quarters for a leisurely walk, or buying his favorite candy from the general store. None of that mattered because he had the greatest privilege of all. Each July to November, he shared a tree with the most beautiful girl he would ever meet. Each year, from the time she was thirteen through the age of nineteen, Iris dutifully went to the farm and worked. Each year, as they grew and changed, the one thing that remained the same was their love for each other.

HOWEVER, THE WORLD AROUND them was changing. For one, President Abraham Lincoln had declared the Emancipation Proclamation in 1863. In northern Georgia, the slave owners were not readily fond of the Emancipation and many ignored it. Without Union support, they still bound the slaves. Some things in the South would not change without a fight. On December 18, 1865, they signed the Thirteenth Amendment and slavery was abolished. It wasn't long after, most of the remaining farmers of northern Georgia gave up ownership of their slaves, including Iris's grandfather.

Many of the slaves on her grandfather's farm left and headed north, including Frederick's parents. But not Frederick, his dreams had nothing to do with a good job in the north. Frederick stayed in the same, small quarters. He worked just as hard and never asked for a cent of pay. He requested his usual two meals a day, a bed and his clothing needs; two pairs of shirts, pants and knitted socks, straw hat, a pair of overalls, leather boots and a jacket. He owned nothing, yet he felt richer than any plantation owner.

As a matter of fact, he couldn't even say he owned the clothes on his back. But, it didn't matter. There was only one thing that mattered to him in this world. It was much more precious than any material thing. As long as Iris loved him, he could live on apple seeds and a few ladles of soup each day. Interestingly, his blind approach to hard work attracted the attention of none other than Iris's usually malevolent grandfather. It wasn't too many seasons before Iris's grandfather took notice of Frederick's hard work and rewarded his loyalty with a position as assistant foreman, a new bed and a small but decent amount of pay. Frederick praised the Lord for his good fortune. For the grandfather, it was more of a self-serving promotion. At the time, good workers were hard to find and harder to keep. Black or white, Frederick was the hardest working man he ever met. Besides, had he hired a white man to fill the position, it would have cost him double.

For Frederick, the new position reduced the time he could spend with Iris and he thought hard about turning down the promotion. But, he knew this would be more than suspicious and also knew the future value of saving every single cent he earned. One day, the money would provide the start for a new life with Iris. Ironically, if the real truth behind his motive for staying were exposed, the reward would have been much, much different.

. . .

AS CHANGE IS INEVITABLE, Iris finally "learned her lesson" and upon her twentieth birthday, advised she no longer had to work her grandfather's farm. Her father used his influence to employ Iris at the local bank as a teller girl. The bank teller job was considered very reputable for a young lady. The job was steady with long hours, credible pay for a woman her age, respectable, but at the same time... devastating to Iris. Each day, her thoughts revolved around running away with Frederick and starting a new life, not counting simple coin and hearing people complain about their position in the world.

One benefit of Frederick's job as an assistant foreman and a free man was the ability to do as he pleased after work. He could leave the farm alone and without chains. To his surprise, he was even provided the use of Bell, the old mule of the farm. So it was, each weekend, Frederick would head down the mountain and secretly meet Iris. They had a special place all their own where he would camp for the weekend, she would stay until curfew and their love would bloom along with the wild flowers.

Even in a time of new freedom, Frederick knew the inherent danger in their relationship. With great caution, he planned his trips down the mountain and took every measure to conceal the location of his weekend camp. As an additional measure, he did not take the traveled road, instead forging a path down the mountain with a hatchet, axe and hard labor. The path was winding and fragile. At some points, even treacherous to cross but well worth the risk.

EACH FRIDAY EVENING, IRIS would sneak out of her room and walk through a small path into the woods. It was a beautiful uphill hike through fresh pine, wildflowers and a small stream meandering its way down the hill. She would emerge into a meadow, high in the hills, clear of any trees. At the far end of the meadow, a large rock sat high above the ground. It was there she climbed and waited, watching for a sign of Frederick's journey down the mountain. From her perch, she had a clear view of the trail above her and when she saw the light of Frederick's lantern, carefully winding its way down the mountain, her heart would light up. She would sit, anxious with excitement and watch the light slowly descend toward her until the flame extinguished from sight below the tree line. A short while later, Frederick would come bounding through the meadow.

She always wanted to light her own lantern to shine her love back and let him know she waited but Frederick convinced her there was no need. He knew she would always be waiting and the risk of exposure was too great. Even though he was a free man, the consequences of getting caught with Iris would surely doom their future plans for a life together in the north. Their passion-filled weekends together fueled them for the week of hard work while apart and were the most precious times of Iris's life. They would take walks in the forest, skinny dip in the creek, pick flowers and gather berries among other simple yet pleasurable pursuits.

And, of course, one of Frederick's favorite pastimes was his love of a good tall tale. He loved hearing them and he loved spinning them. There was many a night, they would lie in the meadow under a moonlit sky and Frederick would spin his tall tales to the delight of Iris. On one occasion, they even planted seeds for two apple trees based on one of his tales. Frederick loved the story and told the wild tale of a sailor carrying secret apple seeds many times; according to Frederick, the sailor was on a ship lost at sea before striking the shores of Australia. The trust in their Captain lost, the sailor and his friend refused to re-board when the ship was ready to continue its journey and left behind. They found themselves wandering the local town, earnest in their efforts to find a new toil, albeit after a respite at the nearest tavern. It was the morning after, when their wanderings led them to a small wooden booth, where they met a lady named Maria Smith who was selling apples and home-made apple pie at a local street market.

The friend couldn't get enough of the apple pie and offered the lady a challenge. He stated if he could eat 50 apples before the market closed, she would have to give him the recipe for her apple pie. The elderly lady had never seen such a thing and accepted the offer. The vigorous sailor wasted no time and devoured apple after apple. By the time he reached twenty apples he was getting a little dizzy. By the time he reached forty apples he was not feeling so good and his stomach looked like he had consumed a large watermelon. And when he reached fifty apples, Ms. Smith was more than astonished as he had not only eaten the pulp of each apple, he ate the whole apple. She had no choice but to turn over her recipe to the entrepreneurial, now green-colored, young man.

As luck would have it, the sailor's found a ship later that day and managed a commission on the ship. It was less than a day into their voyage toward America when fate reared its ugly head as the apple-eating champion became violently sick, suffering from stomach distress. Apparently, the consumption of 50 whole apples was not a wise idea. His friend died a short time later. However, he didn't die without giving his best friend, the sailor, the secret recipe for the apple pie.

When the sailor arrived in America, he decided to give up the sea, start a farm and plant his secret apple seeds. He headed inland until he found a nice piece of land in northern Georgia. But, he soon learned he wasn't cut out for farming. The lady of the sea called to him and he struggled to resist her charm. The life of a farmer was much more difficult than he ever thought.

It was during this critical period, the sailor crossed paths with Frederick.

According to Frederick, he found the sailor during one of his supply runs into town. The sailor sat by the side of the road with a broken-down wagon and a look of hunger on his face. He was in a poor state of affairs. Frederick helped fix his wagon and gave him a few days' supply of food. The sailor thanked him and announced he was heading straight back to Savannah. The sailor gave up farming and felt the need to heed the call of the lady, but not before giving Frederick the secret seeds and the recipe for the apple pie as a form of gratitude.

Upon completion of his latest yarn, Frederick held open his hand, exposing two apple seeds. Iris told Frederick she did not believe a word of his story. She never heard of a sailor who became a farmer in their neck of the woods. Why, the only sailors she ever heard of were at the ports in Savannah, and that was a long way from their little, nowhere town. Bless his heart, she had never even heard of anybody ever going to or coming from Australia. The thought was absurd. Finally, she looked him in the eye and noted the friend had only given the sailor the recipe for the apple pie before he died... not the seeds. How then, did the sailor get the seeds?

Frederick sheepishly looked at the ground as Iris contemplated her own question. It was only a moment before her eyes lit up and she smacked Frederick on the shoulder while declaring there was no way in tarnation she was going to touch those seeds. He would have to plant them himself. Frederick laughed at her and promised she may not be willing to touch the seeds but sure would enjoy the apples one day. He promised, one day the seeds would grow into two, beautiful apple trees and she better learn how to make those apples into that secret recipe pie, right quick. He sure loved a good apple pie. With that, Frederick dug a couple of holes, close to each other, tenderly covered them with dirt and offered a prayer. Each time he came down the mountain, Frederick tended to the apple seeds and before long the two apple trees grew, side-by-side. Frederick loved their secret apple trees and nurtured them like one would nurture a baby. Two years passed and Iris felt it was time to allow their trees to bear fruit but Frederick wouldn't allow it. He told her next season would be the season they would feast on their very own super-secret, green apple pie.

IT WAS IN THE third year of their weekends in the meadow when the winds of change really showed their force. Over the winter, Iris's father had a heart attack and died a short time later at the local hospital. With her father gone, Iris waited until the spring to tell her mother she was in love and planned to move north in the coming fall, with her beloved Frederick.

Her mother responded by squeezing her daughter tight and softly crying in her arms. She told Iris she knew about Frederick for several years. Iris's grandmother had warned her mother many summers ago of the love growing between her and Frederick. Iris couldn't believe what she heard and further astonished to learn her grandma had scolded her ornery, old grandpa into giving Bell the mule to Frederick.

Her mother and grandmother kept the love a secret. All those years. There is no doubt Frederick would have met a gruesome end had the Stanfield men found out about the affair. Iris asked her mother why they helped, and her mother stated because love is not a choice, only God's blessing at work.

THAT WEEKEND, IRIS LEFT the house with a lantern in hand and excitedly perched the warm flame of the lantern close by her side as she sat on the rock. She daydreamed about her future with Frederick. She viewed him splitting the logs, felled by his own hand, clearing a place for their future home. She could see herself bringing him a warm bowl of broth with a square of homemade cornbread. She viewed them lying atop their bear rug, in the cozy cabin built by their own hands, tendrils of orange flame from the fireplace, warming their wiggling toes. She lulled herself into a state of dreaminess. She never felt so happy in her entire life.

She regained her senses when she viewed the familiar flicker of Frederick's lantern burning a hole in the path from the top of the mountain. Even though it was far away, it blanketed her with warmth. She couldn't wait to tell him the news. As she watched the glow work its way down the fragile path, she continued to think about what her future would look like with Frederick by her side. She couldn't see a single obstacle that would stop them from living their moment in time, together forever.

He wasn't far into his journey down the mountain when she saw a small flickering of light at the top of the mountain, above Frederick. It drew her immediate attention as it was the first time she viewed another light. The light soon grew into several small lights and created a trail. The warmth left Iris's body and the rock she sat upon grew cold under her legs. Iris looked at Frederick's light again. It was continuing to work slowly down the mountain. She looked above him. The trail of lights were moving down the mountain at a quicker pace.

SHE WANTED to shout to Frederick, *hurry my love... HURRY, HURRY!*

IT WAS NO USE. Even if her voice worked, he would be too far away to hear her cries. She shrank within herself and trembled, wrapping her arms around her body for comfort, pretending they were the hands of Frederick. Iris kept looking up and down, calculating whether the lights would catch Frederick's light. There was no doubt in her mind. They were going to catch him.

. . .

Run Frederick... my dear love... run.

THE FIRST TORCH of light reached the light of Frederick. Soon, the rest of the glowing aberrations from above arrived and formed a semi-circle around the single, life-giving torch of her dear love. Iris watched in horror as the lights closed around Frederick. She stood up on the rock and her hand extended toward Frederick. She wanted his light to jump into her palm, where she could close her hand and create a safe womb, a refuge from terror. The torches merged closer. She focused on Frederick's light. It fell. It flickered several times as it made its jagged and merciless descent.

AND THEN... the light was gone.

SHE CRUMBLED into her own misshapen form and held motionless on the rock, afraid to breathe, unable to make a sound. She trembled and never felt colder. She looked down and her own lantern had extinguished on the ground. She strained to see and hear into the night. She prayed for anything, any sign of Frederick at all. With desperation, she prayed to see the light just one more time.

THEY FOUND HIS BODY several days later, battered and bruised with the lantern still clutched in his hand and old Bell the mule nearby. When Iris received word of Frederick's death, she wanted nothing more than to end it all and rejoin Frederick in the Heavens. However, the thought of ending the life of the baby growing inside helped her cling to mortal life and decide against giving up. Before the birth of their baby, Iris changed her last name to Earl. She delivered a healthy boy. She named him Frederick Earl II.

Each year, Iris and Frederick II would travel through the path and into the meadow where the two apple trees stood, side-by-side. Each time, they would harvest their fill of apples to make delicious green apple pies. Before they left, each would plant one beautiful Iris and say a prayer. Iris wanted Frederick to know her love and the love of their child surrounded him. She never moved to the north, and she visited their apple trees with Frederick II every year until she died.

And Frederick was right, the apples from their trees made the best apple pies anywhere in the land. There wasn't a soul alive, who was lucky enough to taste one of her pies, that wouldn't beg to know where she found the apples to fill her delicious pies. It wasn't until her deathbed, she gave Frederick II permission to germinate the seeds of the trees and make her pie available for the masses. Frederick Earl II became quite wealthy with his apple orchard... and his mother's famous Granny Smith Apple Pie.

CHAPTER 2

ert and Gertie

HE HESITATED TO PRESS the button on his Nutone intercom as he knew the inevitable outcome from the other side. Instead, he gazed around his small office in search of comfort only derived from familiar surroundings, sights, smells and sounds.

He gazed at the picture on the wall behind his desk, a black and white photo of the tiny kitchen he and his wife Gertie worked from to create the first batches of their now famous "Gertie's Scrumptious Chunk" chocolate ice cream. They were both smiling in the picture with one of his hands covered in chocolate and dripping onto the floor. As she was taller than him, she stood to one side with one arm draped over his shoulder and around his neck in an affectionate hug. Long hours side by side with his wife, laughing and flinging failed samples at each other in delight. Those were the days.

He fell into a deep trance reminiscing, but before long

someone brought him back to the present by the intercom coming to life. "Bert? Are you in there, Bert?" The voice sounded urgent and impatient. He paused and hesitated to answer before the intercom came to life again. "Bert, you stop your daydreaming and get going... NOW!"

Bert's shoulders sagged. He pressed the Nutone button. "Yes dear." His voice sounded meek and fearful.

He paused at the door of his small office and listened for activity outside. Once he felt satisfied with the silence, he opened the door and silently worked his way outside of their large manufacturing plant, feeling anxious as the fear of someone approaching him remained imminent.

Once in the parking lot, he kept his head down and shot straight for the comfort of his 1959 Apache short bed truck. He rejoiced in the beauty of his vehicle. The truck was his baby and the one and only vehicle he had owned and driven since 1959. A few years ago, his wife talked him into "fixing" up the truck and with great reluctance he agreed, and the results were amazing. The auto restoration company paired a crate 350 V8 to an automatic transmission with power-steering, power front disc brakes, deep sounding dual exhaust and aluminum radiator. The ice-cold air conditioning was an added relief to the hot days, and he loved the custom interior. The truck was repainted with a sea foam, metallic, flat paint with white custom detailing and pin striping to finish out the look in style. Every time he looked at the truck he fell in love with it again.

He revved the engine twice for enjoyment and then crept his way past the sea of parked employee vehicles and alongside the warehouse where ice cream of assorted flavors were created, boxed and readied for shipment to stores nationwide. He marveled at the sheer size of the facility, at once proud and saddened over the loss of the "old days".

· · ·

HE SMILED AT THE thought of how it all began, it seemed such a struggle, yet now seemed like the happiest days of his life. He was so proud of himself when he built their first portable ice cream parlor. It was simple, really. With each small profit from each batch of ice cream created and then raced to local stores in ice, he saved enough to buy a used Coldspot freezer. He surrounded the cooler in reclaimed wood and painted the wood. Unknowingly, he created the now famous "Gertie's Scrumptious Chunk" slogan.

He hid the contraption until he had enough squirreled away money to buy a used 1950s Kohler US Army Signal Corps Generator. He mounted everything onto the bed of his pickup truck and wrapped the generator in reclaimed wood and drew a big ice cream cone on the side. Oh, how he thought he had broken his back that late night evening, loading the oversized items onto his truck. He was sore for a week afterwards.

But it was all worth it. He presented his new "ice cream" truck to Gertie on their wedding anniversary and he will never forget the smile that spread so wide across her face. Of course, it was followed by a smack to the back of his head and teasing accusation of employee theft to pay for the oversized contraption.

Regardless, even though he did not know it at the time; he created the path that led to the end of their many hours side by side in their small kitchen, churning away into the night.

HE STIRRED FROM HIS memories as he drove into the parking lot of the Abernathy Medical Hospital and the anxiety started to build in him. His life was a paradox of fear and anxiety. He absolutely cherished people and his love for others was steadfast, yet, he felt terrified of the normal, everyday interactions that usually led to a mutual bond. Biological children would have solved that problem. He always felt the need to hug and to hold and knew he would embrace his own child, absent of fear or anxiety.

THEY TRIED AND TRIED… and tried. But it never happened.

THE YEARS TICKED by and the attempts at life turned to rituals of despair. Modern medicine solved the mystery and Bert and Gertie learned they would never have biological children of their own. By then, time had aged both of them and their business had grown into a small empire. It was almost a relief when they found out. It was as if they spent years, mourning the pending death of a loved one and once the final act occurred, the healing could begin. It was a tough period for Bert. Gertie always seemed to handle the disappointments better.

For Bert, he had already spread his love in his own way throughout their company of "children" but the tragic news released him from any guilt he harbored at his lack of ability to fertilize. Bert knew every employee. He knew every one of his employee's spouses and children. He felt like they were his children and his family. However, nobody really knew Bert. He could not break from the paralysis of fear that gripped him whenever he had to interact with anyone other than his beloved Gertie. She was the super glue that held him together. She was the slogan, the face and the spokesperson for their company.

Besides their own employee records, Bert spent many hours a day "spying" on his children through modern conveniences like Facebook and Instagram. He would rejoice in their posts of happiness and fun and feel their pain when the messenger brought news of hardship or loss. Behind the scenes, he worked very hard to create a positive family working environment. He took great pride in the fact they had a waiting list in the hundreds for people desirous of a job within their company because of the benefit and insurance packages he created and maintained with strict diligence. It was their belief that wealth and good fortune should be shared and there is a reward for a good, old-fashioned work ethic.

He trudged up the stairs to the third floor of the medical building and before entering the office area, took a deep breath to calm down, just as Gertie had advised. He walked into the office and approached the counter. The receptionist positioned her body away from the greeting desk as she engaged in a colorful conversation on the phone with what sounded like a close friend. This was working out great, he thought. He found the sign-in sheet and looked for a pen. He wouldn't even have to talk to the receptionist. However, there was no pen. He looked on the counter, looked on her desk to see if there was one within reach he could silently grab... nothing. He knew he didn't have a pen and now he felt stuck. He froze in place. He didn't want to talk to her but he needed a pen.

So, he waited... and waited... and waited. She knew he was there. She glanced his way several times. Apparently, the phone conversation involving what Sheila did to James after she found a picture of him and an unknown girl sitting at a bar together was much too important to forego and address her latest patient's needs.

Finally, it appeared today's drama had reached a conclusion. The receptionist hung up and squared an impatient gaze, directly at Bert. "Can I help you?" The irritation in her voice was grinding.

He could not find words in his mouth and after several seconds used his hand to imitate writing. She got the picture, removed a pen from her drawer, tossed it onto the counter with an exasperated look and turned away from him as if he no longer existed. Bert snuck up to the desk like a careful mouse wary of a predator. He grabbed the pen and scrawled his name in near illegible words as the encounter had caused his hands to shake. He moved to a corner of the room and buried his head in a copy of Southern Living magazine. He liked that magazine. All the offices always had at least one new copy of the magazine and several older ones. He really enjoyed that. He waited and watched under cover of the magazine as other patients arrived and he studied them, hoping their lives were well and their condition not too serious. One hour passed, then a second hour. Patients that arrived after him were ushered into the doctor's room, yet there he sat, unwavering in his patience.

He was reading a recipe for a southern lemon tart, his mouth pleasantly puckering, when his phone rang. He looked at the caller ID and his mouth puckered some more.

"Sam already picked up your truck and Reginald is waiting outside to drive you home, Bert. Why aren't you waiting outside?" Gertie asked.

"Gertie, Dr. Ying hasn't seen me yet. I'm still waiting," he replied.

"What? What is going on there Bert? The colonoscopy should be done and you should be done. Tell me what is going on!"

"The receptionist hasn't called me in yet, Gertie. Can you please come here... please?"

"Bert... you know I can't do that. Now get yourself up there and demand to know the reason for the holdup... and do it now Bert," she stated and then hung up on him.

Bert took a deep breath and approached the counter. He viewed the receptionist heavily engaged in a conversation involving what James did to Sheila after she sold his prized golf clubs for a dollar at her garage sale. It was retribution for her shoddy husband taking a picture with a lovely young lass at a well-known bar for loose women and adulterous indulgences. Apparently, James wasn't too happy about the unplanned sale of his golf clubs and in retaliation, cancelled their trip to the U.S.

Virgin Islands. His reason being, he couldn't afford the trip and new clubs at the same time.

The receptionist continued to ignore Bert for several minutes until satisfied she had discussed all the juicy details of James and Sheila's lives together. She finally hung up and turned to Bert, looking him dead in the eye. "Can I help you?" She inquired with that same look of irritation.

"I... I... I... was... uh... is Dr. Ying... here?" Bert stammered.

"Well, of course he is, you do have an appointment—don't you?" She continued to glare at him as he stood—speechless. "But seeing as how you couldn't even take the time to write your name legibly, so I could possibly read it, I didn't have the time to figure it out." She provided an amazing re-enactment of a woman scorned, clearly missing her calling as an acclaimed off-Broadway actress. "I couldn't send you back there, when I don't even know who you are!" She glared at him as if he had violently offended her in some way.

Bert shrunk, fears surfacing like a breaching whale, before turning and walking out of the office with his head stuck to his chest. He withdrew his cellphone. It shook in his hand. He couldn't stop trembling as he tried to tap the phone number. It took four attempts before he successfully put in all the numbers and another few minutes before he tapped the send button. But... he made the dreaded call. "Gertie, I'm not going to see Dr. Ying today."

"What? You tell me what happened and you tell me now," she demanded.

AND SO HE DID... recounting the entire ordeal.

WHEN HE FINISHED, there was a moment of silence followed by her calm voice, almost soothing. "Now Bert, you wait five minutes and then you walk back into that office. If that receptionist does not have the door held open for you to see Dr. Ying, then you can come home... that, I promise."

Bert waited not five but fifteen minutes, weighing his options as he dearly did not want to face the receptionist again. However, worse, he did not want to face Gertie if he didn't follow her command. He trudged up the steps like his feet were stuck in mud and meekly re-entered the office.

The receptionist immediately met him. "Oh... I'm so sorry, sir. I'm so, so sorry. I had no idea. I never usually treat people like that. I'm going through a rough time and I'm so sorry... please forgive my rudeness." She talked as she held his elbow and walked him toward the patient rooms. Her hand was unnecessarily firm on his arm. It hurt. He didn't say anything. She held the door open for him.

"It's okay. I understand. We all have bad days," Bert mumbled. He entered patient room four, and she closed the door behind him. He could hear her voice, growing weaker, as she continued to yammer away while walking back to her desk.

It was a matter of seconds before Dr. Ying entered the room, apologized, and the procedure was in progress. Before he knew it, he woke up to the familiar face of Reginald, the colonoscopy completed and time to go home.

CHAPTER 3

ess

BESS SAT IN THE patient room… uncomfortable. She didn't enjoy sitting on the examination table but had trouble squeezing into the small chair with the armrests in the corner. She squeezed into this one, but if not for her bad knees, she would rather have stood and waited for Dr. Anthony Welborough. Luckily, per his standard practice, she did not have to wait long.

Dr. Welborough half-knocked on the door, entered immediately, took a seat on the swiveling stool, did one full spin and faced her with a warm smile. "How are you feeling Mrs. Wolo?"

"Well, Dr. Good Looking, I'm bouncing on top of the world —now," she replied.

Dr. Welborough blushed and smiled again. He paused before he began again on a more personal level. "Bess, the last time we talked, I thought we came to an agreement. We were going to commit to our plan. Can you tell me what's going on?" He looked into her eyes. She saw and felt the compassion.

"Well... I was there, I really was. Every morning I was starting my day with our shake. I killed that kale, slayed that spinach, chopped that chia and buried those berries," she pronounced as she imitated each movement like a samurai swordsman, laughing heartily along the way.

Dr. Welborough couldn't help but laugh with her as Bess had pretty much the greatest laugh he'd ever heard. She laughed with great heartiness and true happiness. Her laugh boomed with life. However, once she settled down, he refused to let her out of the hot seat and waited with a sense of caring patience.

She looked at him and realized Dr. Good Looking was not letting her off the hook. She sighed, a crease of guilt crossing her face. "Well... you know how we went camping the other weekend?" She paused for confirmation and then continued, "well... first... we didn't have an electrical outlet and then at night I made my famous S'more Sandwiches. The first night I resisted. I really did. But the second night was just too much. I had one and then I had s'more and s'more and s'more." And then she laughed again at her own joke.

Dr. Welborough smiled with her but the worry showed on his face.

She looked at him once more and then her eyes lowered to the glossy floor. "I know... well... I kind of lost control after that again."

They both sat silent, stuck in their own thoughts. Dr. Welborough felt frustrated, he wished he could give Bess the strength to resist the temptations of sweetness while Bess wished she could relieve him of his guilt for not helping her enough. She knew eating was her problem, and she felt responsible for her poor decisions. It was her fault. Other than living in her refrigerator to stop her from indulging her cravings, there was nothing Dr. Welborough could do for her. He broke the silence by pointing to the counter in the corner. She looked and noticed his latest gravity-defying monument.

"Take a closer look," he said.

She wiggled herself out of her chair and upon closer examination discovered his latest wonder. Q-Tips were at the base forming a teepee structure with one, cotton ball near the top of the Q-Tips which all rested around the one, cotton ball. A single Q-Tip stood up straight from on top of the cotton ball. To top it off, a single Band-Aid package lay flat across the very top. Once again, she looked in awe at his latest gravity defying feat and wondered how the feat was possible. She bent over, looking closer, studying the precarious pillar, trying to dissect a clue to its foundation.

"No glue... nothing but Q-Tips, cotton and a Band-Aid." He let her look at it a little longer. "I'll make you a deal. If you come in next time around our projected target—for the first time ever, I'll let you in on one of my industry secrets and tell you how this is possible." He smiled as he waved broadly across the structure. He kept his palm extended, waiting for acceptance of the offer.

Bess pushed her hands off her knees, stood up and slapped his hand in agreement. "Ok Doc, I sure will try this time. I know I can do it." She started to turn away then turned back, wiggling a finger in the air. "Wait, a minute. Does this mean I'll have to give up my chewy, candy sours?"

He nodded his head and chuckled.

"That's really asking a lot Dr. Good Looking, but for you... I'll try."

"Bess, no good can come of chewy candy sours. I think you know that," said Dr. Welborough.

"DON'T UNDERESTIMATE the power of the chewy candy sour," said Bess with a devilish smile.

. . .

HE GAVE it his best shot and fired a stern look of disapproval. She laughed again, with her usual vigor. She knew he cared, and she felt bad.

It was so easy and tempting to let it go, to just enjoy being around her. She brought light to the world. Dr.Welborough felt torn between selfishly lapping up her essence and committing to his role as her concerned physician with a patient in a health crisis. "Bess... your numbers are not good. I'm really worried about you. How can I help you understand how important it is to follow a nutrition plan?"

She studied his face. He wasn't going to let her off the hook this time. He was serious. "I know," she replied with a face full of doubt. "I'll leave here and head straight to Whole Foods. I know I can do this... I just need to keep it up..." she smacked her hands together in prayer and looked at the ceiling. As her head fell from prayer, she whispered, "I think I can."

DR. WELBOROUGH WAS no stranger to the power of words. He heard the whisper, "I think I can" and it opened the door for future failure. It didn't signify commitment. "Bess, I'm sorry... but we are really past the point of kind of sticking to a nutrition plan. You are one of the most beautiful people I've ever met but you're in danger of killing yourself." He looked at the ground in frustration for several seconds before gazing back in her eyes. "I'm sorry, but we're at the point of no return here."

She grabbed his hand and squeezed it. Even though they were about the same age, she held his hand like a mother warmly comforting a child when traumatized. "I'm going to be all right. Thank you for being so sweet."

He looked at her, he couldn't hide the concern. He stood up and turned to grab her medical file off the counter. Just then, a loud "SMACK" resonated off the walls as she took advantage of the moment and spanked his rear end. She roared with laughter, giddy in delight at her good fortune. Dr. Welborough turned beet red and couldn't help but smile ear-to-ear at the boldness of his special patient.

As he walked out of the room, she yelled out to him, "now don't go on and forget my barbecue this Saturday because you're too busy being Dr. Good Looking." They could hear the sounds of her laughter in all the patient rooms.

AS PROMISED, SHE DROVE straight to the Whole Foods near her house to load up on all things good and nutritious. It's not like she didn't like his nutrition plan. She liked any nutrition plan that involved eating food. In truth, she didn't eat out of sorrow or depression. She ate because she loved making food, she loved serving food and she loved eating food. There was not too much in the way of food in this world she did not like. She could pretty much take any vegetable, meat, fish or even dirt and turn it into something delicious and mouth-watering. It hurt in the fact, in the process of raising several children, there was a never-ending plethora of delicious leftovers on the plate of at least one child. She made excuses to herself as she looked forward to and savored the extra bits of morsels left unattended by deserting children. After all the hard work, it would be a shame to let the food meet their demise at the bottom of a garbage disposal when she would enjoy it so much more. And besides, does a bite here or there really matter that much... she would think to herself? Deep down she knew the answer to that question but one of her problem-solving methods was to avoid mirrors at all costs. She knew she was obese and probably "fat ugly" looking to some people but she also knew she was beautiful and full of love on the inside. And thank her parents and the

Lord above, she could see her inner-beauty... and let it shine unto others.

She had a particular addiction to sweets. Not just chocolates, peppermints or chewy sours but all sweets. And perhaps, that is where the real problem lied. She thought about what the Doctor said and it worried her, however briefly. She was a firm believer that a healthy, positive attitude will always bring a return of a healthy, positive life. So, the worry within her was short, as she was more mesmerized by the thoughts of the menu she was preparing for her monthly barbecue party on Saturday. She finished shopping and left with a cart filled to the brim.

SHE ARRIVED HOME TO a state of chaos, the kind considered by most people to be unnerving, irritable, unsettling and more than likely unacceptable.

BUT TO BESS... it was the sound of music.

YOU SEE... the house she created was the house of life. She and her husband had seven, wonderfully original children and added to that was an ever-present crew of assorted neighbors, visiting friends and wayward children. Bess would have it no other way. It was as if the bigger the household full of children, the more life breathed into her soul.

She started bringing in the bags of groceries and it wasn't long before her most responsible child, 16-year-old Emma, showed up to help and unpacked the bags. Bess gave her a kiss on the back of her head before heading back to the car. Emma was the quiet one and of all the children, Bess had the hardest time knowing if Emma was feeling her motherly love. Sometimes she worried.

It was probably around the fifth trip in when her most irresponsible child, 3 1/2-year-old Louise, affectionately nicknamed Cheese, made her presence known in her own special way. Bess and her husband Tim owned a two story, split colonial and when you walk in the front door, the office was immediately to the left and the dining room opposite right. Past that was the staircase to the second floor and across from the staircase landing was a large foyer closet.

Bess had just passed the staircase and turned right to head into the kitchen when a small voice screamed out, "hhhiii mooommm" followed by a small body whizzing past her as it slid down the railing of the staircase. The body shot off the end of the railing, flew across the hall and disappeared into the darkest recesses of the open closet.

Bess let out a shriek while dropping the bag of corn on the cob and peaches. She did her own stunt-work as she warbled across the rolling peaches and corn now strewn across the floor and raced to the closet with her hand clutching her chest. And there she was, lying on her back, sprawled across the bed of pillows the stunt pilot had constructed to receive her inevitable doomed flight.

A sigh of relief escaped Bess as her voice grew with concern. "Cheese."

She pointed her finger at her little daredevil and could not bring herself to anger as the sight of her little angel with head poking out of a bed of white pillows was just too precious a sight to behold. Cheese dug herself out with a smile of joy and Bess couldn't help laugh and playfully smack her little one on the rear. "Now you little daredevil, see if you can juggle my peaches all the way to the kitchen without dropping them."

Bess walked back into the kitchen to see Emma trying to balance a sour pickle on her finger before eating it and grabbing another from the jar. She thought to herself how different each one of their children lived life. In almost the same moment, one is flying down a staircase with reckless abandon and another child is performing one of her most reckless stunts, balancing a sour pickle on a finger. The two had similar beginnings yet grew in vastly different ways.

BESS'S MIND FLASHBACKED TO when she had Emma. It was a traumatic time for her and Tim as Emma was a premature delivery and her odds of survival were not good. She knew the pediatricians at Abernathy Medical Center were some of the best in the world, but the fear she felt is one only a mother could understand. Bess could still remember the feeling of holding Emma for hours and hours at a time. Little Emma, with her tiny finger, held onto Bess's finger and refused to let go. Bess believed in the energy of love and poured everything she had into that little girl. It was weeks before little Emma could leave the hospital and in all those weeks, Bess had only left her side for no more than a few minutes at a time. She refused to leave the hospital.

Tim was there, too. In between working two jobs, he would watch the two loves of his life while sitting in a little chair in the corner before falling into an uncomfortable sleep. Bess knew he was getting little sleep, but Tim never complained. They were a good team. Bess liked the rocker by the window and would rock and rock her little girl for hours and hours. It wasn't easy, for a number of reasons. And one big reason, nearly broke Bess. Almost the entire time, she fell under the attack of a Nazi type nurse who demanded Bess only hold little Emma for brief periods of time. The nurse would not relent, ordering Bess to put Emma back in her incubator, over and over again. And in return, Bess refused. She believed in kangaroo care (skin to skin warming) and breastfeeding. When necessary, she rebuffed the nurse's attacks, continuing her own idea of care. This did not please the nurse.

The "NICU Nazi" as Bess would call her, would bring nurses to her unit and stand where Bess could see them through the windows. She would point and talk in harsh, meant to be over-heard whispers. The NICU Nazi even told Bess she could kill Emma if she continued to do it her way. Bess knew she disgusted the domineering nurse. She didn't care. Bess believed in what she was doing and nobody was going to pry her beautiful little girl from her arms without an all-out, tactical assault. Bess absorbed the verbal beatings by the nurse, reluctant to involve Tim and upset him. However, he did find out. It was near the end of their stay when Tim got wind of the behavior of the NICU Nazi. And it was something.

Bess smiled at the thought.

She was a god-fearing woman who loved the world but in this particular case, she found a little joy in another's comeuppance. Another nurse had filled Tim in on the abuse his wife was receiving at the hands of the NICU Nazi and the moment he found out, it was clear things were going to change. The tell-all nurse seemed pleased to let Tim know the disgruntled nurse would be arriving soon for her scheduled shift. Tim called in and notified his supervisor he would be late and paced the outside of the NICU unit, waiting for the mean nurse. By the time she arrived for her shift, there were an unusual number of workers on the floor. Apparently, word had spread there might be a long-awaited battle with the demeaning nurse.

Tim was checking on Bess and Emma when he viewed the NICU Nazi through the window. He charged out of the room. The nurse would not be allowed to even come close to Bess. He intercepted the nurse and let her know in no uncertain terms how he felt about her treatment of his wife. Tim dressed her down to the bones, right outside the windows of the NICU unit. Bess could hear his voice booming through the glass and see the demeanor of the NICU Nazi diminish from one of defiance and domination to a broken, sobbing, apologetic mess. Bess could also see from the group of her fellow workers standing by and watching the scene, the lesson was well-deserved and needed. He finished, re-entered the room and sagged into the rocking chair. The moment emotionally and physically drained him. He felt spent. Bess walked over and kissed him on the forehead, scratching his scalp. She felt so proud of her husband. He was quiet, yet such a strong man, when you needed him the most. Needless to say, the experience of their first birth was very traumatic and stressful. So much so, it gave Tim pause when Bess talked about a second child. It was during those early discussions, the one and only time, Tim asked Bess to lose weight. Initially, the words deeply hurt Bess, even though she knew the reasoning behind it was fair and came from a place of love. Her doctor warned her when she became pregnant with Emma her weight could create pregnancy issues. One of them was the chance of a premature birth. Lo and behold, the doctor's prophecy rang true.

So, here they were again and Bess had gained weight since the birth of Emma, even though both her and Tim had agreed she would lose weight before considering another pregnancy. Bess tried, she really did. In the first year and a half after Emma was born, she lost weight. But the truth of the weight loss was revealed when she stopped breastfeeding. It only took a week and Bess started to put on the pounds.

The decision to go forward with a second pregnancy was really made by her without the full consent of Tim. She had agreed to lose weight before a second pregnancy and did not. Tim really wanted another child but wanted her more. He also felt she would have sacrificed and lost the necessary weight. When she didn't and gained weight, it was a very frustrating period for him. He felt like he had no control over his future and it erupted one night whereupon he exploded in frustration and stomped out of the house, disappearing for two straight days.

When he came back, he folded into her arms and they made love. It was that very night, Bess became pregnant with their second child, Tyler. She didn't tell him for three whole months, afraid she would disappoint her husband again. There was no need. When she finally told him, he felt the strength of their love would prohibit the unthinkable. The sheer force of their combined will, fending off tragedy.

Tyler was born without a hitch. The birth was an easy one and even better... the NICU Nazi was nowhere to be found. The joy of the added child opened their cavernous hearts even more and Bess and Tim continued to produce children for the next several years. After Tyler came Katherine, then Matt, John and Tommy. It wasn't until Cheese, the old problems emerged and threatened the harmony of their parenting. Early in her pregnancy, Bess found out Cheese was going to have problems. The threat of an early pregnancy went from a possibility to a probability as Bess grew and sensed her body was in trouble.

The doctors did everything they could but Cheese was born a preemie at 30 weeks old. Immediately, Tim and Bess knew something was terribly wrong. The first sign was the lack of a cry at birth... a baby's, healthy loudspeaker announcing their arrival into a fresh, new world. The second, even more obvious sign was the stiffness. Bess had enough babies to know something was wrong with her little, newborn beauty. Tim knew too, his face showing no emotion but his hand trembling in Bess's.

Tim stayed with Bess the first three days, twenty-four hours a day. Bess didn't think he slept more than a couple of hours those first few nights. Worse, after the first three days he had to work a double. Times were tough and Tim could not afford to lose a job. His high school education did not afford him the luxury of choosing a career path. He took what he could get and tried to make up for his lack of effort when he was young and foolish. However, when Tim left, Emma stepped in and filled the gap. Right from the beginning, she begged and demanded to help until Tim relented and dropped her with an overnight bag at the hospital on his way to work.

Emma sat outside the NICU for several days before the staff realized she would not leave. They tried their best to convince her that prayers would suffice from home, but Emma would have none of it. She would not leave her mother and her newborn sister. Even if she wasn't allowed in the room, she wanted her mother to know she was there for her and Cheese. No matter what. Finally, they received special authorization to let her in the NICU and be with her mother. Emma continued like a workhorse, getting Bess water, snacks and whatever else Bess needed for support. It was only when Cheese was in the incubator, did Emma curl up in her mother's arms for a little, much needed rest. The nurses referred to Emma as the Iron Angel. It was probably a little more than a week into the hospital stay when Emma sat exhausted on Bess's lap and wanted nothing more than to curl up and go to sleep but Bess wanted to tend the baby. Bess was trying to calm the exhausted worker down when she heard an old, but familiar voice.

"So... THIS MUST BE EMMA."

EVEN THOUGH IT had been several years, Bess knew the voice all too well and couldn't hide the cringing effect throughout her whole body. It was a voice that haunted her dreams for several years. It took more than an ounce of courage to look up and into the eyes of the NICU Nazi. She was older now and her eyes and face seemed softer than in the past. They stared at each other, unsure and searching. There was forgiveness behind Bess's eyes that reflected off the sorrow in the NICU Nazi's eyes.

The once horrid nurse extended her hand. "I am so sorry."

Bess looked at her and knew the apology was real. She extended her own hand and grabbed the NICU Nazi's hand. She smiled at her in a sign of forgiveness. The once taciturn nurse pulled a chair next to Bess's and sat down. She stroked the back of Emma's hair as she said, "I remember when you were born. You were the most beautiful baby I had ever seen and you are just as beautiful today." Emma looked at her and beamed. "C'mon now... into my lap. I need a cozy blanket to warm my old body."

Emma climbed into her lap and fell fast asleep to the soothing hums of the transformed nurse. The nurse watched as Bess picked up Cheese, wrapped her in her bosom and let the baby feed. The nurse smiled with understanding and approval.

Something happened during that hospital stay. Nobody could say for sure how it happened. But Cheese left the hospital and for all intents and purposes, showed no signs of the cerebral palsy the doctors were absolutely sure she had when removed from the womb. But Bess knew... it was love. Pure and simple. They flooded the little miracle child with the love of Tim and Bess, the love of Emma and the unexpected love of the NICU Nazi, better known as Nurse Roberta Pender. A nurse who spent years hoping she would have the chance to show the family she once scorned that they had saved and renewed her faith in the power of love.

For unbeknownst to Tim and Bess, nurse Roberta had lost the love of her life not long before the original meeting with them. The loss was beyond devastating and Roberta felt betrayed by God and bitter at the world. She could not deal with the reality that none of her training and skills would save her husband from death. She never released the pain, and it had been slowly destroying her, carving a deep jagged path across her heart.

It took the power of Tim and Bess's love for each other to wake her from her coma of despair. She would never forget that moment in her life, when Tim protected his wife from her, like she was some form of the devil. She cried for a week straight after the confrontation. His love shook her to the core. It was just what she needed. She emerged like a newborn butterfly fresh from her cocoon. She had successfully released the pain and allowed herself to grieve... and forgive.

NURSE ROBERTA TOOK the liberty of adding herself to the long list of friends who cherished the Wolo family. And they welcomed her with love.

CHAPTER 4

oberta

HE DROVE DOWN THE busy two-lane highway, divided in the center, and the largest artery connecting the suburbs from the main highway. It provided daily access for people, in and out of the town of Iris Valley.

The growing city clung to the small-town feel but because of the success of Gertie's Ice Cream plant, secondary businesses had sprung up and created choking points for the aged, highway infrastructure. The success of the town threatened to forever change the bones of the city. He had several miles to go in congested traffic when he found himself in the right lane behind a small, yellow Ford. The bright morning sun pierced through his windshield and added to his aggravation. He felt stuck behind the little yellow Ford and grew more frustrated as the car would not speed up when each opportunity presented itself, puttering along and oblivious to the "real" rules of the road. Finally, after another torturous mile, he saw an opening, veered left and struck down on the gas pedal with his foot. As he passed the yellow Ford, he viewed an old lady with grey hair, both hands rooted to the wheel, classic ten and two position.

He sneered as he thought to himself, *why the hell do they let those people drive?*

It wasn't long before he found himself behind another vehicle in the left lane, traveling at a speed he felt was ridiculously slow for the passing lane. He made his feelings known, proceeding to perch the front end of his big, black truck on the rear end of the vehicle in front of him. His truck was too high to see into the rear of the vehicle where he could visually intimidate the driver, so he watched for the driver to look into their side-view mirror. He was prepared to provide them with a visual statement of the displeasure he felt at their obscene rudeness. After a few seconds, the other driver abated and moved to the right lane, whereupon, he struck down on the accelerator at full throttle, speeding to the rear end of the next vehicle in the left lane.

As he drove, he imagined slamming his truck into the rear of the vehicles and watching as the driver's heads snapped back before hanging like the dangling head of a piñata horse. One more strike, head falls off and all the candy belongs to him. It wasn't possible, though. Not because he didn't have a strong desire to inflict damage but the thought of damaging his perfect truck was too much for him. The truck created an image, one in which he felt he earned.

One day, I will buy a piece of crap with no plates and ram these people off the road, he daydreamed.

Ahead of him and down the hill he could see there was no way he was going to make the next light. He began counting the cars in the left lane and then the right. As the vehicles slowed for the red light, he realized he had to be in the right lane. Without no more than a slight glance, he swerved into the right lane, causing the unknown driver in the right to brake for their life. He was oblivious to this, because he realized, he was now behind the little yellow Ford again.

How is this possible?

The anger swelled now, and he charged his vehicle with his custom, steel bull bars within inches of the little Ford's rear bumper.

"DAMN HER!" He bellowed in despair.

They stopped for the red light and upon the green signal, she slowly accelerated to just under the posted speed limit of 45 miles per hour.

"DAMN HER TO HELL!" He ranted again.

The insanity of not driving the speed limit was almost too much for him to bear, yet there he was, stuck behind this old lady—screwing his day over. The opportunity to pass arrived, and he moved to the left lane, accelerated, and cruised alongside the old lady. He sneered at her through his window, desperately trying to let her know how close she had come to being rammed off the road. She never looked at him, hands on ten and two, eyes straight ahead, no facial expression at all.

"EEERRRGGGHHH!" He growled.

He felt the anger reaching a boiling point. He swerved his black truck into her lane, stopping inches from striking her vehicle. He decided he would take the pleasure of slowly driving her off the road into a pole. He glanced ahead.

"DAMN IT!" He was losing ground with other vehicles. "CRAGGY OLD HAG!" He shouted as he drove off, leaving her in his wake.

He raced and caught up to the vehicle in the left lane in front of him. While steaming with anger, he thought about the ways he would like to make the world pay for his problems. His thoughts searched for a release from the anger and he thought of ways to relieve the boiling inferno inside. But no, it wasn't working. He felt it coming on but he couldn't stop it.

His thoughts drifted back to childhood and the anger he felt toward his sister. He deserved the attention from their parents but she was always the good one, the one who received their attention, who received... everything. He thought about the time he "accidentally" killed her hamster and the sorrow his sister felt over the loss. The justice he felt then, still brought a sense of satisfaction today. He chuckled as he recalled the look of horror on his sister's face. She deserved it. She deserved the pain. The memory, just what he needed to bring down his blood pressure. In his world, people paid for their selfishness... sooner or later. And if he had anything to say about it... the bills were past due and ready for immediate collection.

In the meantime, the dead memory of Fuzzy the hamster worked, creasing a smile across his face, lifting his black moment. He scanned the traffic ahead and although the entry to the freeway was within sight, he calculated he could pass one more vehicle on the right before veering over and jumping onto the freeway.

HE WAS WRONG.

FOR SOME SINISTER force was at play and the traffic in the left lane inexplicably slowed. He was now in danger of losing ground. It was possible a vehicle might pass him and that was unacceptable. The temporary joy he felt vaporized, replaced by a frantic study of the traffic with rising anger. He realized he could not pass again and cursed as he resigned himself to entering the right lane.

What the hell?

Out of nowhere, there she was... the little old lady in the small yellow Ford... filling up the right lane and blocking his lane change.

Cold fury drove a deep dagger in his heart as he swerved

toward her vehicle, revving his engine and coming within an inch of striking her vehicle. He stared at her with laser eyes and received nothing in return except hands on ten and two. She was a zombie woman. He looked ahead of her vehicle for room to swerve in and noticed the old lady drove within inches of the vehicle in front of her. There was no room for his truck. Not a chance.

She is blind as a frigging bat, he thought.

The entrance to the freeway stood yards away, and he realized he would have to fall back, lose ground and pull in behind her or he would miss his entrance. In one last-ditch attempt, he rolled down his passenger window and drove alongside the old lady's Ford. He screamed bloody murder at her with everything he had, veins in his forehead popping like an engorged river and his mind boiling over with anger.

Nothing. No reaction at all from the evil and ancient one. It was now or never. He had to fall back or miss the entrance. He couldn't afford to be late for work again. He slowed down at the last possible second as the ramp opened up and worked to swerve into a position behind the yellow Ford. But, to his surprise, as he slowed his truck... the old lady slowed her vehicle. He floored it... she floored it. She blocked him out.

"WHAT THE HELL?" He screamed at the top of his lungs. *Is she screwing with me?*

He swerved at her vehicle, fighting his inner demons with his desire to drive her into a wall and his greedy desire to avoid damage to his truck. The freeway entrance loomed, and he had one last chance to force her off the road and enter the freeway, his knuckles turned white while gripping the steering wheel... it was now or never.

Goodbye!

As he missed his entrance, he screamed at the top of his lungs, promising revenge of an epic scale if he ever saw the little, old lady in the little, yellow Ford again... EVER!!! The last view he saw of his newly sworn enemy was the vehicle rounding the curve and disappearing... on his freeway.

WHAT HE COULDN'T SEE as the yellow Ford rounded the curve, was that same old lady glance at her driver's side mirror and a devilish smile crease her face as she deserted her new friend in the big, black truck.

HE ALSO DID NOT KNOW her name... Roberta.

AND THE FACT she loves the Bee Gees, her ice-cold SweetWater Georgia Brown beer and out-sweating her younger counterparts in cardio yoga sessions at the local gym. In a carefree manner, her right hand dropped from the two-position on the steering wheel as she cranked the dial to listen to one of her favorite songs. The smile continued as she sang along and did her own, albeit-seated, Tony Manero disco dance.

 harles and Ida

CHARLES EARL STARED AT the clock with the anticipation of an earnest young boy, ready to run down the frosty stairs in bare feet and peek from the wall's corner to view the Christmas presents under the tree. Finally, after the fifth look, he noted the time had arrived. He walked out the back door of his small ranch home and felt the warmth of the morning sunlight against his forehead and shoulders. It was going to be another bright and beautiful day. He crossed his rear lawn, heading toward the back door of his neighbor Ida's house, situated directly behind his residence. As he crossed from his brown weeded lawn onto hers, he noticed the immediate contrast between the two lawns. Her lawn was thick and green, plush like a furry blanket... inviting.

Even her lawn is perfect, he thought.

He reached the back door, raising his fist to knock, when he remembered her repeated request "Don't knock, just come inside." As he tended to be forgetful, she had asked him count-less times to enter without knocking to avoid waking her son, Percy. He slipped in, quiet as a mouse, and entered the kitchen where she stood waiting, coffee in hand.

"Good morning, Chew," she whispered. Her words were soft and sweet, defined by affection.

"Good morning, Ida. So, how far you going, today?" Charles asked.

"Oh… just the usual."

He couldn't help but stare at her when she turned away to put her coffee mug in the sink. Really… he could stare at her all day, every day, for the rest of his life. But, he didn't want to get caught staring because he would never want her to think he was a pervert. And he wasn't. He thought she was the most beautiful thing he had ever seen and who wouldn't want to stare at that. She put her hand on his shoulder as she passed him, brushing her wrist against the top of his shirt. A simple gesture that added to the list of a thousand things he loved about her. He smiled back at her, another day speechless and she left through the kitchen door for her morning run. The moment she left, he couldn't help but pull the shirt to his nose and soak in the fragrance she left behind.

She even smells perfect, he thought as he swam in dreams of everlasting bliss.

He glanced down and his dreams of marriage were cut short when he viewed the familiar object poking out of the top of the glass, sitting on the kitchen counter. It was an extremely impor-tant gift he gave her… a Tigerlight Non-Lethal Defense System. He snatched it up and raced out the front door, finding Ida on the lawn, doing a last-minute calf stretch.

"You forgot your Tigerlight, silly," he teased her with the look of the quintessential mother hen.

She smiled at him and slid the wrist strap around her hand. "You're always looking out for me, my knight in shining armor." With that she sped off, soon lost in the morning haze.

Charles re-entered the front door of the house, feeling good and dreamy when a familiar sound made him freeze in his tracks. It was the sound of somebody racking the chamber of a gun. In silence, he reached into his waistband and drew his own weapon and silently worked his way toward the back bedroom, the probable source of the threat. He turned the corner and was no more than a few feet down the narrow hallway when he came face to face with the cold end of the barrel of an EE-3 rifle.

He froze in place and raised his hands, trying to give the impression he was going to give up. But in reality, he was just trying to bring his own weapon, a Blas-tech DL44, to target and fire on his shadowy assailant. It was a valiant plan but doomed from the start as the assailant seemed to read his mind. Before Charles could fire a single round, the assailant fired a barrage of penetrating blasts, striking Charles in the front of his body. Charles dropped his weapon and clutched his chest, before falling to the ground in a pronounced thud. The assailant entered the hallway and approached with a visible grin across his face.

"I GOT YOU STORMTROOPER!" The assailant giggled with joy.

Charles squinted out of one eye at Percy and continued to play dead until Percy drew closer, at which time Charles grabbed one of his ankles. Percy unleashed another volley of Nerf darts and Charles jerked up and down off the ground, finally coming to rest in an ultimate death spiral. Percy responded by laughing as only a child can laugh.

. . .

IDA USED THE TIGERLIGHT to light up her path as she ran her morning route over some cracked areas of concrete sidewalk. Now was not the time to suffer a twisted or broken ankle. As she ran, she thought about Chew. He was kind and gentle and a wonderful father figure for Percy. There is no man that ever treated her better. She knew how he felt about her. It was obvious. But, try as she might—she didn't feel attracted to him. She felt awful and vain she allowed physical attraction to be a barrier between her and such a good man but she couldn't help it. Ida realized early on she loved him, but could not love him.

She thought back to the few men she ever had a relationship with and like it or not, they were all strong, physically attractive and considered a man's man. As much as she laughed and enjoyed Chew's childlike interactions with Percy, they were just that... childlike. She often looked at him like a child. He was not dumb, but he kept things simple. He was an easy read, there was no spice. Just... simple, and of course, extremely loyal. In contrast, the men in her life were strong. They never seemed childlike or weak. Percy's biological father, he was extremely strong... or she thought. He showed no weakness until the very end, and if not for the letter, she would have never known a side of his character he never revealed during their time together. She thought about the letter and the pain breached the surface of the water again.

Knock it off, she thought to herself as she slapped her thigh. *Get back in the moment... remember what the doctor said... live in the moment.* She gathered herself with a quick inner pep talk. *Look how far you have come since then... a loving mother... a journalist... an aspiring television reporter. You can do it girl!* With that she burst up the hill and over the crest, headed to the park.

THE TOWN OF IRIS VALLEY was a great place to live,

however odd, in its geographical formation and development. The roots and actual town of Iris Valley were on the south side. Small businesses and residences covered the east and west borders while Gertie's Ice Cream Plant covered the northern border.

Many years ago, the Abernathy family purchased hundreds of acres of undeveloped land just north of town. In what many investors considered a foolish idea, they turned around and donated the land to the town of Iris Valley under one condition; the land must be turned into a nature park and remain a park for a thousand years. The Abernathy's even set up an annual fund to help the town cover the costs of maintaining and improving the park. Eventually, as the town prospered, they built developments around the circumference of the park. This turned out to be a brilliant idea by the Abernathy's, creating enjoyment and recreation for ages and attracting immigration to the area.

PERHAPS, ON ANY GIVEN day, the driver of the panel van could be delivering mail, or looking for an address, or maybe even enveloped in a text conversation more important than the safe operation of a motor vehicle.

BUT... no. The driver of the van had another plan, another sole purpose. His entire existence hinged on it.

IT HAD nothing to do with helping, serving or working in the community. The driver was not delivering mail, looking for an address or carelessly texting. This driver had other plans for the day. Plans, if successful, that would bring much needed peace and happiness to his twisted, inner world. Inside, the lone man drove with one hand anxiously gripping the steering wheel and the other hand clutching a pair of handcuffs, swallowed in the size of his hand. As he drove, he methodically set the tension on the hinged handcuffs and then using his thumb, pushed the locking bar through the gears, spinning it around back to the same tension point. He did this repeatedly without thought as his concentration focused on the activities of the runner ahead. He reached the crest of the hill and could see she was running her usual route, headed for Iris Valley Park. The slightest crease of a smile emerged as he salivated and whistled the words to one of his favorite songs, involving a bluebird on a shoulder.

He stopped whistling as she drew closer to the park and the sound of the whirring handcuff blade sped up as the heightened anxiety of the moment revealed itself. She entered the park, running dutifully toward the wooded trail way, disappearing from sight. He sped ahead of her on the road, adjoining the trail. He felt everything in perfect harmony. Time to start the second verse. He whistled again and read the words in his head.

He was through a few bars when he stopped, lips puckered, mind racing for information. He slammed on the brakes and the screeching tires echoed in the narrow cavity of the tree-lined street. He screamed in fury. Again, he could not remember the next verse of the song. He frantically searched his brain. It felt blank and hollow. He tried and tried but the frustration grew and the intellectual side of his brain faded while the rage took over and manifested itself. He slammed the unhinged pair of handcuffs down, again and again upon the dashboard. The hard plastic, already abused, gave way and cracked with puncture wounds. He continued to slam the handcuffs as the cracked edges of the dashboard sliced and diced his hand. With each strike, the blood spattered back up in his face and turned the inside of his van into a Jackson Pollock canvass.

The sweat and exhaustion finally broke him and he slumped down in his seat with a ragged sigh. He looked at his mangled right hand and realized he was losing a lot of blood. He searched between the seats, blood dripping onto the rubber floor. The glint of silver, stuck out from under the passenger seat. He reached down and grabbed the duct tape. It wasn't planned for this use but he had no choice. He pressed the skin of the open wounds together and duct-taped around and around his hand until the blood stopped oozing out.

When finished, he looked around the passenger compartment of his van, accidentally catching his reflection in the rear-view mirror. His face was splattered, torn circles and smears of red blood, some losing their hold and dripping down his cheeks, creating the illusion of crying. They were tears of blood. He couldn't help but stare at his visage and feel an immediate sense of comfort. He grabbed his cell phone and took a picture of himself, wishing he could look like that forever. The beauty of the thought reduced his anxiety and brought him closer to a place of peace.

With regret, he scooped the blood off his face with his left forefinger, and sucked the warm juices from his thick finger like a child with a melting ice cream cone. He let the blood linger and rejoice in his mouth. With his face cleansed of all traces of fiery red, he looked away from the rear-view mirror and took another long look at the picture of himself in the phone. He sighed in tranquility before calmly driving away, foiled mission erased from his memory.

IDA ARRIVED HOME, SWEATY and invigorated from the morning run. She slipped in the back door, walked down the hallway and stopped outside of Percy's open door. She could hear them playing in the room.

Yoda Percy said, "I hear... a new apprentice you have, Emperor... OR, should I call you, DARTH Sidious?"

Palpatine Chew responded, "Master Yoda... you survived."

"Surprised?" Master Yoda asked.

"Your arrogance blinds you Master Yoda, now you will experience the full power of the dark side," said Palpatine.

Ida peeked in the room to see Palpatine raise his arms at Master Yoda, making lightning strike sounds as Percy flung himself across the room, against the wall, and settle on the bedroom floor, lifeless.

Ida felt it would be a good time to interrupt the battle. "It looks like the dark side won this round."

Immediately, Percy jumped to life. "MOOOUUUMMM! The dark side never wins. The hero always saves the day—right Chew?"

"That's right, Master Yoda. Should I take this one to the Mind Eraser?" Chew said as he grabbed Ida's arm.

Percy gave his mother the deep frown look. "Aaawww, it won't do any good. She has never even seen a Star Wars movie. Girls... sheesh!"

"HEY, that's not true. That Han Solo, now that's what I'm talking about. He's all man," said Ida.

"MMMOOOMMM, HE DOESN'T LIKE GIRLS."

Chew and Ida laughed at their little Yoda. The harmonious affection they had for Percy did not go unnoticed by Ida. After he left, Ida took a shower and found herself sitting on her bed, reflecting on her life. She had worked hard to erase bad memories but somehow, they would find ways to creep up and leave her with a deep sense of sadness. She couldn't help it, she still missed him.

DEMARCO WAS HER HERO. Whenever she was around

him, she always felt safe. There was no better word to describe it. Ida first noticed him when she transferred high schools and went to her first football game. He wasn't the standout running back or quarterback. He wasn't flashy or smooth. He was the defensive player who hit so hard, the crack of football gear striking each other, rose above the chorus of football cheers and cheerleader chants. She found herself attracted to the sheer power in which he played football. The next week, in school, she knew the dominant figure walking down the hall had to be the same football player. It was the way he carried himself. His bearing was so strong, it was palpable. As he walked down the hall, the other students moved out of the way. Except they didn't look scared, it was more like a show of respect. He nodded and high-fived several students but never stopped until he was upon her.

"I apologize, Ms. Ida."

It startled her. She didn't expect him to recognize her existence, let alone call her by name. "Apologize... for what?"

He continued, "I forgot to check my student assignment in the leadership class. I didn't realize they assigned me as your student liaison."

Ida had a quizzical look on her face. "My student liaison?"

"Why yes, ma'am. I have to go now but I surely would like to see you in the library at first lunch." He turned and as he walked away, stated, "name is Demarco. See you there."

He disappeared down the hall while Ida stood frozen, in a rare moment of bewilderment. She wasn't sure what just happened, but it affected something deep within her. One thing she could comprehend... she knew where she was going to have lunch. The rest is history. They became an item and were together non-stop, from that point forward.

Not only was he manly and good-looking but he also had a gentle and funny side. He used to tease her a lot and very importantly, she knew he would be a great father one day. Whenever they were around, children just gravitated toward him. He was like a big, moving, jungle gym. The little kids would climb on him and he would wrestle and play with them for what seemed like hours or until he tuckered them out. She loved watching him interact with children.

Ida always told him he should teach elementary school. It was only then, a flash of weakness in his confidence would emerge, as he felt his grades and intelligence would not carry him to the esteemed position of an educator of children. Of course, Ida felt that was nonsense, he could conquer anything. Everything was so right in her world during that time. For her, she viewed high school as an adventurous opportunity that filled her mind with knowledge and non-stop events in her social calendar. She wasn't your typical student, unsure of life and the future. She knew she was on the right path to achieve her dreams. And with Demarco, he filled the last void making her feel empowered and safe. She saw Demarco as a big, strong furry bear. She would curl up in her furry bear and the world could never hurt her... as long as he held her... forever.

BUT, forever is a big word with a lot of land and life in between. Forever is a dream.

DEMARCO WANTED FOREVER, too. But, he also had a dream, more of an unbreakable conviction. Demarco felt it was his honor bound duty to serve his country. And not even the love of his life could stop him from joining the military and protecting their great home, the United States of America. Ida begged him to go to college with her but he was adamant in serving his country first. He was a loyal American and nothing she said could sway him from his self-proclaimed mission. Little did she know, the sacrifice to his country would involve more than just a tour of duty overseas.

The minute she realized he would not change his mind, she counted down the days to his deployment, and each day found herself more and more reluctant to let him go. She embraced her big, protective bear with a sense of clingy desperation. She found herself using words like "you can't" and "what about us" and "who comes first." They were words meant to evoke guilt and regrettably, they worked on both sides. Through it all, he was patient and kind yet would not change his mind. Finally, it was the day of his deployment when he let her in on a little secret he had carried with him since the day she met him in the school hallway;

There was no student liaison club.

He confessed he noticed her in the stands at the football game and could not stop thinking about her from that day forward. He couldn't wait to go to school the next week and each day walked the halls during breaks until he found her. He said there was not a chance he would take no for an answer if she did not want to date him. He could not explain why but he felt drawn to her the moment he saw her and it would never change. She would never forget that moment. She had never felt more loved in her entire life.

It didn't make his leaving any easier. She went from pure happiness to a curled-up ball of tears as his plane faded from view. If not for the kindness of the Captain, she would have sat in the airport for days, futilely hoping the whole thing was a mistake and her big, strong bear would return home. She was sitting there, a wastebasket full of crumpled up tissues in her lap, when the older, grey-haired man sat down next to her.

"It was so many years ago… yet I remember the scene as if it was yesterday," he said like he was making a quiet announcement to the window in front of him. "I plastered my face against the small window of the plane and I could see my wife, pregnant with our first child, pressed against the glass, just like this glass, in the small airport."

Her head remained sunken, but the tears stopped as her attention became focused on the Captain's words.

"I had never seen that kind of fear in my wife before... ever. It made me doubt everything I was doing and everything I stood for. I wanted to run for the emergency exit and jump out of the plane." He paused as his mind replayed the moment. "I cried, quietly—I didn't want anybody to hear me. And for a moment, I was lost in my sadness. But then, I heard the quiet weeping of other soldiers, just like me. I looked around... and young men all around me... were looking out their own small window at their own loved ones. Each one, lost in a little window of grief and doubt." He stopped talking and sat in silence. He was a comforting presence, a compassionate and dear friend during a time of great need.

"Why then?" Ida whispered.

He sat silent for a moment and let her ponder her own answer. "For me... I have always believed there was something greater that I wanted to be a part of. I felt drawn to serve our country and do my part to protect my friend, my neighbor, my country... and above all else—my family."

She sat there, wrapped in his words. She understood. She knew what kind of man she loved... and she was proud of him. The Captain stood up to leave, and she grabbed his hand. She looked into his warm face. There was no need for verbal words of gratitude. He nodded and softly patted her hand. Ida knew she wasn't alone. We are all in this together.

The first tour seemed like it lasted forever. When Demarco arrived home, he wasn't very different. He was bigger, even more muscular and carried himself with a more powerful presence. She loved him even more and life fell into a steady, happy rhythm. She dreaded the thought of another deployment. But, deployment was unavoidable. He served a second, then a third and finally a fourth tour of duty. Each time, he changed a little more. He grew quieter... darker.

BUT IT WAS his return from his fourth and final tour of duty where the change was immediate and drastic, a change that turned the word "forever" into a forbidden thought in her sealed heart.

CHAPTER 6

 avid Sweeney

DAVID WAS WALKING INTO the Starbucks to buy his daily grande, Caramel Macchiato when he noticed the black Audi pull into the parking lot. The sleek and bold Audi; an immediate symbol of success that he couldn't help but dream of owning one day. He expected to see a middle-aged, balding executive type exit the vehicle but to his surprise, stared at a stunning, mid-30's woman, with flowing black hair and a business type suit that didn't come from Target. He nearly walked into the glass door, fumbling for the handle. He entered, approached the counter and mentally kicked himself. He missed the opportunity to hold the door open for the stunner. He watched as she grabbed the door and pulled it open with ease. She was athletic. He turned away and faced the counter as she entered but could almost feel her breath on the backside of his neck as they waited in line.

"Good morning, David," said Sydney the barista.

"Good morning, Sydney, and aren't you looking even more lovely than yesterday," David said.

She smiled. It was clear she liked the compliment. "Thank you. Now, let me guess... a grande Caramel Macchiato?

"You got it," he said, flashing the charm.

She wrote his name on a coffee cup before wishing him a wonderful day. While waiting to pay the cashier, he heard the stunning woman behind him order one of those fancy drinks you never see on the menu. He stood to the side waiting for someone to call his name and to his surprise, the woman paid for her drink and stood right next to him. Before long, he caught her eye and commented, "do you ever notice, how most of us men walk into Starbucks and order a black coffee or one of the simple drinks on the menu. While women walk in and seem to have some secret Starbucks language, ordering from a different menu?"

She thought for a moment, looked at him and laughed. "You're right about that. I never thought about it before."

David continued, "you know, I've been coming here for five years now and I still haven't made it past the menu on the board. I wonder if that relates to my educational level?" David smiled at her as he attempted to self-deprecate.

"It might, or maybe you know a good thing when you have it," she replied.

He felt pretty good about reading people. Her words sounded flirtatious. He laughed. "My name is..."

She cut him off. "David... and your coffee is ready."

He looked and yes, the coffee was ready. Count on Starbucks to be efficient in their delivery. He sighed internally as he smiled at her, retrieved his macchiato from Joseph and turned back toward the woman. The window evaporated. She had turned away from him, talking on her cell phone.

"Buy 500 if the price drops to 450."

He overheard her words, choosing to believe he wasn't eavesdropping. David lingered for a couple of minutes, pretending to read a local advertisement for a bogo tan at a nearby salon. It was no use. She received her coffee and sat at a table in the corner, staring out the window, heavy in conversation. David left and sat in his truck, staring at the woman's Audi. Whatever success he achieved, he felt dwarfed by this woman. If his guess was right, she was talking about buying stock, and at $450 dollars a share, she was dropping $225,000 on a single purchase.

Is she using her own money?

As he contemplated, he watched as she confidently walked out of the Starbucks with fancy drink in hand and left in her prized vehicle. He sat there for a few more minutes, sipping on his coffee before he realized he would be late for work. And even more dire, miss the beginning of the general manager's meeting.

DAVID ONLY MADE IT a couple of miles before he viewed steam rising through the front hood of his truck. He pulled over and parked, exasperated. He popped the hood and remembered what the oil change guy told him, just last week. He cursed at himself for not listening to the guy. But, how could he? Every time he ever received an oil change, they tried to scam him into buying one thing or the other. He took pride in not being one of the suckers out there. Unfortunately, on this occasion, the oil change guy told the truth. His truck was low on radiator fluid.

As luck would have it, hope wasn't lost. David looked around and of all things, his eyes caught a glimpse of a local auto parts store. As he strode across the street, he felt relieved the mysterious woman in the Audi left first. If not, she may have run across him and his broken vehicle. And how would that look? He bought enough antifreeze to fill his truck and threw the extra fluid in the back of the cab for future use. Once the truck cooled down, he was off and running.

ON ARRIVAL AT WORK, David greeted Constance, the head secretary, with a smile and a wink as he grabbed a file folder off her desk and whisked by, her eyes trailing him. He knew she wanted him. She made no secret of it on many occasions. If the timing was right, he might be interested, but for now, he felt it best to continue with the innocent flirtation.

He walked into the meeting room with a confident swagger. Everybody was there, seated and waiting for his arrival, including the General Manager, Mr. Hashbrack. David pretended not to notice as Mr. Hashbrack adjusted his yellow, round glasses, aligning them to a habitual position of disappointment. David held the file folder with one hand up in the air and dropped it in dramatic fashion onto the board table with a thud. He looked squarely at Mr. Hashbrack.

"I apologize for my tardiness, sir. I had to run back and get this project I'm working on. I haven't figured out all the numbers yet, but I was just too excited to let it wait."

Mr. Hashbrack adjusted his glasses to the more centered, approval position. "Well, arightee' then… let's pass that report around and see what you got."

Without missing a beat, David replied. "Oh… I wouldn't embarrass myself like that Mr. Hashbrack. This file is what I call my chicken scratch. Besides myself, the only one I think could understand my language, is my third grade English teacher… and she wanted to send me back to the second grade." David laughed at himself and noticed Mr. Hashbrack lightening up.

"Please, tell me your idea, David," Mr. Hashbrack encouraged.

"Sir, since we opened our last store, I've been taking some time aside whenever I've had a free moment, to crunch some numbers. Because of the volume of sales in our frozen foods section, I think we can make some immediate changes, which will save our company at least 3% in frozen food costs and open our store up to new growth at the exact same time."

Mr. Hashbrack took a long look at David and leaned forward, lowering his glasses to the best position possible. "Well now... that is interesting. Tell us more."

"Sure," said David. He paused, sharing a confident look amongst the team. "Since we opened our fifth Old General Store, I had Bob here..." and he looked and pointed to his assistant manager Bob, "provide me with our sales in all areas of our frozen section. I then connected with the other stores looking at their inventory and output. Once I finished the rather tedious job of putting it all together, I felt we were able to leverage a better deal with some of our sources." David paused and realized he had everyone's attention, especially Bob's.

Except Bob had a different look on his face. David wasn't sure how to read him. His lips were pursed and his hands, intertwined on top of the table, were clenched tight.

"Basically, we are big enough where we represent a comfortable margin of profit for at least nine of our distributors. I took it upon myself to contact our vendors for each of these companies and with very little leveraging, they have agreed to several modifications to our current contract. These include additional deliveries, increased stock inventory and the icing on the cake." David performed another theater pause. "Currently, five out of nine of these vendors have agreed to stock our frozen food section, using their own employees. The end result—we will need less frozen food space for storage and keep less food on the shelves because they will re-stock on a more frequent basis. Because of this change, we can reduce our own manpower because they will stock our shelves for us." As David finished, he gave his best humble pie look of charm.

The room went silent, waiting for Mr. Hashbrack's reply. He propped his chin on his hand and sat in thought. He looked beyond his glasses. "David... you are one of the main reasons this company is doing so well. That is brilliant... just brilliant!"

David looked on in mock humility while quietly sliding the file folder into his lap, lest someone take an interest and want to look at his "chicken scratch". The meeting went on for another hour with little more fanfare and ended with Mr. Hashbrack requesting David meet for a few minutes after the meeting. As the managers left the office, David couldn't help but notice Bob's cold stare of silence toward him.

What is that all about? I mentioned his name in there, it's not my fault Mr. Hashbrack only commended me, David thought.

When they were alone, Mr. Hashbrack advised David he had been looking for a self-motivated individual as a general manager candidate for the next store. David thanked Mr. Hashbrack for his kind words and stated he would continue to work hard for the company, as he was a very loyal employee. As David left the meeting room, he viewed Bob talking to Constance. He lingered around until Bob walked out of the main office.

David made his move and hovered around her desk, just long enough to slip the file folder back on Constance's desk and place his finger to his lips. She knew David and knew the best thing to do would be to go along with whatever he was planning. David left the office and walked out onto the floor of the big box store. He scanned the aisles of the massive warehouse that sold everything from corn dogs to barbell collars for weight sets. As he finished surveying the entire store, he felt like extending his arms wide, like the place was his for the taking.

One day, this will all be mine.

In the few short years he had been with the company, he had risen from a shipping and receiving grunt to a full-time manager. He believed his success was because of his conviction toward his fellow employees. He felt he bent over backwards for his peers and supervisors and now it was paying off. With the success of each store, there was no doubt further expansion was inevitable. Today's victory, another notch in his belt, putting him closer to the coveted position; General Manager. There was nothing that would stop him from that. From there, part ownership and who knows... maybe even CEO. Why not?

He walked into the bathroom to relieve himself at the urinal and to his unpleasant surprise, Bob walked in and joined him at the next urinal. He tried to focus straight ahead but could feel Bob's glaring stare, burning into him. David wished he wouldn't have consumed so much coffee. The silence broke.

"How could you do that?" Bob asked. The tone felt sharp and hostile.

David turned red. The feeling was so overwhelming and uncomfortable, he zipped up, spraying his underwear and pants with his own urine. "I don't know what you're talking about, Bob," he muttered as he exited the bathroom, never looking at his surprise adversary. He rushed to his office, shut the blinds and locked himself inside, feelings of anger boiling up.

How could Bob treat me like that... I'm his boss... who does he think he is? Does he know who I am?

As the thoughts raced through his head, the anger grew, and David felt the immediate need to find his blue stress ball in the bottom drawer of his desk. He squeezed and squeezed until his anxiety leveled out.

I always treat these guys so well, is this how it is? Is my kindness a sign of weakness? Am I really that weak?

. . .

63

FOR THE NEXT HOUR, he tried to focus on work, but felt an overwhelming urge... a need, to feel better. And he couldn't do it alone. He had to find Valerie. She always made him feel better. She was his confidante ever since Diana left the company. He missed Diana. Whenever he needed to talk to somebody, she was always there. There were many nights, the responsibilities of being the manager would trouble him and Diana would stay after work and comfort him.

He always tried to repay her for her kindness. There were times she called in sick and he covered for her. There were times he helped her out in other ways, too. He remembered the time she didn't have money to pay for some doctor's bills. She had come to him, desperate and frantic for help. The story going around that she was a loose woman and needed to deal with an unwanted pregnancy. This was none of his business. He wanted to help someone in need, so he paid half the bill out of his own pocket.

And then suddenly, Diana disappeared. She didn't call, didn't show up for work and when he finally looked for her at her residence, discovered she had moved out with no forwarding address. It was another incident where he felt, because he showed kindness and weakness, she took advantage of him and he was left holding the bag.

Luckily, not too long after, he met Valerie at a local Taqueria Mercado where she worked as a waitress. Her English was poor at the time, but he felt she would be a good fit for the company, so he talked her into working for him. He knew she was working back in freight and knew she always welcomed a break with him. He texted her and waited for a reply. He opened his door and waited several minutes. He was about to go find her when his phone beeped the reply "ok". He sat back down and waited for her arrival. A few minutes later, she slipped quietly into the office and locked the door behind her. He dropped his blue stress ball into the drawer and closed it. He no longer needed it.

LATER, after she left, he sat in his office, pondering the events of the day. He knew he had to make some changes in his life. It might as well start now.

CHAPTER 7

ert the Spy

JENNY BEGAN WORKING FOR Bert and Gertie when she was 16-years-old. She was thin and fresh-faced with a perpetual smile on her face. Bert liked her from the start. One of his habits, was to stow away in a position where he could watch employees enter the plant. It meant a lot when he would see them entering the plant, relaxed and happy, ready to enjoy another day making ice cream. To Bert, not only was ice cream one of the greatest delicacies ever created but the life of an ice cream maker had granted him and Gertie years of success and happiness. So much so, that he wished every one of his employees could feel the same joy and prosperity.

Jenny's joy for ice cream making was clear from the very first day. On a regular basis, as she exited her car, a pleasurable smile grew on her face. Other employees were keen to point out how much fun they had working with Jenny. Over the years, she had worked in multiple departments and currently occupied one of the most coveted positions in the factory, the enviable role of Flavor Expert.

As a Flavor Expert, Jenny and others had the privilege of daily samplings of ice cream flavors. They were part of a very special, quality control team. The team also met with Gertie, once a month, to sample new flavors and combinations for possible, future brand flavors. Their palates were finely tuned to the subtle nuances of each flavor. Jenny had one of the more famous palates. One of her more well-known quality control discoveries was the time she noticed the slightest change in flavor of a sliver of pistachio found in their pistachio mint ice cream. As it turned out, the batch of nuts were diseased. The ice cream, if manufactured, would have caused stomach distress and discomfort for thousands of pistachio mint ice cream lovers across the country. Instead, Jenny and her team bravely suffered the consequences. They were all proud to be a part of maintaining and protecting the reputation of their ice cream family.

There was one other drawback to this job. If one were not careful, the addition of a few pounds was easy to find. Jenny managed her weight well but found herself a little more rounded over the years. She was the first to tell anyone that would listen; she did not know of any other drawback to the company than a little extra love inside. She was a genuine sweetheart.

With that being said, a few months ago, Bert became focused on Jenny entering the plant because she didn't look the same. She looked different. She looked sad. It took some time and some digging but he finally noticed it—her young daughter, Lulu. Bert had to go back and forth through the Facebook pictures several times to really get it, but he did. In the August photo of Lulu at the park—she had very short, thin blond hair parted to the side with what looked like a small red bow on top.

A few, short months later, on Christmas Day, a picture was posted of Lulu and she had long, blond hair extending down her back. Jenny had taken the picture as Lulu appeared to be walking away from her and Lulu was looking back, sadly. Bert stared at the picture and his heart sank. There was no way the little girl grew her hair that quick. It had to be a wig. He suspected what could be wrong and personally knew the heartbreak Jenny may be feeling.

He typed an email to his secret connection at Abernathy Medical Hospital and a short time later, received the devastating news. Lulu had cancer, the rare and aggressive kind, standard care could not treat. Unfortunately, Abernathy Medical Center did not have the requirements or ability to start experimental therapy. Worse, Bert did some more research and discovered the insurance his company carried would not cover the experimental treatment.

Bert felt heartsick. Could this be true? Is this how it really works? How come nobody can help this little girl? Somebody has to help her. He spent the next hour contemplating life before forcing himself to move on.

HE WENT BACK TO the Facebook news feed. It wasn't long before a random post put a smile across his face. Right there, in the news feed, was a group of his very own employees taking pictures of each other in the plant. It looked like they had taken a romp through a mud field as something covered them in dark brown splotches. They were all laughing and smiling. In one picture, Cindy was slathering what could only be Gertie's Scrumptious Chunk ice cream on Tim's face while unbeknownst to Cindy, there stood Ralph behind her about to cream her with his own handful of chocolate ice cream. Bert couldn't get enough of the pictures and shuffled back and forth through them trying to relive the moment. He giggled with joy as he imagined himself there, slinging his own chunks of ice cream.

He couldn't help himself and buzzed Gertie to share the moment with her. "Gertie, Gertie…" he called on the Nutone.

"Yes, Bert?"

"Did you see Cindy and Ralph and Tim and Sheila and Joy and Jesus and Tashawna and Garrett having a giant ice cream fight?" His words were fast and stuttered. He felt too excited to talk. He should have waited a few minutes to calm down.

"I heard about it Bert… quite a mess they stirred up," she responded. Her words were slow and measured, with no sign of enthusiasm.

"Doesn't it remind you of the good ol' days, Gert?" His words were tinged with hope.

"Now Bert, you need to move on from the good ol' days. I told you that already."

"I just thought you might like it… that's all." With each word, the sound of his voice faded.

"Bert…" she paused, and he could hear a deep sigh. "I need y'all to focus on the future. Can ya' do that for me, Bert?"

"Well, would you have a scoop of Raspberry Burst ice cream with me this evening for old time's sake?" Bert asked.

Another long pause. "I'm leaving in a few minutes, Bert, and besides… you know I can't do that anymore."

Bert stared down at his finger for a long moment as sadness overcame him. He felt like he was standing under a shadow of a large cloud, blocking out the sun. No matter what he did, he couldn't get out from under the dark shadow and feel the warmth and brightness of life. The feeling left him reeling with emptiness. Finally, he pressed the button and said with a heavy sigh, "yes dear."

Who knows if she was still there to hear him? Bert kept his finger on the Nutone button for several minutes before spinning around and staring at the old picture of him and Gertie again. *I don't want to live in the future.* He stared at the picture for at least another hour, thoughts of the past swirling in his head. *I just want my Gertie back... please, God.* He buried his head in his arms and sunk into the desk.

OUT ON THE PLANT FLOOR, in the break room, another conversation was taking place with several of the employees.

"Did y'all hear Bert wants to cancel the company picnic this year?" Renee asked.

"I heard that but I don't know, we've done had the picnic goin' on at least twenty years," replied Ralph.

"Does that mean the bonuses won't be handed out this year, then?" Reginald asked.

"I don't know," said Ralph.

"Well, I don't know about y'all but if they can't pay it this year because of what's goin' on then I don't need it," said Ralph. He got up and threw his paper lunch plate in the recycling bin. "I don't need a picnic to know y'all are family and I sure ain't leavin' this place because I don't get some bonus."

"I'm with you Ralph, but you think there'll be a company much longer with what's goin' on with Bert and Gertie?" Renee asked.

"Reginald, you've been round here the longest. You even know Bert pretty good. Whatt'ya think is gonna happen?" Ralph asked.

"I don't know. I just pray every day. That's all I can do," sighed Reginald.

"You know, I've been here 13 years and I've never even spoken to Bert. How come he won't talk to us Reginald?" Renee asked and before he could answer, she added, "he doesn't like his employees?"

"Bert is a good man. In fact, one of the finest men I've ever met in my life. He's just quiet, that's all."

"Quiet is one thing, ignoring us is another," said Ralph. He paused while swallowing a chocolate chip cookie, whole. "I've been here over twenty years and the only time I ever talked to him was by accident when I saw him walking past my house one day."

"You saw him walking by your house?" Renee asked.

"Yeah, tell him, Tim. You saw him that day, too... or somethin' like it if I remember correctly," said Ralph.

Up to that point, Tim had sat in the corner in silence, eating his lunch, enjoying the company. By nature, he wasn't much of a talker, and it didn't help in Bess, he had one of the most outgoing people in the world. With her around, there was no need to talk. But he was a man well-respected, and if he had something to say, people listened.

"I walked out front with my lawn mower and there he was strolling by like he didn't have a care in the world. Which was strange, because when I asked him, he said he was on his way to walk the trails at Iris Valley Park," said Tim.

"Why is that strange?" Reginald asked.

"Because I live nowhere near Iris Valley Park. Why would he be walking in my neighborhood on his way to walk in the park?"

"That is strange... did you help him?" Renee asked.

"I offered, but he refused... and then just walked away," said Tim. He took another bite of his sandwich.

"That's it?" Renee asked. Her question was too quick. She had to wait as he thoroughly chewed and swallowed the bite of sandwich. He was too much of a gentleman to talk with his mouth full.

"That's it. Something was up—I'm sure of it, but I never figured it out," said Tim.

"I sure didn't," said Ralph.

"Are you still in that house, Tim?" Reginald asked.

"Of course we are—heck, we'll die in that home. It's our dream house. You know how hard it was to get that house? We had to go through five banks before one of them would approve us. And you know what?"

"What?" Ralph asked.

"We've never missed a payment." A rare sign of posterity shown on Tim's face. It wasn't pompous, but he was proud of how hard they had worked to get ahead in life.

THE DAY PASSED QUICKLY as Bert's secretary inundated him with paperwork, some of which he'd never seen before. He sat scratching his head over and over and if not for the help of Barbara, the secretary for Gertie, he would never have completed the odd array of forms, authorizations, bills, etc. It didn't help that Bert was a man of great imagination and short attention span. He found his wandering mind much more pleasing than authorizing such nonsense as a bill for shipping containers or calculating the costs of replacing mop heads.

In fact, he was authorizing a memorandum for the change to their Raspberry Burst Ice Cream packaging when it reminded him of the incident that created the name. It was years earlier and Gertie had just about nailed down the recipe for a delicious raspberry ice cream. However, as much as she tried, she kept ending up with different tasting ice cream with each batch. Now to the average person, the taste difference was negligible. But to Gertie's keen sense of smell and taste, the difference was entirely unacceptable.

A little investigative questioning and she discovered Bert had been picking raspberries from two different farms, one on the west side of town and one on the east side. Why? Good question and nobody, not even Bert, could answer that one. Just one thing he liked to do. So, they scheduled an afternoon to visit both raspberry-picking places. Their first stop was the west end farm. It took Gertie only two hand-picked raspberries to confirm the west end farm, was the culprit for her distasteful batches of ice cream.

However, Bert convinced her to drive to the east end farm, just to make sure. Secretly, he loved the farm and the old goat that ran it was more than a hoot... that was for sure. The farm was down a long-ago carved, dirt road in poor shape that more than likely felled more than its share of automobiles over the years. When they arrived at the farm, Gertie could see the farm wasn't much better off. The house was a typical two-story ranch house, white, with a wrap-around porch. The boards on the porch were dried out, cracked and unsafe to set even a rocking chair. The roof had undergone multiple patch jobs and was more than ready for a complete overhaul. One section even had a blue tarp covering it. Yet, the house had the charm of history on its side and one could tell it was a beauty in disguise.

Bert led Gertie to the side of the house where a bell hung. He rang the bell once and stood next to it. Nothing happened. After a few minutes he rang the bell again and stood by it. Nothing happened. It was on the third ring, Gertie did not notice Bert lowering himself and sitting on the ground, against the wall of the wrap-around porch. Several minutes passed and just as she was moving into position to ring the bell a fourth time, she heard the distinct voice of an older gentleman, yelling from inside the screen door.

"WHAT! YOU THINK I'M DEAF? GIT YER HANDS OFF MUH BELL!"

The screen door opened, and a curmudgeonly old coot came shuffling out, one suspender hanging by his side, wearing wool trousers and a red checkered, long sleeve shirt that looked as old as dirt. He looked down at Gertie with a steel glint in his eye. "Darnation woman, a man shouldn't be disturbed when he's tendin' to his mornin' constitution. Now git off my property!"

It startled Gertie, she turned and walked a few steps toward their truck. But, the shock wore off, and the spunky attitude of

Gertie emerged. She turned back to face the old coot. "I shall do no such thing, Sir. Now you speak to me as a gentleman or I'm not leaving!"

The old coot turned red in the face and shook his fist at the gumption of this young, rude woman. "I said... GIT OFF MUH PROPERTY... NOW!"

She didn't move a muscle, eyes locked on the old farmer. The most epic of stare downs and Bert with the best seat in the house. Or so he thought... because after a couple of tense minutes, Gertie dropped her gaze down to him... and Bert knew that look. Regrettably, he stood up and positioned himself so the old coot could see him.

"What in... didn't I kick you off muh farm last week?" The old coot said to Bert.

Bert shrugged. "Yes, sir... but it was after I bought them delicious raspberries you sold me."

The old coot stared a good long stare at Bert. "Y'all need to teach your woman to speak her mind whilst sitting alone... in a closet somewheres. Now git your raspberries and leave muh money in the bucket." The old coot turned around and shuffled back into the house, all the while muttering, "darnation youngun's. Got no manners these days."

Bert was turning toward Gertie when he received the slap upside the head. "Bert Abernathy. You knew what you were doing... didn't you?" Bert sheepishly looked up at Gertie and a smile crossed his face. Gertie furnished a good hard stare and then they laughed all the way to the barn.

The barn was red, weathered and held together by the efficiency of laboring men who took pride in their daily work, a trait often lacking in today's cookie-cutter housing for maximum profit mindset. As a matter of fact, everything about the house and barn looked old with only patches of repairs when necessary. There were no signs of modern conveniences, tools or farm equipment. It held its place in time and one could see why Bert loved the place. Just inside the barn doors sat an old wooden, berry crate, along the wall. Inside the crate, were perhaps thirty small, wooden baskets. Each one, stained with fruit from years of picking duty.

Bert gave Gertie two of the baskets and ambitiously stacked six, for his picking plans. He smiled, as the simple thought of spending an afternoon picking berries with his wife, brought him an immediate sense of bliss. The berry patch was located a good distance from the house, so they loaded up in Bert's truck and drove there. Along the way, lay barren fields of earth, once used to grow rows and rows of green leafy plants, colorful vegetables and succulent fruit. Now, Mother Nature had reclaimed the land with prairie grass, weeds, and wildflowers.

"Gertie, can you imagine what an amazing place this must have been when the fields were tilled and plants and vegetables were springing to life?" Bert asked as they drove to the berry patch.

"I can... this is a wonderful place, Bert. I can see why you wanted me to come here. Thank you." She squeezed his hand.

Bert pulled up to the field of raspberries and it was amazing. Rows and rows of raspberries, plump, juicy and red, begging for harvest. The old coot had long ago lost his ability to keep up the farm but Mother Nature had not and her hand blessed the grounds with an abundance of thriving, juicy raspberries.

Bert watched Gertie's eyes light up as she carefully examined row after row of raspberries. Her enthusiasm made him feel good inside. Finally, she grabbed his hand and dragged him excitedly to a patch of floricanes planted north to south and agreeable to the afternoon shade from the large overgrown neighbor of trees. She zeroed in on one particular bush and picked a ripe, red berry and popped it into her mouth. She closed her eyes, savored the fresh taste and a deep smile emerged.

It was picking time.

She started on one side and Bert started on the other. With Gertie, it wasn't long before the harvesting became a race to the end of the row and the casual picking became a serious affair. To make it even more fun and check the taste of each plant, they had to eat at least one raspberry from each plant as they were picking. The pace grew fast and furious as they worked their way down the row, with one or the other offering a well-timed butt bump. All is fair in love and war.

They arrived at the end of the row with Gertie edging out Bert by a bush. She raised her hands in the air and turned to Bert. He looked and her cheeks were swollen twice their size with raspberry juice escaping down one side of her mouth. She looked like the happiest chipmunk that just found the biggest acorn in the woods. Bert snorted heartily as Gertie fought to contain her laughter. Bert saw an opportunity and imitated the body language of the old coot, while repeating, "darnation woman!"

Gertie couldn't hold it in any longer and the berries burst from her mouth as she exploded with laughter. Bert became the unintended recipient of a spray of raspberries and juice, splattered handsomely in the face and chest. Immediately, she regretted her unladylike response, covered her mouth albeit a little too late and froze. Bert wiped a sizable chunk off his brow and swatted it to the ground, looking at Gertie. He was a splattered mess of dripping berries and splotchy color... his white shirt a most certain poor choice for raspberry picking.

She looked at him and they both just laughed and laughed. Finally, she gave him a kiss on his forehead and they went back to their picking, this time at a more leisurely pace. When it came time to name their ice cream, Raspberry Burst seemed like the perfect fit. Even better, every time someone inquired as to the name's origin, Bert and Gertie giggled with their little secret.

The raspberry picking became an annual ritual for several

years until the old, flavorful coot passed away and the new owner established his reputation as a not so friendly person. As much as they begged, the new owner would not let them on his property. He even told Gertie on one occasion, he was real fond of shooting bothersome critters. It was probably something you shouldn't tell a woman of her nature. Gertie did not forget that remark.

It was years later, when success had crossed their doorstep, that Gertie planned a special surprise trip to that same farm.

She heard the cranky owner was trying to replace a large beam by himself, seeing as how nobody would help him, and had dropped the beam onto his leg. It shattered in several places. The end result being his inability to continue maintaining the farm, in the poor manner it had become accustomed to under his care.

Gertie, unbeknownst to Bert, personally negotiated with the owner and his attorney, purchasing the farm for mere pennies on the dollar. As a way of saying thanks, she had a painting done of a deer holding a shotgun. Interestingly, the barrel pointed at a man who looked a lot like the former owner. The caption above the deer read 'Get off muh property!' The former owner did not appear to be all that keen of the special gift.

Gertie hired a caretaker family for the farm and immediately put a plan in place to bring the farm back to its original glory. She checked on the progress of the farm every chance she had, checking in while under the premise of "shopping" excursions with the ladies, Bert failing to notice she never brought home any new items.

It was a good two years later when the special trip to the farm arrived. Bert had been asking Gertie for a week why she was so "jumpity" as she could barely contain her secret. As they drove to the farm, it challenged Bert's memory, as the surroundings looked familiar but the newly paved road off the main highway did not. The freshly painted wooden fencing along the side of the road did not look familiar, either. He could see the house in the distance and as they drew closer, his memory rustled up some fond images. However, it wasn't until he saw the roadside sign, he knew just what Gertie had up her sleeve. The tears flowed the minute he read the large wooden sign, 'Bert's Raspberry Farm' next to the driveway.

All he could muster was a whisper under his breath, "Gertie" and embrace her across the seat of his truck. He had no words to describe the happiness inside of him.

They spent hours at the farm with Gertie going over every minute detail of the restoration of the house, the barn and the rest of the farm. She felt so proud and so happy for Bert. They concluded the visit with a huge outdoor meal at the picnic table built for twenty under the big old Oak. Bert and Gertie ate dinner with the caretaker family, and they finished the meal with a granny smith apple pie topped with a healthy scoop of Raspberry Burst ice cream.

BERT NEVER FELT SO comfortable in his life than that day... that is, of course... after he loosened up his belt a notch or two. It was a show of love Bert would never forget.

CHAPTER 8

 Bess Party

BESS STOOD ON THE 17th tee box, a long par 3 over "water" to a two-tiered green fronting back to front. The hole was famous for gobbling balls and nearly swallowing golfers whole, whoever dare come close to its murky waters... no known golf balls ever rescued from its grasp.

The last golfer that lost his balance and stepped backward into the water was quickly swallowed up to his chest in quicksand like muck and if not for his partner pulling him to safety with a sand wedge, who knows how deep the tipsy golfer would have sunk to a black, murky death. Bess and Tim knew the hole very well as they lived in the golf course community and the hole was only a short walk from their home.

It was a miracle, they lived in such a nice neighborhood. They were renting a two-bedroom, one-bath ranch on the outskirts of Iris Valley, when they found out about the new golf course community being built in a prime location in Iris Valley.

Try as they might, bank after bank turned down their request for a mortgage loan. It was heartbreaking. Then, out of nowhere, the bank they kept their meager amount of savings in, called and said they changed their mind and would finance their mortgage. Tim and Bess had never heard of a bank calling people to express a change of heart, so they went to the bank and addressed the lender. They were advised the builder of the new golf community wanted to close out his sales and move on to his next project. Somehow, their name came up, and the bank wanted to help them. Before they knew it, they were in a home they never dreamed of owning in a million years. The whole thing was a blur; sign here, sign there, sign everywhere. Tim and Bess didn't know what to think but had a deep faith in karma and just went with it. They never found out how and why they were chosen to receive the deal of a lifetime. It was a true blessing for their growing family.

On the first day at their new home, they met Ralph, who later became affectionately known as Cannonball Ralph. He was a large, friendly man who told Tim and Bess he developed his girth from the love of the greatest job on Earth. He was a flavor expert at Gertie's ice cream plant. It was Ralph who sponsored Tim's employment into the ice cream business. Prior to that, Tim repaired cars at a restoration shop. He took great pride in his work, but it was long hours and it really wasn't for him. Coincidentally, he was part of the team that restored Bert's treasured pickup truck.

So here they were, living down the street from a beautiful par-three hole. It was a dream come true and there was not a chance Bess would not take advantage of the new, wonderful living environment. Many an evening, they would walk down with their children and practice on the hole. Once in a while, a golf cart ranger would come around and watch their play. Normally, a person would be kicked off the course for trespassing, but in Bess's case, she had long ago bribed Gerald the ranger with her old-fashioned oatmeal cookies and Fred the ranger with her triple berry pie. Anybody else that came along knew the score; accept Bess's delicious delights and let her play the hole or... let her play the hole. Either way, nobody was kicking Bess off the golf course. It was an unspoken rule handed down over several years.

In all the years, Bess had never hit one in the "tar pit" and had no plans for such nonsense, today. She looked at the green with the pin cut center and viewed her husband Tim's ball twenty feet from the cup, a great shot by any standard.

"Go ahead Bess, you can do it. Don't worry about the big, black, ugly, huge tar-pit. I know you can do it," mocked Tim in fake encouragement as he awaited her shot. Tim was brimming with excitement because it had been several years since he had beat his wife in a round of golf and here they were... at the seventeenth hole and tied in the match. Even better, his ball was in a great position to snag a birdie and go at least one up into the last hole.

She responded with her usual hearty laugh and for good measure, not only waggled her club but gave him a good waggle of her behind as well. He smiled and knew he couldn't shake her. Bess took one last look at the hole, zeroed in her focus and swung away with complete abandon. It was a sure representation of her zest for life. She had an unusually fluid swing for a woman of her size and coupled with her confidence, enabled her to surprise most people who challenged her to a match. Tim had played with Bess enough and was not surprised when she stuck her shot inside of his own ball, coming to rest only six feet from the hole.

Ooohhh, here it comes, he thought.

When she was done admiring her handiwork, she turned to Tim and tossed her club to her new "caddie" and followed with the infamous Bess swagger back to the cart.

God, I love her. She is something else, he thought.

He cleaned her hybrid iron, returned it to her bag and sat down in the driver's seat of the golf cart next to her. Before he could come up with something clever to say she drawled, "proceed James."

We all know how it ended, Tim missed his birdie putt and Bess poured hers in, destroying any chance he had of finally beating his highly competitive wife. She laughed with joy as the putt dropped into the cup and followed that up with a good smack to Tim's behind as he bent over to scoop her ball out of the hole.

The humiliation, he thought and laughed. Only Bess.

They finished the round with Tim listening to Bess give him the needle and took the short drive from the clubhouse to their home. On arrival, she gave Tim a hearty kiss and then pronounced she would always love him, even if he was a horrible, shameful and downtrodden wannabe golfer. She had a way with words.

IT WAS TIME TO ready for the afternoon pool party and barbecue. They walked into a house full of busy bees. Emma looked up from vacuuming the living room, nodded and playfully ran the vacuum at Bess. Cheese was picking up toys scattered throughout the house. Tyler was outside blowing the leaves from the pool deck. The rest of the children... Katherine, Matt, John and Tommy were on bathroom and bedroom duties.

Everybody moved in synchronicity as Bess had parties just about every weekend to celebrate just about anything. Bess loved people, people loved Bess and the more the merrier. The house of Bess was always moving, always busy and never alone. Bess had a thing about being alone and long ago had decided she would never be alone again. She needed to be close to people and fortunately, people needed her. Her huge heart was filled with an all-consuming warmth and felt immediately by anybody that spent more than a moment with her.

When Cheese saw her father, she looked at him and immediately gave the thumbs up sign. He smiled and gave her the thumbs down sign. She responded by squatting and pretending to go number two.

BESS, he screamed in his head.

Outplayed again, his wife had already taught their smallest child how to stick it to him. Knowing he met his match in his wife, he responded by posing in his own poop stance with a sad face and nodding head. Cheese giggled at her funny daddy before continuing her wanderings, picking up loose toys.

Tim headed out to the backyard behind the garage and the scent of smoked meats provided the symphony of smell he was expecting. He was up at four in the morning loading his secret recipe ribs into their large smoker and the payoff was almost here. A couple more hours and the ribs would be falling off the bone and melting in the mouth of cherished family and friends. He went into the garage and grabbed an ice-cold Sam Adams from the refrigerator. As he walked toward the back of the garage, he looked up at the sun. It was going to be a great day. He found his favorite chair and settled in.

Years ago, he set up his own cooking zone with a zero-gravity chair, umbrella and outdoor pillow, which sat in the backyard's corner. From there, he could see the pool, the kids playing and watch his smoker and barbecue grill. It was his special spot. Nobody sat there, nobody in his family and not even Bess. Even his guests respected his space. He sunk deeper into the chair and watched the wafts of delicious smoke rise into the air. His eyes soon grew heavy, and he was fast asleep.

Tim woke up to the feeling of water splashing on him. He groggily looked towards the pool and Ralph, their 300lb. neighbor, surfaced from under the water with a big grin on his face.

Yes, Cannonball Ralph struck again.

Tim sat up. "I tell you what Ralph. One day, I'm going to eat all these delicious ribs myself and when I get up to about 350, I'm going to pay a visit to your bathtub." Tim gave him a mock look of sincerity.

Ralph laughed and responded, "I don't think that's going to happen anytime soon, Tim. Why, I'm looking at you right now and you couldn't be more than a buck 50 soaking wet." With that, he turned and swam away doing his best imitation of a languid manatee.

Tim smiled again and looking around, realized the afternoon's barbecue was in full swing. It wasn't uncommon for Tim to wake up to a house full of guests. He was a hard-working husband and father and with his limited education found the need to work two jobs to meet the demands of his large family. It was a sacrifice he accepted, and he never felt sorry for his position. Like Bess, he looked around and felt filled by the love of his family and friends. Unlike Bess, he was quieter about his feelings and demeanor but everyone knew Tim was a committed, heartfelt person.

He looked deeper into the pool and there was Bess mowing over several sacrificial children as she drove toward the pool basketball net for one of her power dunks. With great merriment, children bounced off her as they tried to tackle, climb, trip and swipe the ball from her grasp. She returned the attempts with gentle stiff arms, hip bumps, body shakes, twists and turns. There was no stopping her.

Looking past her, he really wondered how long he had been sleeping because the party was in full swing, with at least 30 guests milled around the pool area. Several people were even holding empty plates in their hands or their laps as they sat in a motley assembly of chairs, waiting for the dinner bell.

As Tim continued to look around and soak up the scene, he noticed Emma sitting alone under the eave of the unattached garage. She had a look of sadness on her face and did not seem to even notice the guests swirling around her. He studied her for a moment and felt the look demanded some attention. He waded his way past the pool splashes, the hellos and the assorted greetings. He was within a few feet of Emma when Ralph enveloped the space in front of him with a big, quizzical look.

"Tim, now I know you can smell those ribs of yours... where you going?" He took a great sniff of air as he put his arm around Tim's shoulder and nudged him in the correct direction. "You need some help with taking them out?"

Tim turned back towards the smoker, took one long inhalation through his nose and realized Ralph was right. The ribs were ready. He looked around and knew his guests were anxiously awaiting the bell for lunch. He looked past Ralph at Emma, hesitated for a moment and decided he would talk with her later when it was more private. On the back corner of his garage, he had an old-fashioned dinner bell hanging from the wall. Per tradition, he was the official bell-ringer. He grabbed the rope and pulled hard. He enjoyed doing it. It was his moment. The attention he needed. The crowd roared their approval. It was no surprise, waiting first in line, was none other than Cannonball Ralph.

Later, once things settled down, Dr. Welborough sat down next to Tim with a full plate of ribs, sauce dripping off the sides of the plate onto the concrete driveway. "I tell you, every time I come here it gets harder and harder to find a seat in this place," he said to Tim. He used his finger to wipe the side of his plate and added, "you should think about a reservation system."

Tim smiled as he put down a gnawed rib of his own. "Yeah, we are pretty blessed."

"Tim... did Bess tell you she was in my office the other day?" Dr. Welborough asked.

"She did. She said there was nothing out of the ordinary going on. Why do you ask?" Tim responded.

"I guess, in a way, she was telling the truth," said Dr. Welborough.

Tim didn't like what he saw in Dr. Welborough's face. "What's going on, Doc?"

Dr. Welborough paused for a moment while he wiped his hands with a napkin. When he was done, he shifted in his seat so he faced Tim. "She's not doing very well, Tim. Her blood pressure is through the roof. She has a higher level of insulin output, which indicates entry into a diabetes problem." Dr.Welborough sighed as he watched Bess for a moment, busy entertaining a small group of friends near the pool. "She has already had one heart catheterization. The medication can only do so much if she is unwilling to follow a healthy lifestyle."

Tim sat and stared at the ground. He was a simple man and problems like these were hard for him to digest. He had talked to Bess, begged and pleaded with her to work on a healthier lifestyle. However, food was Bess and Bess was food.

"I will talk to her, Doc. I just don't know if she can do it. Bess loves food too much," said Tim.

"We all love Bess. Do what you can Tim and I will try my best too," said Dr. Welborough as he put his arm around Tim.

"Okay Doc... thanks," said Tim with a sigh as his shoulders sunk down.

THEY FINISHED UP THEIR conversation just in time as one of the epic battles in history was shaping up in the nearby pool. One could only guess where Cannonball Ralph developed the courage to face Bess in an epic water basketball match... the likes of which had never been seen before. Perhaps it was the mile-high plate of ribs, three cobs of corn and half a dozen buttermilk biscuits that gave him the gumption and reserve to take on the undefeated Bess in all her greatness. Perhaps it was just a fool's dream. Either way, someone threw the challenge down and the pool cleared, lest the innocent fall as collateral damage in the quest for the righteous title of Ruler of the Pool.

Kids scrambled for the best seats in the house... the courtside seats just outside of the pool behind the basketball net. Tim viewed a couple of the moms rubbing Bess's back as if she was a prizefighter about to enter the ring. Dads were standing off to the side, scrambling to find money in their wife's purses or their own pockets. They chose Dr. Welborough as the most honest man to hold all the bets and it looked like the match was about dead even at the bell.

Bess was all business right away as she faced off in front of Cannonball Ralph. The visitor enjoyed first possession and Bess sent a message right away. She pretended she was going to hand the ball to Ralph, instead bouncing the rubber ball off his forehead and back into her hands. The crowd laughed with approval just above the roar of Bess's own mischievous guffaw.

However, when she settled down, Ralph was more than ready. No sooner than she tossed the ball back to him, then Ralph charged forward and right. Bess took the bait and tried to lunge his way, finding herself off-balance. Ralph was waiting for this and cut back, giving her a big, hairy, belly bump. Bess was caught off-guard and fell backwards sending a small tidal wave of water over the side of the pool and onto the strategically positioned children.

As Bess worked to regain her footing, Ralph casually waded up and waited to dunk for the first score until Bess surfaced from under the water.

Tim noticed the look on Bess's face and chuckled to himself. There would be no need for him to exact revenge on Cannonball Ralph for splashing him earlier because his wife was going to provide Ralph with a lesson he would remember for a long, long time.

Ralph and Bess squared off again with possession belonging to Bess. He looked at her and felt a little sheepish for his aggressive behavior in his host's pool. Not to mention, he knew Bess's reputation and could see... he woke the beast. Bess started forward and turned sideways into Ralph. With live elbows, she pushed her way forward then suddenly fell back. She lobbed a shot for a perfect swish into the net as she fell into the water. The kids went crazy and the parents betting on Bess cheered with delight.

And so they went... back and forth.

They were two gladiators showing uncommon agility and grit, neither one willing to accept the inevitable loss. Finally, the game came down to one last point. Ralph and Bess were tied with possession belonging to Ralph. One more basket and he would be the new Ruler of the Pool. As Bess was positioning herself in front of Ralph, he couldn't help but glance at the large chair at the head of the pool. The chair Bess had governed over countless volleyball, Marco Polo and basketball games over the years. He was one point away from the coveted chair.

He knew what he was going to do, it worked before and it would work again. He would run the same play as the very first one, the Triple B. He had not used it again the entire game and she would never see it coming. Bess settled into her position like an indomitable mountain. Nothing would pass through her watch. Ralph might as well zip himself into a body bag and save hassling others with the task. Warily, she tossed the ball to Ralph, and he sprung forward and to the right, like a leopard pouncing on his prey; albeit a rather large male leopard who looked like they swallowed a hot-air balloon.

Bess took the bait and lunged in the same direction. Ralph turned back and sent the mightiest of belly bumps her way... only to find air as she expected the copycat move and side-stepped. The weight of his mighty belly sent him uncontrollably forward and as he fell face forward into the water, he threw up a last-ditch Hail Mary in the direction of the basket. The shot was nearly perfect, a miracle in the making. But alas, the ball struck the backboard, the rim and by the tiniest of margins, slid off the side into the water.

Ralph emerged, with false hope in his heart, only to be greeted with the smug smile of Bess... The Cannonball Killer. She turned away and went to her starting position for her own attempt at a victory. Ralph wasn't done. Oh no, he didn't come this far to lose the crown. He summoned the memories of his college football years and with a grind of his teeth and a growl from the depths of his soul, readied himself in front of Bess like an all-star lineman on Super Bowl Sunday. A hush fell over the crowd, the excitement over the intensity of the battle creating a fever of energy.

Ralph tossed the ball to Bess, and she returned the favor by charging right at him like a mad rhino. He braced himself and they collided, sending an aftershock of water in all directions to the delight of the crowd. He lost very little ground during the first exchange and bumped her back to almost the same starting position. Both would not give up their position and charged each other. It was like watching the two greatest Sumo wrestlers in the world exercising their craft in a turbulent ocean.

Finally, after several exchanges they retreated from each other a few steps, gasping for air. The crowd squeezed in as they sensed the battle had reached a turning point. Bess regained her steely composition and looked beyond Ralph to the net. Ralph took one more deep breath and settled into his impenetrable stance. Bess charged. As she approached Ralph, she suddenly jumped. To a fault, witnesses recalling that day swear she didn't jump... she flew.

Her body broke the surface like a hungry, great white shark lunging for a doomed seal. Bess towered up and over Ralph with her ample bosom devouring the top of Ralph's head and sending him reeling backwards into the farthest depths of the pool. She came crashing down on top of him and as she entered the water, sent her own Hail Mary to the gates of heaven for entry.

BOTH RALPH and Bess surfaced to the sounds of a crowd gone wild, witness to one of the greatest sports matches ever held... with the reigning champion due her seat on the throne.

CHAPTER 9

 oberta's Lucky Day

ROBERTA CONTINUED ON HER path to work while listening to her favorite oldie's radio station, led by the eternally gorgeous, Duke of Disco.

"All right listeners, we already gave you a clue to our next challenge. Here's the trivia question of the day… we all know John Travolta starred in the movie, Staying Alive… but… who wrote and directed the movie? Ok listeners, we're going to take the tenth caller. Good luck!" He blasted off.

"Siri, call the Duke of Disco right now," called out Roberta to her phone pal.

As Siri dialed, the next song, titled Eyes of the Tiger by Survivor started to play on the radio and Roberta immediately knew she had the right answer. She dropped her hand from the two-position and cranked up the song as she hopefully waited for the Duke on the other line.

The song came to an end and no sooner than she turned the

radio down, she heard the familiar sound of the Duke himself—
ON HER CELL PHONE.

She quietly squealed in delight as he came alive on her
phone. "Congratulations, you have reached the one and only
Duke of Disco, delight the audience and give me your name,
lucky caller number 10."

"My name is Roberta and I've been a fan of yours well over
20 years now," Roberta stated excitedly.

"Well, I don't know how that's possible darlin', you don't
sound a bit over 25."

"Oh Duke, you shouldn't be charmin' an old broad like me
unless you mean to follow through," said Roberta.

"Now, if you've been a listener for a long time, you know
what instruments I like to play with, darlin'."

"I do… and if y'all ever get tired of playing with that little ol'
woodwind section, I have the string, brass and percussion
sections just waitin' to create our own symphony," said Roberta.

The listeners heard the Duke start chuckling at the boldness
of this special lady and after a pause he replied. "Well, I bet you
would little lady… I bet you would. All right, now let's get down
to business… the trivia question of the day. Who wrote and
directed the moving Staying Alive? Do you have the answer,
sweet Roberta?"

"I sure do, Duke, the answer is Sylvester Stallone," she
responded confidently.

"Congratulations Roberta, you are most certainly right!"

She again quietly squealed in delight at her good fortune.

The Duke continued, "you my darlin' have won one of our
more unique and exciting prizes of the day. We are going to
send you on an adventure you won't soon forget… an all-
expenses paid adventure to Robert's Swampland, where y'all
come face to face with nature in all its glory. Why, y'all see birds
and reptiles, coral snakes and green sea turtles and most
exciting of all… speed through the wilds of the Everglades with

your own personal airboat tour guide. And you know what you're going to face? The infamous el legarto... better known as the Florida alligator. Now how does that sound to you, Roberta? Are you game for a little adventure?"

"I sure am Duke. I always wanted to go on one of those airboat rides," Roberta responded.

"Well, good luck to you, thanks for being one of my greatest fans and don't forget to stay on the line after I hang up to get your prize. Best wishes Darlin'."

"Best wishes to you too, Duke. And don't forget my offer."

"Oh, I don't think I'll be forgetting you anytime soon darlin'. That's for sure," he said as he chuckled and hung up. "Well, there you have it folks, the ol' Duke thinking about the string section for the first time in a long, long time. Bless that charmer, Roberta," said the Duke into the radio before the next song started its track.

Before Roberta could even wrap up the details of her prize with Duke's staff, she was hit with a text message from her dear friend Bess;

YOU ARE ONE SAUCY GRANDMA. Luv you gal

ROBERTA SMILED as she returned to ten and two on the steering wheel to complete her journey to work, without a care in the world. She pulled into the employee parking lot at Abernathy Medical Center with a fond wave from Joe the guard. At first, her routine was the same. Grab a coffee, greet her co-workers, examine the patient charts and prepare for rounds. But, she wasn't at work for long in the ICU unit when she knew word had spread of her good fortune. Indeed, Roberta was a saucy woman. She liked sass, a good joke, and she liked a flare for boldness. What she didn't like, was political correctness. At her stage of the game, she felt she didn't have time to tell it any other way, then up front and honest. Everyone knew her and everyone loved her, even though at times, the truth could be painful. Roberta had been a nurse longer than some residents were alive. It wasn't the doctors who ran the ICU. It was Roberta. And she ran it with selfless devotion and tireless efforts where she expected everyone to pitch in to care for patients and see them to recovery.

There was only one short moment in her career where she faltered and she swore it would never happen again. It was the roughest personal period in her life, but she refused to allow that to be an excuse. Her behavior was inexcusable and the lesson she learned that straightened her out was one of the best lessons of her life. So, Roberta held herself to a very high standard and demanded the same from everybody else.

As such, it was more of an honor to be derailed by Roberta than a disappointment. As intelligent as the doctors were, they were no match for her sharp wit and humor. So, when a rare opening presented itself, the doctors took great joy in teasing her. And by no surprise, Dr. Lee Cassidy was the first one of the day to give it to her.

Dr. Lee Cassidy was notoriously known for picking the cream of the crop of good looking, young, stud-like men. Roberta had no problem accusing Dr. Lee Cassidy of picking his men, absent of any quantifiable I.Q. In reality, Dr. Cassidy was charming, good-looking and definitely going places. In other words, he had no problem attracting potential mates.

Roberta was quietly talking to Stan, one of her patients recovering from cancer surgery, when Dr. Cassidy walked in, holding a rolled-up piece of paper. One end was in his mouth and the body held like that of a golden flute. Dr. Cassidy said nothing, as he hummed the sounds of a tune on his paper flute, floating around the room.

Roberta looked at him sideways and let him enjoy the

moment. After a couple of twirls, Dr. Cassidy settled in on Stan and inquired on his health.

After getting the all-thumbs up from one hand while Roberta sat bedside and held his other hand, the good Dr. Cassidy asked his weathered patient, "Stan, do you play any musical instruments?"

"I used to play a pretty mean piano back in the day," replied Stan.

Dr. Cassidy continued. "Yeah, I pretty much have stuck to the woodwind instruments my whole life, like this flute here. Sometimes I'll switch though and play with one of my bigger woodwinds like an English horn. And if I really need the music to fill me up—I might even try a saxophone." A smirk spread across his face.

The straight-faced Stan responded with pure innocence, "you know... I always thought about playing the Saxophone but with my lung problems, I never thought I could blow hard enough."

With that, Dr. Cassidy turned away and essentially keeled over in a wheezing hysterical fit as he tried to mask his laughter with fake coughing. Roberta turned her head down, away from Stan, summoning everything in her to keep from losing it with the mischievous doctor.

When the good doctor recovered, he returned to his normal upright position and looked at Roberta. "How about you Roberta, would you like to try my flute?"

Roberta never missed a beat. "I doubt I would ever be interested in your flute, Dr. Cassidy. I pretty much favor a Bassoon as my woodwind of choice." And as she said it, she stared directly at his belt line.

"Oh my..." Dr. Cassidy responded, and the rest of the words were lost as he sheepishly turned away and exited her patient's room.

She called after him loud enough for the desk staff to hear, "good day, Dr. Cassidy. Nice to see you and your little flute."

She turned back to Stan as he asked her, "Roberta, do you think with my new lung, I might be able to play the saxophone one day?"

She smiled and while caressing his hand responded, "these days you never know Stan... you never know."

Roberta left Stan when he fell into a relaxed state of much needed sleep. Roberta knew the secret for Stan and most, if not all of her patients. All Stan needed was a true moment of compassion and care to alleviate the fear and anxiety in his heart. There were very few people Roberta ever met that could lie in a hospital bed and feel right at home, healthy and safe. She more than understood the fear a patient feels in the uncertainty of their own health. The immense trust that must be created to allow strangers to physically invade their bodies around the clock and the realization that life is a blessing. Each day may bring gifts of joy and happiness or gifts of heartache, pain and even death. Unfortunately, for most people, it is only when death is knocking at the door do they ever pause and smell the flowers.

Roberta completed her morning rounds with a visit to sweet, little old Elaine. For the past week, Elaine had ever so politely indicated her pillow was too hard and she could not sleep. Each shift, Roberta had searched high and low for just the right pillow. After a week of trying to no avail, she switched her strategy and took an existing pillow, stuffed it with three large bags of cotton balls and sealed the end so they wouldn't tumble out. She walked in and immediately saw the results. Elaine was sitting up in her bed for the first time, with a look of a person who gave Rip Van Winkle a run for his money. She smiled at Roberta and motioned her bedside. Roberta asked her if she needed anything and Elaine insisted she come closer. Roberta bent over and Elaine gave her a kiss on the cheek, usually reserved for the best of grandchildren. It was a heartfelt moment and the reason Roberta would never stop being a nurse.

ROBERTA LEFT A SHORT time later and headed to the cafeteria to meet her friend, Bess. On the way, she was ambushed by Dr. Joe in the service elevator and Calvin from maintenance. Both of them heard the exchange on the radio and gave her the needle. She returned in kind as only she could do.

In the cafeteria, she picked up a Cobb salad, a peach iced tea and a well-deserved double, chocolate-chip cookie and sat down with Bess. "Thanks for coming down to meet me for lunch."

"Good afternoon Ms. Sassy," chimed Bess with a sly grin.

"Yeah, yeah, yeah. Go ahead and give it to me," said Roberta.

"I don't need to give it to you. From what I hear around this place, you've been getting it good all day," said Bess and laughed. Roberta couldn't help but laugh at the folly of it all, too.

"When are you going to go down and experience this great swamp adventure?" Bess asked.

Roberta responded, "I know... right. Only I would win an all-expense paid trip to a swamp. Couldn't have been St. Croix, Hawaii or even a trip to Branson, Missouri. I guess it fits my personality."

They talked a bit longer on the subject when Bess remembered to bring up the latest juicy gossip related to Roberta. "Have you heard who keeps talking about you?"

"Don't go there, Bess. And how would you know anyway?"

"You know I have friends in low places. You know I know."

"I'm not interested," responded Roberta. She knew where Bess was going with this line of questioning.

"ROBERTA! You are a single gal and a great catch. It is time to move on. He is kind, and he is the head of surgery. You will be well taken care of for the rest of your life," pushed Bess.

"I told you, I'm not interested. You know that. I had the love of my life." Roberta absentmindedly took a bite of salad as sad memories surfaced. "He's gone now," said Roberta, finishing with a whisper.

"That is pure nonsense and you know it," said Bess. She lifted Roberta's chin up with her fingers and looked her in the eye. "I suppose you only love one of your patient's? And the rest are treated like dogs in a kennel cage?"

"Don't be ridiculous," said Roberta.

"Ok... then don't be ridiculous either, girl."

They looked at each other as only two best friends can. Roberta understood the warmth behind the criticism.

"It's not your fault you fell in love with a man twenty-some years older than you, but the odds were, he would be leaving us first. You knew that going in," said Bess.

"I know... I still miss him though," Roberta said and sighed. She took a nibble of cookie and a sip of her tea. "I tell you what... when another man makes me forget him... even for a moment... I will move on."

Bess looked her friend in the eye and charged, "you better not be pullin' my britches... Roberta the Recluse."

Roberta laughed at her friend and assured Bess she would do her best to keep her eyes open for the next man of her dreams.

CHAPTER 10

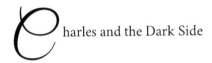harles and the Dark Side

IT WAS WELL BEFORE DAWN, dark and cold with the morning chill as he sat in the back of his van on the small bench, using a flashlight to stare at the face in front of him. He looked around the cabin of the van, enticed by the shadows. They created varying waves of light and darkness, hiding areas and exposing others. He imagined hiding in the darkness and then springing into the light. The light responding with shock at his grotesque features. And then he grabs the light like a tug-of-war rope, pulling the light into his fists... until all is dark. Nobody deserves the light.

He looked at the mask in front of him again. He had stuck together several stretches of duct tape, so it created one piece that would cover the entire face of a smaller-sized person. Once that was accomplished, he carefully put one longer strip at the top and hung the strip from the ceiling of his van, so it dangled down in front of him. He carefully used markers to create a face on the empty, grey canvass. The face, inspired by the photograph of his own face, from the blood-filled photo taken the other day. He drew his new face on the smooth side of the duct tape and the sticky side was left untouched. He finished his artwork and stared at it. Something was missing.

"WHAT IS IT?" He screamed.

HE KNEW he was running out of time and lifted his wrist to look at his watch. When he did so, he breathed heavily on the face of the watch, creating a small fog across the face. The answer clicked. He studied his duct tape face once again and using his imagination, took an educated guess where the improvement was needed. He grabbed his extreme combat knife and with the tip of the ultra-sharp knife, twisted two small holes around the center of the macabre mask. The perfect spot for two, small breathing holes. He sat back and stared again at his work of art. He felt giddy.

IT'S PERFECT. A crooked grin spread across his face.

CHEW COULDN'T WAIT ANY LONGER. He decided to walk over a little early and talk to Ida about the big day. Hopefully, she was awake and in the kitchen with her morning coffee. He quietly entered the back door per their understanding and immediately picked up the faint sound of pleasant humming coming from down the hallway. He knew the sweet and melodious sound could only be emanating from Ida's perfectly formed lips. He found himself entering the hallway like an entranced child following the Pied Piper. The light was dim in the hallway but he could see the bathroom light on at the end of the corridor and the door halfway open. He just couldn't stop himself... he inched closer and closer, her voice intoxicating, drawing him in, until afforded a reckless view. He caught Ida's reflection in the mirror. Her hands were overhead as she lowered her sports bra over her naked bosom. He froze in fear and immediately flooded with guilt and pleasure, regret and joy, back and forth.

They're perfect... and I'm a pervert. He couldn't help but imagine his face buried in those caramel mounds of joy. *She would hate me forever if I get caught.* He gingerly took a step back as the reflection revealed her brushing her long, dark brown hair. He made it back to the kitchen and sat down as beads of sweat dripped down his face. *Do I tell her?*

It wasn't long before she came spiritedly into the kitchen with a morning smile on her face. She took one look at Chew with the rose-colored cheeks and sweaty brow and had to ask, "did you work out before me? That's not like you." She moved past him toward the coffee pot. "Are you all right?"

Chew responded without turning toward her. "Uh... yeah. I figured it was time for me to lose a few pounds... uuummm... how bout you... are you done with your workout yet?"

"What? What are you talking about? You know I haven't even left the house yet. What's gotten into you?"

Chew responded faint-heartedly, "I think I'm a little dizzy. I haven't seen a workout like that in a long time."

"Well, don't take on too much, too soon. You don't want to have a heart attack you know. Who's going to watch my baby then?" She stated and laughed.

"Oh, I don't think I'll do this again for a long, long time," he lamented.

She smiled while putting her arm around his back and gave him a big, playful squeeze. "Today is the big day, Chew. I'm going to look for you, so be ready. I already told Johnny I want a close up of you... IN ACTION!" As she said action, she swept her arms wide.

He laughed and with his best Terminator voice returned, "I'll be ready." He did a little robot dance, albeit while seated, before continuing, "do you know if you guys want to film a particular section of the park?"

"It's a three-minute piece. So, we'll get a lot of coverage. Johnny already has 2 minutes of recorded footage ready to go and we're going to do about a minute of live coverage, right at 12:15 p.m. Then it will be replayed at 6 and 11." She bent down and started tying her shoes as she talked. "I think your boss is going to be very grateful you worked so hard to get the free publicity," she said as she popped up. "And I'm really grateful." She reached in and gave him a one-arm hug. "This is the longest segment I've been assigned to handle so far."

Chew reacted with a glowing smile.

She smiled sweetly at him and took one more drink of coffee before heading toward the door. As she exited, Chew called out, "and don't forget what I'll be wearing."

"I won't," he heard as the voice faded away.

Chew felt so excited, he could hardly contain himself. The thought of being seen as a provider and somebody that would look out for her, made him feel wonderful inside. *Did she look at me different? Maybe, she does know I would do anything for her and Percy... ANYTHING.* His thoughts drifted back to his earlier transgression and the possibility he was seen spying on her... *DID she look at me different?*

For the moment, Chew felt glued to the kitchen chair. His mind couldn't stop alternating between the feeling he had when seeing her in the state of undress and the shame associated with his act of voyeurism. He sat quietly in a state of heightened anxiety before forcing his mind off the subject. He was the protector. His thoughts changed, and he wondered if she remembered to take her Tigerlight defense alert device (D.A.D.)

with her. He really worried about her running alone and in the early morning, sometimes while it was still pitch black out. He knew it was in her blood and he couldn't sway her from her morning runs so he gave up on that idea. Chew wanted to run with her each morning, to protect her, but that wasn't even a remote possibility. He could probably make it a few hundred yards before he would be gasping for life.

It was somebody at work, who mentioned their daughter was saved from a date rape situation, because she had a Tigerlight. It was a really neat gadget, small and unobtrusive. Whoever thought of the Tigerlight, must have a lot of daughters in their brood. It was a handheld flashlight that contained a powerful pepper spray, easy to use and could be strapped to a person's hand while walking or running. Even more amazing? It had an emergency GPS signal alert that would broadcast the user's location in case of emergency. Chew made sure he was on Ida's emergency cell phone alert list. If the spray activated, or she depressed the alert button, he would immediately be notified of her location and could come to her aid.

He knew, at times, she looked at him like a child. But, the fantasy of being her hero one day, was omnipresent in his mind. Actually, not just one day, he wanted her to look at him the way she occasionally talked about Percy's father. Chew dreamed of Ida seeing him as a strong provider and protector of her little family. As his mind wandered, he glanced at the kitchen counter. He felt relieved to see his badgering paying off, the Tigerlight was gone from the counter top. She must have taken it with her.

Now, in the matter of Percy, it was time for a little payback.

Chew quietly drew his Nerf Doomlands Desolator from his waistband and soft-stepped down the hallway to Percy's bedroom. He peered in the open doorway and saw the shape of his unsuspecting victim huddled beneath his blanket in false comfort. He had a ten Nerf bullet magazine and a spare clip waiting for action. He gave his best Darth Vader impression and stated, "PERCY… I AM YOUR FATHER!"

But Chew didn't offer a hand. He was the earlier, meaner version of Darth Vader. He had revenge on his mind. He quickly unloaded the full, 10 rounds into the blanket covering Percy. The Nerf bullets bounced off the top of the blanket and scattered throughout the room. Chew continued, "OBI-WAN NEVER TOLD YOU THE TRUTH ABOUT YOUR FATHER!" He finished and reached into his waistband for his spare clip when a voice could be heard from the partially open closet.

Percy cried. "THAT'S IMPOSSIBLE… NNNOOO!" He emerged from the closet with Nerf blaster in hand. A big, smug smile could be seen in the dim light.

Chew looked on in mock horror and fumbled for his spare clip as Percy leveled his blaster at him, unloading his own barrage of Nerf bullets at the evil Darth Vader. Chew staggered back, twitching and jerking with each strike to his body before splattering himself against the hallway wall and sliding to the ground in mock death, tongue out for good measure. Percy laughed and laughed at his good fortune and Chew's comic abilities. When he came back to life, Chew asked Percy when he was going to win a battle and be the hero.

Percy responded in his best Yoda voice, "you must UNLEARN what you learned. NO… Try or try not… DO… or do not."

IDA PUT HER HEADPHONES ON, stretched on the front lawn and then headed up the hill toward the park. As much as she wanted to try a different route, she found comfort in her usual morning routine. It was wooded, peaceful and quiet. It was her time to unwind and mentally prepare for her coming day. To her, the physical aspect was not as important as the thirty minutes of mental freedom. Together, running was a strong stress reliever for her body and mind.

She reached the top of the hill and for some reason, felt a strong sensation to look back down the hill. What was it?

She slowed down and peered over her shoulder. She didn't see anybody walking or running behind her. The only thing she saw was a white minivan, driving slowly up the hill. She stopped moving, to study the van a little closer. The van pulled deep into a neighboring driveway and disappeared from sight. Ida quickly dismissed the van as a neighbor coming home from work and started her trek again, toward the park.

It was a dark morning, and the trees cast shadows across the manicured trail. She turned on her Tigerlight as a guide and continued her run, even speeding up a little as one of her favorite dance songs, revved up her eardrums. As she ran, she thought about how she wanted to fill the minute of airtime, later in the day. She was excited to be given complete control of the direction of her piece. Sure, it was a fluff story but people like the fluff and more importantly, if you become likable doing the fluff, then that could open doors to more serious journalism.

She became so engrossed in her thoughts that she didn't see Old Oaks legs protruding above the ground like oversized varicose veins. The tree had been there for hundreds of years and everybody knew where the roots were, yet somebody, like her, was bound to trip on Old Oak now and then. Ida fell hard to the ground, knocking her earphones out and scratching her knees. She stood up and began to wipe the dirt off when she caught the sound of a voice, filled with anger. It was in the distance and muffled by the trees but the frustration in the deep voice could not be mistaken.

She looked to her left, where the sound originated and knew the road was not far from the trail. It was pointless, but she strained to see through the trees and discern the origins of the sound. Suddenly, the angry voice was replaced by the sound of heavy, destructive pounding upon an unknown object. Ida didn't realize she was clinging close to the trunk of Old Oaks, her pulse indicative of a sprinter and not a distance runner. She clutched the tree for several seconds, hesitant to move or make a sound. She realized how fast her heart was pounding and told herself to calm down.

A few seconds later, she heard the sound of tires squealing and a vehicle taking off at a high rate of speed. She never saw the vehicle, due to the thickness of the foliage. Really, she didn't see anything, only the sounds. She realized how ridiculous she was acting, considering whoever was in the van couldn't see her either. There was no way he could know she was there.

And so what if they did? She thought, easing her worry.

She granted herself a sigh of relief and it was then she noticed she had dug claw marks into Old Oak with her fingernails. She apologized to the old tree, and without any further haste, began her trek back home. "You are so silly, girl," she said out loud to herself.

SILLY OR NOT... Ida found herself stowing away her earphones and clutching her Tigerlight a little more secure for the remainder of her run.

CHAPTER 11

$\mathcal{D}$avid at Starbucks

DAVID WAS GROWING TIRED of the hunt and it was costing him at work. For the past month, he had religiously driven to Starbucks each morning, waiting as long as time permitted, in the hope he would meet the mysterious woman again. He hung out there after work and even drove there on the weekends. In the process, achieving three major things, none of which were helping him at all. He was becoming a major Starbucks junkie, going outside his planned budget and worst of all, seeing a little extra macchiato paunch around his middle.

This is it... her last chance, he thought as he drove to Starbucks. *Just one more time... enough is enough.* After today, it would be the start of his new, old routine. No more fantasies involving the mysterious lady and no more late-night television because he was "jonesing" from an overdose of caffeine. He pulled into the Starbucks lot and his heart jumped into his throat.

Her black Audi sat parked in the lot's corner. David wondered if he should wait until the vehicle left that was parked next to the Audi. That might turn out looking bad. He decided against waiting and picked a free spot a few spaces down. He nearly crashed the front end of his prized truck into a parked Subaru as he hurriedly forced the vehicle into the cramped quarters. He did a mirror check, took a deep breath and walked into the coffee shop of dreams.

"Good morning, David," said Sydney and continued smiling. "I'll be honest with you. Since you joined the wild side, I don't know what you want today."

He looked back at her and smiled, "I don't know, either. I feel like a little excitement today. Just surprise me with something different."

"You got it," she responded with the usual Starbucks corporate enthusiasm.

As he waited for his coffee, he did his best acting job of scanning the room, like he didn't care at all but had nothing else to do at the moment. He spotted the dark-haired beauty seated at a corner table by herself, staring into an iPad. He couldn't take his eyes off her.

The gods must have been shining down on David. No sooner than he received his coffee, then the table next to the mysterious woman opened. He filled the seat and pretended to check his email. He could tell she was gazing at the screen of her iPad and wasn't sure whether to disturb her focus. A few seconds later, she withdrew her cell phone and spoke to an unknown person and David couldn't help but eavesdrop the conversation.

"The trials were good except for one marker, however, the FDA just rejected them," she said and then listened to the unknown voice for several seconds. "I know, I know. I agree. There's no doubt." She listened again before continuing, "it's down 22% right now. I think it will drop more, before the end of the week."

David tried to put it together. To the best of his knowledge, he believed she must have been talking about a medical trial that failed and a drug expected to receive FDA approval was rejected.

She lowered her voice as she continued, "I already told you. My source said the only reason they didn't meet approval was because of an analysis contradiction that resulted from misrepresentation by a couple of the subjects in the test group. It's a minor technicality. The drug was a superstar outside of that."

David listened and thought of his own portfolio. The mutual fund of the century, they said. You will be a millionaire by the time you are thirty, they said. *Yeah... right.* As the poor performance of his mutual funds flounder in the stock market and his dreams of wealth erode, the administrator fat cats of the account get a steady paycheck and richer every day. *Man, would I love to beat the system just once.*

"We wait. I will stay on it and before the end of the week, I will make a move," she said and then listened. "No, I'm thinking at least 2.5.," she responded to her unknown phone partner. She listened a few seconds longer, hung up and returned her gaze to her iPad. David watched as she took a strong sip of her even stronger latte.

She is so out of my league... what am I even doing here? He buried his head in his cell phone and gave up on his fantasy. He felt dejected, like the little kid nobody wanted on their ball team. He was almost through his emails when he heard her voice, aimed at him.

"You know, David... I had you pegged as more of a square. You know... grande Caramel Macchiato on Monday, then Tuesday, Wednesday and on and on."

He looked up in shock. She was standing right in front of his table... and talking to him... and she knew his name. David noticed she wore a black skirt with a green, dress shirt tucked smartly inside. *Game time, David—MAN UP.* He absorbed the rub and exchanged the volley. "Well, you never know, a Rubik's cube is square." He smiled. He felt sly.

"So is Pandora's box," she countered without missing a beat.

Holy crap, she's quick. I don't have what it takes to play this game. He changed it up. "You know my name, but I don't think we've properly met," he said as he stood up and shook her hand.

"Deianira." She pointed her finger at him. "Let me ask you something David... you weren't eavesdropping on my conversation, were you?"

David turned at least three shades of red and meekly responded, "I might have accidentally heard something about a medicine or something... but no, not, uh, really."

She laughed at his insecurity and he felt like a little boy caught stealing the cookies from the cookie jar. "Don't worry about it," she assured him with a smile and pointed to the seat across from him.

As she sat down, his spirits took a leap forward. He must have done something right, why else would she sit down with him? Now that he was a short Starbucks table space away, he could really see her true beauty. She had smoldering, dark-green eyes, full lips and dark features accentuated by her long, black hair. He guessed she was Greek or from some area near there, but she was definitely not born and bred in America.

"Again, I apologize... can I buy you the next round?" He offered.

"The next round? I like that David... confidence," she said.

He smiled and brimmed inside with renewed faith.

"Do you like a little excitement—a little risk?" Deianira asked.

"Well, I have to admit, I did hear a little more of your conversation, and if you are talking about taking risks with my money... then no. I'm probably more like your seven day a week, Caramel Macchiato guy."

She laughed at his cleverness and then stared at him with her piercing green eyes. "I like a little risk now and then..." she glanced at her phone again. She looked like she read a short text and did a calculation in her mind before continuing, "so much that I'm going to give you, a total stranger, a little advice." She leaned in toward him. Her scent wafted into his face, containing a scintillating blend of flowers and spice. Two buttons of the dress shirt, open at the top, allowed enough cleavage to spill forward that David could barely function on any intellectual level.

"Can you keep a secret?"

He studied her for a moment, fighting the urge to look at the cleavage rising and falling with each breath, trying to clear the fog that enveloped his reptilian brain. "I sure... um... I know I can."

She smiled at him. It was intoxicating and spellbinding. "My job is to analyze things—businesses, markets, people and more. I work for a broker, mainly behind the scenes and gather information for their clients," she said and then sipped her latte. "Do you play the stock market, David?"

He didn't know squat about the stock market. All he had done for years, was send a part of his paycheck, to somebody at some company who barely made a dime for him. "I like to dabble here and there when I think the timing is right."

"You're in luck then, David. Maybe it's fate for you... who knows," she encouraged. Just then, she received another text message. She glanced at the text, put the top on her latte and apologized. She had to leave. He sat there looking at her, not sure of himself and thus stuck in the uncomfortable feeling of blowing it.

She stood up and moved closer to him before leaning over and whispering into his ear, "take a look at BioPharma, down over 20% in a day because of an FDA rejection of their new drug. It's only a temporary setback. That drug is a step away from approval and I'm sure you can figure out what that means." She leaned back up and walked out the door. He sniffed the air. Her scent lingered.

David was so ensconced in what she told him, he forgot one of the golden rules of standing up when a lady leaves the table. Further, he didn't even remember to ask for her number or any other contact information. *How dumb am I?* Forget the stupidity, he realized he was in danger of being late for work, again. He scooped up his coffee and as he rushed out the door, his mind ballooned with images of a life with the intoxicating woman.

David arrived at work and searched the Internet for the stock market price of BioPharma. He ran a history and Deianira was right, except now, the stock was down over 28%. He jumped to his Fidelity account and calculated his risk. He had worked a lot of years for the money in the account. It was his whole future. Could this stock tip actually be true? Could he have finally gotten the big break he so richly deserved?

How much should I invest?

He stared at the BioPharma stock and stared at his portfolio. He went back and forth, repeatedly, the pain of indecision weighing on him. About twenty minutes into his indecision, he gambled. He wasn't a Caramel Macchiato guy. He would prove it. He decided, since the stock was down 28%, he would invest 28% of his net worth. He typed in the order, clicked to the preview page and was about to submit the order when Mr. Hashbrack came crashing into his office, a look of exasperation and fear on his face.

"I HAVE to talk to you about Bob… NOW!" He croaked.

CHAPTER 12

*B*ert plans for a Picnic

OOOHHH, THIS IS SO exciting, thought Bert as he scanned the back pasture behind the plant, where workers were busy setting up the annual company picnic. He could barely contain his excitement. There were always so many happy faces. It was the one time a year their whole "family" came together to celebrate and bless each other. Bert felt every single employee, every child of an employee, every relative of every employee were part of his and Gertie's family.

The picnic had grown a little each year to the point it was now a full-fledged festival, entertaining hundreds of family and friends for one special day. It had started so small. It was an idea born out of love for children, dreams and family.

MANY YEARS AGO, HE and Gertie spent one day a year, secluded from the outside world. They would share their feelings and their dreams in a private setting, enveloped by nature and God's creatures. They would load up camping equipment, other supplies and even some superb old-fashioned candies in his pickup truck and they would drive out into the wilderness.

On their very first trip, Bert and Gertie drove with no intentional path or direction. It was enough to be together and let the good Lord find their way. Bert happily drove until Gertie told him to stop and park in a small clearing just off the roadway. Gertie said she did not understand why but something told her—it was the place. A small path revealed itself through the rays of sun, basking the floor of the forest. It was a beautiful uphill hike through fresh pine, wildflowers and a small stream meandering its way down the hill.

They knew it the moment they emerged into the clearing, a piece of heaven on earth. It was a meadow high in the hills and clear of any large trees except two apple trees, bearing granny smith apples. They were in the perfect position to swing a hammock built for two. Stunning, flowering Iris's, Gertie's favorite flower, surrounded the trees.

Every year, the same thing happened when they reached their secret, private meadow. Gertie would look out on the field of yellow and blue bearded irises and a pure, joyful sigh would escape her lips, each and every time. Bert would sit and stare at her, knowing he had found the place where her heart lied. As a result, his own heart soared.

The Iris flowers anther and standards were soft shades of yellow and the beards fluffy fingers danced in the wind. The falls, which were the larger outer petals, were saturated with striking shades of blue, nature's testament to the beauty of the world.

Once she had soaked herself in the sun's warmth and the embrace of the iris's, she would give his hand a squeeze and they would walk in silence to their little slice of heaven, at the highest point of the meadow. During one trip, Bert had built a fire pit surrounded by rocks, a short distance from the two apple trees. On arrival, his first annual chore was to check the integrity of the pit and clear any unnecessary debris.

While he built a fire, Gertie would be busy stringing the homemade hammock between the trees and prepare the meal. Gertie took great pride in the ingenuity of her hammock. Over time, she accumulated several burlap sacks, a result of their forced appetite for potatoes. There were many days, because of poverty, Bert and Gertie feasted on baked potatoes, French fried potatoes, mashed potatoes, potato soup and more. It was a true testament to Gertie's creative cooking and Bert's iron stomach they survived that era of their lives. She stitched the burlap together until she had fashioned a hammock just big enough for two. She used to tease Bert about his ice cream eating habits and warn him if he continued to gain weight, he would have to sleep underneath her on the ground.

Once the site was set up for the evening, it wasn't long before they were sharing a special meal together and a bottle of their favorite wine. The first half of the evening they would talk about their accomplishments, laugh, share memories and rejoice in their blessings. When the moon and stars arrived, they would cozy up in their little homemade hammock and each would talk about their future dreams for themselves, each other and their eventual children.

Unfortunately, they continued to talk about the dream of having children until Gertie was well past the age of fertility. Their secret place felt magical to them. But, no matter how special and mystical, the stars would not make all of their dreams come true. Their business success grew with each passing year, but they talked less and less as their dreams of birthing children faded, like a dark cloud drifting into significance and extinguishing the light of the stars, one by one.

Bert did his best to never feel victimized. He refused to live life in that manner. There were too many other blessings. For one, the continuous growth of their company provided him with many, many children and grandchildren in his eyes. He felt blessed.

There was only one experience, during one of their short retreats, that shook them and changed their future habits. And it was a lesson well learned. Normally, Bert would take any leftover vittles, secure them in a sack and hang the sack from a tree down at the bottom of the meadow. However, there was one year Bert brought two bottles of wine and they did a little more drinking than eating. As a result, he forgot to hang the sack of vittles in a tree and left them on the ground between the fire pit and the hammock.

It was about three in the morning when they awoke to the sounds of a big old bear finishing Gertie's fresh Granny Smith apple pie. Apparently, the bear liked to eat dessert first. As soon as he finished, he lifted his nose in the air and sniffed out the main course hanging from the apple trees. Bert and Gertie's only defense was a knife, stuck in the ground by the fire pit. So, unless the bear was the gentleman type and handed them the knife, there was no way they would retrieve it.

They decided their only chance of survival was to play possum. So, they rolled the hammock around them to create a tight cocoon, hoping the burlap sack would be found less than appetizing. The bear pressed its nose against the wall of the cocoon, deeply sniffed and appeared to be unsure of just what type of meal hung from the trees. He took a second, longer sniff and promptly sneezed. It was full and hearty.

Bert and Gertie did not figure it out right away. It wasn't until later, looking back on their adventure with the unwanted dinner guest, were they able to figure out the reason the bear kept sneezing. It was a small act of love by Gertie, repeated each year, for her beloved Bert. In all the years, Gertie prepared for each retreat with a little spritz of Bert's favorite fragrance, a 1952 bottle of Gourielli's Moonlight Mist.

Apparently, the bear was not as fond of the fragrance as Bert.

On the infamous night of the sneezing bear, the furry hunter pushed the hammock with his nose and head, irritated by the new fragrance filling his nose. The hammock swung a little. He pushed again, and the hammock swung a little more. Inside, Bert had his arms wrapped around Gertie as they swung back and forth in the night's darkness. Bert could feel the head of the large bear pushing him in the side as they tried not to move or make any sounds. The bear pushed one too many times, and the hammock swung just hard enough to come back and smack the bear straight on the nose. The bear wailed in surprise and in a show of strength and fury rose to its full height on two legs. The bear would show the smelly cocoon who was the boss.

The bear promptly shoved the hammock with its two large paws, sending the hammock with the tipsy occupants, swinging away from it with great force. Bert and Gertie flew up in the air and thought they would flip over or fall out, leaving them exposed on the ground underneath. Bert squeezed Gertie so hard, she later found bruising on her sides.

But no... as Isaac Newton would have it... what goes up must come down. The hammock swung back with equal force and struck the inhospitable bear in the chest, sending the animal rolling backward and landing butt first... right on top of the smoldering ashes of the campfire. The bear let out quite an indignant roar of pain and humiliation as it scurried out of the fire pit and escaped the wrath of the big cocoon thing, smoke rising from its hind end as it fled to the safety of the forest.

Bert and Gertie watched in surprise as the trail of billowing, butt smoke receded from sight. From that point forward, Gertie declared there would only be one bottle of wine a year. Bert agreed, under the condition she would never forget the spritz of Moonlight Mist.

Eventually, they bought the land with the apple trees and

many more acres around it. And for many years, they secretly went off to their slice of heaven. But, in the end... even that stopped. Life was too busy, their extended family too large and a new responsibility hung around every corner. Bert missed those trips—dearly. He always felt close to Gertie. But, it was during those times in the meadow and amongst the two apple trees, when their hearts would grow stronger roots in the rich soil of their lives.

NOW, THE EMPLOYEES OF the ice cream plant were their children, the company picnic replacing their secret excursion. It was one of their ways to make the manufacturing facility much more than just a place to collect a paycheck. They wanted the plant to be a place for friends to enjoy the process of creating something special... together. Bert understood the importance of memories... even some of the bad ones.

Over the years, the picnic had grown so big, they broke the areas off into sections. There was the stage area and wooden, dance floor for the hoedown. The picnic table area, bathrooms and the inflatable wonderland of which both kids and adults played. Then there were the carnival games, Bert's personal favorite. Over the years, he had collected numerous antique games from yesteryear and put them to good use for their extravaganza.

Each year, Bert liked to add something new, fun and interesting for the company picnic. This year was no different. A few weeks before the picnic, he was lucky enough to acquire an original 1930s High Striker. The rather simple contraption was composed of a tower with a bell at the top and a puck attached to a lever at the bottom. Carny's would entice egotistical men with shouts of "step right up" and "who thinks they are a strongman?"

The "mark" would use a mallet to strike the lever as hard as they could to force the puck from the bottom to the top, striking the bell and winning the prize. However, many High Striker's in the 1930s were rigged, so a small Carny could show how easy it was to hit the bell. However, when a "mark" tried to hit the bell, the Carny would rig the High Striker, so it was impossible to ring. Thus, the "mark", would lose their money and the Carny keep their prize supply.

Bert well knew of this con game and hoped most of his employees were too young to know of such a thing. He couldn't wait to watch the fun when one of his strong deliverymen tried in vain to ring the bell and then watch in surprise as a child as young as nine ring the bell with ease. "That should create some memories," he whispered to himself and chuckled as he sat and stared at the pre-production efforts. Someone cut his daydreaming short when he felt a tap on his shoulder. It was Reginald.

"Excuse me, sir," said Reginald.

"Yes, Reginald?"

"Ms. Gertie would like you to call her."

Bert gave Reginald a concerned look, a silent request for information but Reginald provided no clue, his face blank. "Okay, I sure will. Right away."

Bert dropped out of his secret perch overlooking the preparations and headed to his office, preferring to call Gertie in private. He dialed Gertie's number, the phone connected, and he didn't even have time to say hello.

"Bert, I know what you've been doing. Stop yer' daydreaming and get ready for the meeting."

Bert ran his hand through his thick head of gray hair and rambled, "but Gertie... you said, you would be there."

"Now Bert, I said no such thing. Now be a man, review the notes I gave you and run the meeting," she ordered and then emphasized, "I will not be there, Bert."

The thought of being the center of attention and running the monthly activity meeting brought shivers up and down his spine. *I can't do it.*

"But Gertie…"

She cut him off with an even more stern warning. "BUT NOTHING… do it Bert." And then she hung up.

He sat back in his chair and felt like crying. *Keep it together, Bert.* He looked down at his desk. The meeting notes were neatly arranged on his desk, prepared by Gertie and delivered by her secretary. Regrettably, he spent the next few minutes reviewing her carefully constructed notes. It wasn't long, though, before he turned around and stared again at his favorite picture of him and Gertie in their old house and in their humble kitchen. He looked at her arm around his neck and shoulders. He loved the way she cuddled him… shielded him from harm.

It took a while, but the picture brought him back to his happy place. His thoughts turned back to the picnic and the biggest surprise of all. He painstakingly planned the surprise—all by himself. Quite shocking, at least so far, all evidence would indicate Gertie did not know of his secret planning. He believed the surprise would please everyone but would mean so much more to his beloved Gertie. It was not an easy task at all for him and the process of meeting people, taking charge, organizing the surprise… it severely drained him.

IT WILL all be worth it. He looked up and prayed out loud, "please… please Lord… let this moment happen."

CHAPTER 13

 ess and Family

BESS QUIETLY LEFT HER HUSBAND, snoring in their small
bedroom and tiptoed her way to the kitchen. It was late at night
but the lure of leftovers from the barbecue sent waves of desire
through her stomach and she simply did not have the willpower
to resist. She listened for the sound of any movement or listless
children who might stir in the night. She knew her husband had
teamed with the children to help control her food appetite and
she didn't want to be caught on her midnight run for a little
taste of goodness.

She made it into the kitchen and murmured in delight at the
sight of their LG double door-in-door "mega-capacity" refrigerator. A much-needed commodity to handle not only her needs
but also the rest of the family. And, let's not forget, the needs of
probably half the neighborhood. Bess froze for a moment and
listened. All quiet on the western front, nothing stirring, not

even a mouse. Bess opened the refrigerator. The soft glow illuminated wide, bright eyes and a voracious smile. She studied the contents of the refrigerator. She wanted to choose wisely from all the delicious offerings. Finally, she could wait no longer and went straight for the big plate of country ribs and bowl of cole slaw.

No sooner than her thumb sank into a gob of barbecue sauce as she grabbed the plate, then a voice came out of nowhere.

"Hi, mom."

Bess, quite startled, jumped back a good few feet while nearly pulling the tray of ribs onto the floor with her. She put her hand to her heart and tried to peer through the illumination of the refrigerator to see what made the noise.

A little voice came from above, shining through the light. "Are you supposed to be in the fridge, mom?"

Bess shut the refrigerator and there sitting on top of the refrigerator was her daughter Cheese, with legs crossed, elbows on knees and hands on chin.

"Well, you little dickens... what are you doin' up?" Bess asked.

"I'm your guardian angel, mom," she replied. Her tone was confident and sincere. "I look out for you."

Bess looked at her little ball of love and she didn't feel hungry anymore. She reached up and scooped Cheese into her arms and gave her a big momma squeeze that would make a Boa Constrictor jealous. "I love you, my beautiful little girl," Bess said.

"I love you too mommy," Cheese replied.

As Bess played spider fingers with her hand, chasing her fingers around Cheese's body and tickling, she looked around and soon felt perplexed as to how Cheese could have found herself on top of the refrigerator. There was nothing to stand on, nothing next to the refrigerator to climb up, nothing... just the refrigerator. "Cheese, how did you get up on the fridge?"

Bess looked up and down at the refrigerator again. "Did somebody put you up there and leave you?"

"No, mommy."

"Then, what? But... how did you get there?"

Cheese looked her straight in the eyes, innocent and honest in her words and manner. "It just happened."

"Huh?" Bess responded, still perplexed. She looked around the refrigerator again. She just couldn't figure it out.

"Well, let's get to bed now, sweet Cheese." She started toward the bedrooms when her stomach grumbled. "Except... hey... how about maybe just one of those ribs off that slab?" Bess opened the refrigerator door again. "Do you want to share it?"

"No," replied Cheese. With a look usually reserved for an impatient mother, she restated her meaning. "No ribs."

"Okay, um, well how bout a little cup of slaw? Just an eensie weensie, little bit?" Bess asked while putting her finger and thumb close together.

Cheese nodded no.

"Umm, maybe a little, tiny bowl of Gertie's Scrumptious Chunk. You couldn't possibly say no to that... can you?" Bess asked.

Cheese shook her head no.

"Maybe just one cheese ball... little, teeny, weeny cheese ball?" Bess begged.

Cheese was like a General in the military, holding an impenetrable line. She dropped her chin into her chest and her eyebrows lowered.

"Alright," Bess sighed. "Let me take you up to bed." With that, Bess closed the refrigerator and trudged up the stairs with her tough, little food angel. She laid Cheese in bed, kissed her on the forehead, and quietly slid back in her place, next to Tim. She fell asleep to the competing sounds of Tim's snoring and her growling stomach.

· · ·

BESS WOKE UP THE next morning to the delightful smells of morning coffee, fresh griddle waffles, and chunks of greasy bacon. Add real maple syrup, an assortment of fresh fruit... and it was Sunday.

Ooohhh, how she loved Sundays, the only day of the week Tim was not working and they dedicated the day to time with just their immediate family. It was a chance to splurge their affection and attention on their children. Another thing she liked about Sunday, was the sense of adventure that was born and developed over the years. On each Sunday, a different member of the family chose an activity. It could be something new and different or it could be something as simple as making a big bucket of popcorn and watching a favorite movie together in the den. It didn't matter, it only mattered they spend time together. Bess had just sat down with a waffle and a generous helping of bacon when Tyler announced his planned activity for the day.

"Rock climbing!" Tyler said while his eyes bulged with excitement.

Tim and Bess looked at each other and Bess burst out laughing. "You want me to climb rocks?" Bess asked Tyler.

"Awww, you can do it mom. You can do anything," he responded with a sense of false enthusiasm.

She laughed again and stated, "well, I'll make a deal with this family right here and now," and she waited for everybody's attention. "If I make it to the top of one of those rock-climbing walls—then it is a loaded garlic, cheese-filled crust pizza for dinner tonight. Do we have a deal?"

Everybody grinned. Tim looked down, shook his head while smiling and mumbled, "you sure are something Bess. This I gotta' see."

Breakfast was over too quickly in Bess's mind, not just because of the food but also because of the relaxed atmosphere and the joy of having everyone at the table laughing and joking around. It was the making of treasured memories. Once they cleaned the kitchen, it was off to their weekly church service.

Bess was driving everyone home when she started up again with Tim. "Boy, are you in trouble with the Lord... ummm, ummm, ummm."

Tim looked back at her in mock horror.

"You're going to have to pay for your sins. That's for sure," announced Bess.

When they arrived home, the children had a list of small chores to accomplish before they were allowed to eat lunch and prepare for the start of family adventure day. Tim and Bess had other plans. Today, and each previous week, Bess gathered the children and issued the same declaration. "Now, your daddy has to pray for forgiveness. I'm going to pray with him. There can be no disturbing of our prayers. Get your chores done and we'll be out when we're done praying for his salvation."

With wonderful innocence, Cheese looked at her mother and cast a look of sympathy toward her father. "Momma, how come daddy always sins on Sunday, right after church. Shouldn't he know better?"

The older kids and Tim choked back a laugh as Bess stared them down before focusing her attention on Cheese. "Oh, your father has sinned on a Tuesday, Wednesday, Thursday and Friday. We just like to pray extra special on Sundays... that's all."

She then gave the older children a wink, turned and led her sinner husband into their bedroom for their Sunday prayer session. Tim was going to repent, whether he liked it or not. The ear to ear grin was probably a giveaway of his frame of mind.

· · ·

AFTER CHORES, PRAYER AND lunch, they all loaded up and headed to Mountain Adventures, known for being one of the best indoor rock-climbing venues in the country. It was a massive warehouse where rock walls projected high to the ceiling and even on the ceiling itself. They also had a cardio, pilates/yoga studio and workout room. This was the first trip for their family, so they had to attend the safety orientation class before they were allowed on the floor. The lesson taught the basics of harness and shoe fitting, rules of safety and other guidelines.

The harness fitting did not go so well for Bess. They had two young instructors fitting their family. One of which was a fit, college age girl with abs as hard as the rock walls and an attitude to match. Even before she attempted to put on the harness, Bess caught the young, opinionated instructor looking at her in obvious disgust. The girl's contempt became even more clear as she struggled to fit the harness on Bess.

"Are you sure you want to do this, ma'am?" She said, looking Bess up and down. "I mean... I can see why you might want to just watch."

Beth felt infuriated at the callousness of the young, hot shot. For a moment, memories of her young school years came flooding back, bathing her in shame. Children can be cruel. But, she kept it hidden inside, like so many other times. She calmed herself and tried to make a joke about it to lighten the mood.

"If you can get the harness on this old air balloon, then I don't see why I can't figure out a way to float to the top with all my hot air," she said and laughed.

The girl didn't even come close to recognizing Bess's attempt at healing the situation. "Ma'am, this isn't the place to have fun and make jokes. People like you get hurt here." And with that, she cinched the harness so tight Bess could feel the extra rolls of love drooping over the harness fabric as they tried to break free from their new prison.

Inside, the ever-competitive Bess swore to herself that she was going to show this girl that even a fat woman could conquer the mountain. They finished the session, and the kids scattered, like excited mice in a new, multi-tube cage.

Tim walked up to Bess and put his arm around her, giving her a caring squeeze. "You sure you want to do this, Bess?"

She replied with more than a hint of fear. "I think so."

They walked around and checked out the complex. It was pretty amazing. There were different areas with different heights of walls, marked for complexity and experience. One room contained two large, freestanding boulders with thick mats to catch a wayward climber's fall. The main room must have been at least 150 feet across and ascended to the ceiling at least 75 feet.

In the orientation, they were advised the main room was off limits as only the higher-level mountaineers were allowed to climb the wall. There were no automatic belay systems there. Each climber had to have his or her own personal belayer to assist his or her climb. A personal belayer used a long rope, run through a pulley at the top of the ceiling. They attached one end to the climber's harness system and the belayer on the ground controlled the other end. As a climber worked their way up, the belayer kept the slack out of the rope. If the climber lost their grip and fell, it would only result in a drop of a few feet. The experienced belayer would reel them down to safety or the climber would re-establish a grip on the wall and continue their journey.

Outside of the main room, the walls had multiple automatic belay systems where a human belayer was not needed. They were quite interesting. A rope was attached with a carabiner to the ground. If you wanted to climb the wall, you would release the carabiner and attach the rope to your harness vest. The other end was attached to the belay system itself, which was mounted at the top of the wall. Theoretically, they designed the belay system to automatically adjust to a person's body weight and prevent them from a fast, free-fall descent if they lost their grip on the wall. They designed it to slowly carry a person back to the ground so no injuries would result from a fall.

Tim and Bess walked around and located each one of their children. They watched and encouraged them with words of support. The only one they didn't see on a wall climbing was Emma. They found her sitting alone on a bench... staring out the window. Tim glanced out the same window. There was nothing to see, just a steady stream of anonymous traffic on the local freeway. The thought struck Tim... he never talked to Emma at the barbecue. She had the same look of melancholy. They sat down on each side of her and Tim pulled her hair back toward her ear on one side.

"Hey sweetie."

Emma would not look at them and continued looking down. This time, Tim really looked at his daughter. He studied the thin lines of worry. The tightness in her face... the stress.

"Are you alright?"

"Yeah... I'm ok."

Bess put her arm around her girl. "Are you sure, Emma?"

Emma studied the anonymous cars again. "I think I ate too many waffles at breakfast. I should be fine... in a little bit."

Tim looked at his girl and knew something wasn't right but didn't want to push it. Of all the children, Emma was the quietest and usually reserved in outward displays of emotion. She was a thinker by nature and liked to discuss things on her own timetable. They both knew better than to push her.

Bess leaned closer to their precious child. "We love you, Emma. If you want to talk to me or dad, we'll always be there for you." She rubbed Emma's back and kissed her on the cheek.

"I'm okay. Thanks guys. Now go and climb that mountain, mom," Emma said.

Tim and Bess looked at each other and knew it was best to leave her alone. Bess was also worried about Cheese, their most mischievous child. Tim and Bess did one full lap around the authorized areas of climbing and didn't locate her. They split up with Bess taking a look in the main room, knowing Cheese may have talked someone into helping her climb one of the big walls. Nothing. No Cheese. They decided to do another lap, but this time, gathering all of their children to assist in their search. Everybody searched and then met up in a secondary area away from the main climbing wall. Nobody found Cheese. Tim and Bess were about to notify management when they heard a small voice from above.

"Hi, momma," said Cheese.

They all looked up and there was Cheese at the top of the wall, tucked away in a corner. Somehow, nobody saw her there. She had wedged herself in and was just sitting there, looking as content as somebody lounging by a pool on a sunny afternoon.

"Come up here, momma. Come and be with me," she said. She smiled softly with a look of innocent encouragement.

"Oh... I don't know, honey. Why don't you come down and we can climb something a little smaller?" Bess cajoled.

"No momma, you have to climb this one." She didn't budge.

Bess looked at Tim and they both knew there was no telling when Cheese would come down.

"You know what? Okay... yeah... I CAN DO IT!" Bess said and laughed her wonderful laugh.

Tim smiled with concern while the children cheered.

Bess attached the carabiner to her harness and took a deep breath. She looked up at Cheese and figured she must be at least thirty-feet high. Now that she was standing against the wall and looking up, it seemed overpowering to her. The climbing holds attached to the wall were all color-coded. According to the instructional class, each color represented a different path and a different degree of difficulty. Bess decided it would be in her best interest to stick with the easiest path.

She found the first climbing hold, studied the path and gave herself a pep talk. *You can do it, Bess. You can do anything. It's only a wall.*

Bess took a firm grip and successfully pulled herself up, placing her foot on another hold. She brought her free hand up higher, grabbed another hold and pulled herself up to where she was now on the wall, free of the constraints of the Earth. Bess looked at her lactic acid-filled forearm, beads of sweat were forming and a single bead broke free, running like a roller-coaster from her hand down to her elbow. The next hold was yellow and secured to the wall by two bolts. Bess feared the bolts would give up before her and send her crashing to the ground. She shoved her fear away and reached for the small and malformed plastic. She pushed herself and grabbed the next hold, while her right leg shook under the weight. Bess felt her best option for survival was to keep moving at all times. The next hold was green, she liked green. Green was her friend. She made it but now she gasped for air. Somebody took all the air. She felt like she just climbed 50 floors in a high-rise stairwell. Her shirt was turning a darker shade of color as it absorbed the steady stream of sweat. Now, both of her legs trembled, and she feared her knees would crack in half.

Bess stopped for a moment and looked up, her pint-sized daughter seemed like an eternity away. Cheese looked down at her. There was something, Bess couldn't quite grasp it. On the surface, Cheese seemed unusually calm. But Bess is a mom... and all good moms have a sixth sense. Bess felt like she needed to get up there. She needed to get to her little Cheese.

"I'm here for you, mommy." Cheese extended her little arm toward Bess.

She was nowhere close enough to reach it. Bess became

more determined than ever and mentally shelved the pain. She made it two more steps up the climbing holds and again stopped for air. She was struggling for oxygen and the pain was searing through every part of her body. She went up again. She started to fully realize the immense task she had assigned herself. She looked up at Cheese and for the first time, felt she might not make it. She wouldn't reach her little girl.

Bess never heard or saw the crowd below. Other climbers and members of the gym couldn't help but take notice of the large woman on the wall. The woman who was showing more tenacity and grit than had ever graced any wall in the gym before... or after. Perhaps, at first... they watched to see her fall. But her sheer determination changed them.

Bess gave herself another pep talk and through no small amount of incredible effort, made it up another level. She had now been on the rock for almost twenty agonizing minutes and was only about two-thirds of the way to the top. She looked up at the next climbing hold. Her arms were wracked with pain and her knees felt like they would explode. Yet, she grabbed the next hold. She started to pull herself up and then her grip and her legs simply gave out. There was nothing left in her.

She fell... and she fell hard. The self-adjusting belay system was designed to slow down the fall to a safe speed. Whether the system was faulty or Bess simply weighed too much will never be known. Either way, Bess came crashing down and landed in a lopsided heap. Her right ankle broke sideways, the loud snap sending gasps of horror through the large crowd that had gathered to root her on and watch the outcome.

Before anyone could get to her, the sight of Cheese falling slowly from the sky with her arms outstretched, stopped them in their tracks. Cheese floated down like an angel and landed gracefully on top of her mother like a warm, winter blanket. She rested her head on Bess's shoulder.

Bess stifled her pain and caressed her little angel's head. "I'm so sorry I couldn't reach you, my beautiful girl."

"EVERYTHING IS GONNA BE ALRIGHT, MAMA," she whispered in Bess's ear.

CHAPTER 14

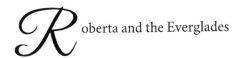
oberta and the Everglades

ROBERTA WAS GETTING TIRED from the drive down to the Everglades when she found herself off the main highway. She was driving down a particularly precarious roadway where mother nature was reclaiming her stolen bounty. She bounced back and forth as she crossed over broken asphalt and deep potholes filled with the larvae of mosquitoes, wallowing in the murky swamp water. She shook her head.

She saw the small, wooden sign. It definitely read, "Roberts Swampland" in faded red letters and had an arrow pointing down the path she occupied, however, the one-lane road seemed to do nothing but lead her deeper and deeper into the swamp. She looked again for a place to turn around. It felt like the jungle would swallow her and her vehicle at any moment. The only way out would be to drive in reverse. Her mind flashed to a recent memory when she hit a pole in the hospital parking lot. Driving was not one of her strong suits. Instead, she slowly trudged forward, hoping to find the mysterious place or at the very least, enough room to turn around and head home. Finally, after what seemed like an eternity, she made a sharp right and the road spread out into a good-sized dirt, parking lot. At least it looked big, compared to the road she just traversed or because there were only three cars in the parking lot.

She parked and looking around, viewed several straw thatch-type huts, none of which looked like a main building or an entrance to the swampland. The place was dirty and unkempt in appearance, more than likely unsanitary. Even so, Roberta couldn't help but feel the buildings were not invading or competing against their surroundings. They seemed to belong there, amongst the overgrown vegetation, the dark and sullied waters of the swamp and large, moss covered oak. The buildings looked like they were co-existing with nature, not fighting against it or destroying it.

As she stood there and studied the place, she nervously thumbed the snap on her Liberty London Tote Bag. In Roberta's opinion, a ridiculously expensive accessory her daughter Kate bought her as a must have purse for her special mom. Secretly, Roberta loved the feel of the dark green, Marlborough Iphis-Print Tote Bag and with a measure of guilt, found the purse in her rotation most of the time. She scanned her surroundings again, looked at her purse, and decided the best course of action would be to secure her purse in the trunk of her car, lest an accident occurr and the purse was lost or damaged on her new adventure.

She unbuttoned the top of her shirt and secured the vehicle key fob in her bra, joking with herself in the fact her age would more than likely prevent interest in any type of body search. Back in the day, she was curvy and quite proud of her bosom. A few hungry mouths to feed and the passage of time took care of that and now they were fashioned more as "soft and comfy pillows" according to her smallest grandchildren. Not that she really minded, she was very proud of the fact she breastfed every one of her children for at least a year. At times, it wasn't easy, but in her opinion, it was absolutely vital for their health and development.

Roberta walked to the nearest of the huts and entered thru a creaking, ramshackle door. She viewed assorted sizes of aquariums with snakes of all different sizes and colors within. There were at least 50 aquarium tanks stuffed into the hut, surprisingly larger than it looked on the outside.

She viewed one particularly large tank and strolled to it as she looked around for any other customers, caretakers or workers. She didn't see anybody. She looked in the aquarium. A large Boa Constrictor, measuring at least twelve feet in length, dozed under a sun lamp. She stood there in amazement at the size of the snake and prayed she wouldn't run across a snake that size on her adventure. Roberta heard the sound of a boot scrape against the wood floor. Out of nowhere, an old, grizzled man popped up from beneath one of the nearby aquariums and walked toward her. His hands were out in front of him, slowly pulsing back and forth, motioning for her to remain still.

"Eiddy, eiddy, eiddy Missy," he seemed to mumble as he approached.

Roberta wasn't sure whether the man had a mouth full of food or spoke an unknown language. She felt the need to move and escape the room but something about the concentrated look on his face drove her feet into the ground. She froze with a combination of fear and interest.

As he approached, he moved slower and slower until sliding his body in front of hers, facing the Boa Constrictor aquarium. Roberta thought he must be a complete oddball but at the same time, sensed something wasn't right.

"Heel back, ma'am, right slow," he said without turning around, his focus on a dark area, underneath the aquarium.

As she moved back, she heard a pop that carried a distinct sound; the sound of someone passing gas.

The nerve, she thought.

Roberta stared at the ogre, ready to give him an earful, when he lifted his right knee into the air and extended his foot toward the underside of the aquarium. It happened so fast, she almost didn't see it. Her mind had to catch up to her eyes. A snake sprung forward from the shadows and sunk its fangs into the sole of the odd man's boot.

She probably wouldn't have processed what happened if not for the fact, one of the snake's fangs embedded itself in the shoe and stuck there. The snake was red and black with yellow rings separating the colors. It would have been a lot more beautiful to look at had the view been one of looking through glass, and Roberta's heart wasn't in her throat.

The man, in one swift motion and uncanny flexibility, lifted his foot up and swiped the snake from his shoe. He held the snake up to his face while holding the head. "Gloria, you aaaa da devil little girl. How you keep scapin' I never know, you sweetheart."

She watched in quiet fascination as he took the snake and dropped it into a nearby aquarium. He sealed the lid before turning his attention back to her. She inspected him and he was a contradiction in terms. His face was weathered and sun dried with at least three days of grizzle. He was missing teeth on one side of his jaw and one of his arms looked like it wouldn't straighten out. Yet, he walked with grace and power and looked more like a bull that wasn't ready for pasture yet than a broken down, old man. He walked up to her as she studied him. Roberta was so busy checking him out, at first, she didn't realize he was doing the same thing. She watched as his eyes measured her from head to toe.

"Eiddy Missy, well this is a real pleasure," he said.

He looked her in the eyes for only a moment. His eyes

drifted down to her bosom. He made no attempt to hide their path. She realized she forgot to button her shirt back up when she secured her car key and her Soma bra was creating a little "days gone by" cleavage.

"A real pleasure," he repeated, making no attempt to hide his delight.

She ignored his obvious rudeness and switched to nurse mode as she buttoned her shirt up. "Are you all right? Did you get bit?"

"Aaahhh no ma'am, that was just Gloria bein' a little feisty, that's all," he said as he pulled a mouse out of his pocket.

She stepped back. *Did he just pull a live mouse out of his pocket? What...*

He moved back to the boa constrictor tank, lifted the lid and dropped the doomed mouse in the tank. The mouse landed on the snake and scurried to a corner as he continued talking.

"She's a good girl. Heck, I like my women a little feisty," he said, flashing a wry, teeth-missing smile.

She ignored the comment. "That snake wasn't dangerous, was it?"

"Well, ol' Gloria is what's known as an Eastern Coral Snake, her bein' one of the deadliest snakes in the world," he said. He walked around as he spoke, looking into the tanks, inspecting each snake and its surroundings. "Ol' Gloria, we have a friendship that goes way back. She was just playin'."

Just then, another scruffy looking but younger man walked in and approached the man. "Excuse me," he said and waited for the odd man to look up from the cages. "Robert, I can't wait any longer for that Bee Gees lady to show up. Mae called, and I got to pick up Etta, done sick from school."

The man replied, "that bitty-bee alright, Jed. I think Ms. Bee Gees is this fine lady right here, and I don't mind atall taking her out in the glades."

"Howdy ma'am," Jed said and nodded his head toward

Roberta. Without waiting for a response, he turned back to the grizzled old man. "I got Ol' Chugger ready, except for gas. I left two tanks of petrol on the deck."

"I got it, I surely do. See ya' Jed," said Robert.

Jed quickly disappeared and Robert turned back to Roberta. "So, pretty lady. Take your time, look around and when y'all feelin' ready, I, Robert McFarland, will be takin' you to see the wondrous sights of my home—the Everglades."

Roberta nodded. She felt strange, oddly drawn to continuing the adventure. The exchange between the two men, however short, revealed something. She felt the young man, Jed, looked at the man, Robert, with a deep sense of respect. In turn, Robert's words and manner were... for lack of better words, affectionate. Yet, they probably weren't father and son.

Robert left the hut and Roberta was once again left alone to wander and discover the interesting ecosystem of the Everglades found in Robert's rough strewn huts. She went through each aquarium and when she came to Ol' Gloria she stared at the magnificent coloring of the snake. It dawned on her, that without a word, Robert had put his body in front of hers and possibly saved her life at the expense of his own.

She couldn't shake the thought... she felt safe the moment she saw him. She allowed him to get physically close to her, immediately. It turned out, he was protecting her. But she had always protected herself. She had always felt confident and safe. Why did she let him, a perfect stranger, get so close?

What's going on with you, Roberta?

She left the hut and entered the next one, which was even bigger inside. It was a museum of stuffed animals native to Florida with short descriptions underneath each display, written on what appeared to be old pieces of barn wood. The museum had an armadillo, marsh rabbits, a gray fox, beaver, bobcat, white-tailed deer and other small critters.

She took her time and studied each one and the description underneath as she had a thirst for any new and interesting knowledge. She made her way toward one corner of the poorly lit hut. As Roberta drew closer, she squinted and realized she was looking at the butt end of a skunk with its tail, raised high in the air. The skunk appeared to be looking back over its shoulder at its intended target.

She couldn't make out the description on the piece of wood, so she moved closer to read the sign, positioned directly underneath the butt of the skunk. As she bent forward, she was suddenly sprayed dead in the face with a fine mist, ejecting from none other than the skunk's rear end. She staggered back and gasped for air, fully expecting to be consumed by the acrid smell of the skunk. Except, there was no smell. No pungent contamination or debilitating attack. And upon further examination, she realized the spray was not the sulfur-containing chemicals from the two glands of the skunk. No... it was nothing but pure old water.

She couldn't help herself... she still had to read the sign. She wiped the mist from her face and this time, she angled her way in from the side until she was close enough to read the wording. The sign read:

Danger:
If you can read this—you are too close
Question:
Why did you put your head up a skunk's butt?

WHY THAT SNEAKY SON-OF-A-GUN.

She left the hut and viewed Robert walking along the long deck, carrying two large cans of gas. She marched toward him with "skunk" water still dripping down her face. "YOU... I want to talk to you, Mr. Swampman!"

"Uh-oh," muttered Robert under his breath and smirked as she approached.

She put a finger in his face. "You own this place, RIGHT? You are responsible?"

"Why, yes ma'am, that'd be right," he answered with the face of an angel. He then appeared to inspect her and a smile spread across his face. "Did you..."

"You bet I did, smart guy," she cut him off.

He took a good, second look at her dripping face and the laughter came up like a Texas oil well, fresh-tapped and bursting into the sky. He laughed so hard, he had to turn away, wheezing for air.

It only took a moment for it all to sink in and Roberta soon found the ridiculousness of this eccentric old fart to be quite amusing. She couldn't help herself. It was absurd... and it was funny. She couldn't help laugh with him.

When they both settled down, she looked him in the eye. "Mr. Robert, there will be a day when ol' Roberta is going to serve up a delicious dish of payback. You best watch your back."

With that, he served up another grin. "Well Ms. Roberta, I might look forward to that atall." He then bowed and pointed his bent arm toward Ol' Chugger, docked at the end of the pier. Everything at Robert's Swampland seemed to be labeled as old, because just about everything was old and outdated, including Robert.

Ol' Chugger was no different. It was a small airboat, maybe 12 feet long. There was a single seat in the front followed by another single, pilot's seat, directly behind the front seat and a few inches higher up. The propeller was wrapped in a red pinwheel, red paint chipped in multiple places and numerous dents and scrapes on the pinwheel. The rest of the boat looked much the same.

She stared at the airboat and if not for the unexplained need to prove to this man that she could handle whatever he threw at her, she would have walked away from the adventure. Even in her best day, she was not a good swimmer, and the boat looked like an ancient shipwreck.

Robert stepped past her and down into the boat. He grabbed a small, orange seat cushion and placed it on the lower seat. Roberta looked at it. It was faded and cracked on one side. He extended his hand from the boat. She looked him square in the eye. She grabbed his hand, accepting the challenge.

"Well now, alrighty... this should be fun," he teased.

"I think you have a pretty good feeling, I don't like getting wet. You watch yourself, Mr. Robert," she cautioned with a stern look.

"Yes ma'am," he replied with confidence. He patted the side of the boat. "Nobody knows better what Ol' Chugger needs then good ol' Robert."

With that, he fired the engine, and they were off. Roberta felt her heart in her throat again but at the same time, felt thrilled by the wind rushing through her hair and the exciting promise of a new adventure. It didn't hurt that she could feel Robert's knees, lightly brushing against her sides. Again, she wondered why there was comfort in his closeness. And why she let it happen.

ROBERTA'S CAR, the huts, the dock and the two large cans of gasoline disappeared from view, as they were enveloped, in the wilds of the Everglades.

CHAPTER 15

harles at the Park

THE CRAZY CAMPERS ADVENTURE PARK was located on the north-east side of Iris Valley. Years ago, the town had rather easily convinced Bert and Gertie to allow construction of a campground in the park, for families and recreational users. As the success of the park grew, they expanded it to include an amusement park, and finally, a water park addition. Bert and Gertie stopped by often to watch the construction of each phase. They supported and loved it.

They wove the developments through the existing topography and preservation of natural habitats were of primary concern. As a result, each new phase of the park wove into the fabric of the land with little movement of dirt and removal of bushes, trees and plants. This made the process of building each phase much more difficult and time consuming. It was no surprise when each budget ballooned well out of the town's fiscal comfort zone.

Each time, the Gertie Ice Cream Company came through with private funding for the projects. The company asked for one thing in return for the funding. Each one of their employees and immediate family members, present and future, receive discounted passes as long as the parks were operational.

CHEW LOOKED IN THE bathroom mirror in the employee washroom at the park and shrieked in mock horror. He looked closely and peered over every inch of his face, neck and head.

I'm so evil looking. He bubbled with energy as he looked for the time. *Uh oh, Chew you gotta go. Man, I hope she likes it.*

Ida was scheduled to arrive any minute, and it was now or never. The clock was ticking. Chew took a deep breath and exited the washroom, determined to make a great impression on her, no matter the circumstances. They had arranged to meet at the water park entrance and he was currently on the amusement park side. He hustled across the park, passing the Moon Rocket Roller Coaster and the Blazin' Dragster. As he walked, he rehearsed his opening lines to Ida, never taking notice of the stares and inquiring looks of interest from passing tourists and even park employees. He turned the corner of the Wheel of Death and spotted Ida, back to him, microphone in one hand and a set of index cards in the other. She never saw him coming.

He snuck up and stood behind her. "Ida, come with me to the dark side."

She turned around and nearly jumped out of her shoes. She expected to see Chew, but instead, faced the sinister Darth Maul, lightsaber in hand. Or rather—an altered version of Darth Maul, after a few too many nights of intergalactic, fast food.

"WOW," exclaimed Ida as she looked him up and down. "You

look awesome, Chew. You nearly scared me half to death, you look so real."

"Thanks, Ida," said Chew gushing. He felt lucky he was already red.

"This is so exciting around here. I can see why you like it so much," Ida said.

"Well, it's usually pretty exciting but being Star Wars day, takes it over the top," said Chew.

"So... do you run this... um... or where do you—I'm sorry, Chew. I just realized I don't know. God, I'm such a lousy friend."

"It's okay. I'm the assistant manager of the water park division but within two years, my manager, Mr. Duncan, said he was retiring and wouldn't leave until he was sure I got his job." Chew looked at Ida for approval. He didn't care if she knew what he did, but he wanted her to know he had plans for his future. She seemed pleased.

Ida looked over at Johnny, who was busy with his camera equipment. He wouldn't be ready to take any shots for several more minutes. She turned back to Chew. "Okay... well, the live spot is in about 30 minutes, so if you'd like, we can practice with a few questions... if that would make you feel more comfortable?"

Chew drew his lightsaber, spun it around and gave his meanest Darth Maul impression. "There is no need for comfort... only pain."

She couldn't help but laugh. He was hilarious. *If only he was...* she looked down at her index cards, feeling guilty in her role as the love of his life. It just couldn't be. She couldn't see it. She focused on the cards and found a question for him. She was about to ask him when she noticed Chew looking at a man, fast approaching on foot.

It was Brian, another manager from the amusement park. "I need you to head over right now and handle TRex Drop. The gate keeper just fell walking up the steps and is on the way to the First Aid station," he said, laboring for breath. "I have no one else right now."

Chew looked at him and stood for a moment in shock. He was the assistant manager. He had not run a gate in several years. WHY NOW? He screamed to himself inside. Chew asked Brian, "Can you get somebody from your side?"

"I'm sorry, Chew. The park is jam packed man, and I tried to get Mr. Duncan's help, but he isn't answering."

"Yeah..." Chew sighed and struck the ground with his lightsaber. "He's off. He wanted me to handle the big crowds today. He thought it would look good for me."

As Chew walked away with head down, Ida and Johnny couldn't help but feel for him. He was so excited. "You know what, Johnny... I don't think the lighting is going to work here." She pretended to look around in disappointment. "I think our shot would look better over by the TRex Drop. What do you think?"

Chew stopped dead in his tracks and looked back at Ida. Johnny looked at Ida, looked at Chew and quickly got the picture. "I think you might be right, Ida."

Chew smiled and spun his lightsaber in delight. "Awesome Sauce! See you guys there." Chew hustled off and when he turned the corner out of sight of Ida he smacked himself in the head with his lightsaber. "Awesome Sauce? What am I? Five years old. Idiot."

IDA AN JOHNNY ARRIVED at the TRex Drop a short time after Chew and the grandeur of the ride amazed them. It wasn't planned but it would serve as an amazing backdrop for her live broadcast. The ride had a water chute starting at the top and running down the face of a volcano with natural and artificial foliage cleverly hiding the stairs. About halfway down, a clear chute appeared for several feet, wound down and around and then disappeared into the mouth of a hungry and waiting, Tyrannosaurus Rex. From the ground, it looked like riders in the chute were being eaten whole by the T-Rex. It was even more terrifying for the riders who came out of pitch darkness and into the light. They shot out of the darkness just in time to see themselves entering the mouth of the sharp-toothed carnivore.

Ida and Johnny discussed shot locations while looking around for Chew. If at all possible, Ida wanted to include him in the background. She knew how much it meant to him. It wasn't long before Johnny found him standing at the top of the TRex platform. They watched him for a moment, trying to figure out how to use him. They assigned him the duty of making sure only one rider entered the dinosaur chute at a time. Chew appeared to be having fun doing it as he kept spinning around and using his lightsaber as a gate to let riders into the chute. It was obvious kids were having a ball finding Darth Maul at the top of their climb.

Ida and Johnny both waved and yelled up at Chew, but he was too busy wielding his mighty lightsaber and having fun with the kids. He forgot about them. Before they knew it, Ida's live feed was seconds away. They decided Johnny would cut to Chew at the top while Ida discussed the T-rex ride, hopeful Chew would notice by then.

"3, 2, 1…" said Johnny.

"Hi Knox," said Ida, responding to in-studio newsman, Knox Fairhoff. She was listening to him via earpiece. "Yes, this is my first time here and I can tell you I'm way more excited than I imagined." She listened to the seasoned vet throw easy softballs her way. It was a nice professional gesture.

"Yes, I think if you really want to see and do it all, a great idea would be to spend a weekend at their campground. What better way to spend time with your family and friends, Knox."

She listened again to Knox and then waved her arm wide. "If you look around, you can not only see the excitement in the children, but the parents as well."

Johnny panned the crowd walking and gathering nearby.

"Today is another extra-special day. As you can see by the numerous costumes, it is Star Wars Day. A super, fan favorite." She listened again then followed up, "we're standing in the water park area in front of the TRex ride... yes, it is scary. See for yourself," and she pointed up. It was her signal for Johnny to include Chew in the shot.

What she didn't know, is Chew was very ready to get in the shot. As a matter of fact, since the airing began, he repeatedly waved, jumped and shouted down to Ida from the platform high above. He had been practicing his Darth Maul moves for months with his lightsaber and was more than ready to show them off, even in his current cramped location.

Johnny did catch his cue and pan to Chew's location on top of the platform. Chew responded by posing in the famous Darth Maul fighting position and spinning the lightsaber with the bravado of a gifted swordsman. Perhaps, it was the excitement of the moment, the shining star syndrome or "camera courage," but what happened next, surprised everyone. Chew felt confident he could do a Darth Maul flip in the air. The odds were against him in a normal environment but to do it on a small, wet platform would be epic. He felt energized, pumped, and this was his moment to shine.

He jumped and generated enough thrust to lift high into the air. However, in his moment of fame, he didn't realize two kids, around twelve-years-old had moved up on the platform and one kid stood on the bottom of his robe.

Chew never stood a chance. He started his ascent, immediately canted right, bounced off the railing, spun around and while attempting to catch his balance; struck both kids with his lightsaber. The sudden attack by Darth Maul sent the children flying backwards into the wading pool and down the water chute, one on top of the other. Chew the hero dived into the pool, a mad and poorly constructed plan to save them. They were just out of his reach and disappeared down the tube.

Meanwhile, Ida broadcast below, without missing a beat. "Darth Maul is here, and it looks like he's won the battle with two young rebels, Knox."

Chew stood up in the wading pool, his clothes and robe heavy with water. He went to step, slipped and crashed down, snapping off part of the lightsaber. He then disappeared from camera view, meeting the same fate as the young rebels.

"I think we're about to see Darth Maul meet TRex," said Ida and Johnny panned to the clear part of the tube before the mouth of the TRex.

Chew slid into view. He looked like a big, black ball with a red lightsaber sticking out of his belly. Somehow, as he approached the mouth, the lightsaber wedged itself into the sides of the water chute and Chew got stuck in the tube. As this was happening, the producer of the segment told Ida and Johnny to continue rolling; her live segment extended to cover the developing, live action.

"It appears Darth Maul is using the force to avoid being eaten by TRex, Knox. Can the forces of evil save Darth Maul or will TRex get his lunch? I think we're going to find out," said Ida.

Meanwhile, Chew was in serious trouble. The weight of his clothes, the robe wrapping around him and the charging water were drowning him. He felt like he was in a straitjacket and being water tortured at the same time. He tried to control his panic as he swallowed water and pushed, pulled and tore with his hands and arms to free the malevolent garments.

"The battle for good and evil is strong, Knox. I don't think we'll be seeing Darth Maul around much longer," said Ida.

Chew was running out of strength and pulled away at his

clothing one last time. He drank enough water to run a marathon and felt like he was going to pass out. His shoulder popped as the robe twisted free. The charging water seized his robe of torture and flushed it down the chute. He had successfully freed himself and a few seconds later, flushed into the mouth of the waiting dinosaur. Unfortunately, there was a price to pay for that freedom. And depending on your viewpoint, it could be a big one.

Ida tried her best to announce the action in the vein of a preplanned scene. Inside, she felt horrible for Chew. "Darth Maul survived the water torture, only for us to find out he secretly wanted to be a rebel, as evidenced by..." she paused. Ida shot a glance at Johnny, he looked ecstatic. She continued, "... his Luke Skywalker... uuummm... bathing suit."

Yes, in the moment Chew freed himself of his restraints, he also declared to the world his true allegiance to the Star Wars universe with his favorite pair of Luke Skywalker, whitey-tightey underwear, pasted to the side of the clear water chute.

Ida heard the producer tell Johnny to zoom in closer on Chew's "position". She couldn't take it any longer. As she moved past Johnny, she pushed his camera down to eye level and stepped back in front of the camera. Johnny got the message; he focused the lens on her for the closing shot.

"As you can see, lots of action and excitement here at Crazy Campers Adventure Park. Come join the fun. I'm Ida Wells, see you next time." Ida lowered the microphone and her head. She breathed a sigh of relief. Her heart was still pounding from the sudden turn of events and she wasn't sure if she captured the moment well or not. Not to mention, she felt awful for her dear friend, Chew.

Johnny lowered the camera, walked next to Ida and put his arm around her. "You did great, Ida. Don't worry. It'll be alright."

He knew how much she wanted to be a successful reporter.

He really hoped she impressed the producer or at the very least, did not embarrass the show too much. It was hard to tell as the turn of events took both of them by complete surprise. Johnny decided he would do his best to step in and take the blame if things went wrong, since he was the one who continued to shoot the action.

Chew waded out of the water at the bottom of the chute. He grabbed his robe and tried to wrap the heavy, soaked garment around his waist to hide his underwear. He forgot about his treasured lightsaber, broken in pieces somewhere in the pool. As he exited the pool, he viewed the cameraman with his arm around Ida. He stood and watched Johnny, not him... comforting Ida. Chew's heart sunk to such a level, he wished he had drowned in the TRex's mouth. He didn't bother approaching her... he couldn't. He turned the other way and headed to the employee offices. He wasn't in the locker room five minutes, when he received a call from the general manager, demanding Chew respond to his office immediately. At the moment, he didn't care what the general manager did to him, he was much more concerned with what he did to his relationship with Ida. She thought he was childish and immature before… what is she thinking now?

IDA WAS DRIVING BACK to the station with Johnny when she received a text to see the producer upon their arrival. She showed Johnny the text, and he shrugged his shoulders, not sure what to tell her. He wanted to tell her she did great, but truthfully, he was so wrapped up in the fun of filming the lunatic, he didn't pay attention to her performance. Personally, he loved the bit and thought it was hilarious. Ida wasn't so sure.

She arrived at the station and wondered why she never noticed how long a walk it was to the producer, Mr. Howell's office. She looked at the pictures of former and current news stars that flanked the walls. She felt like her picture would never be there. She walked into the lobby and his secretary waved her past. She knocked and entered Mr. Howell's office and he motioned her to sit down.

"Ida, glad you could stop by," he said as he closed a file on his desk. He crossed his fingers together and rested his forearms on the desk. He focused on her.

"Yes, sir."

"Let's get right to it—what do you think of your coverage today, Ida?"

Carefully, she tried to measure her words, "well... I think it was an interesting situation, and I tried to adjust as the sequence unfolded."

He studied her for a moment and then said, "to make it as a successful television reporter, you have to think, move and react very quickly. Not only that, but you have to capture the action with words that are in harmony with the visual images that are assaulting the viewer's senses... while it is happening. People don't realize how hard that really is."

"I know, sir. I'm young and that was my first segment where I had to roll with the action—live I mean. I'll do better next time —I promise," she pleaded.

He continued as if he didn't hear a word she said. "A reporter has the ability to take a potentially significant moment in history and destroy it or make it even bigger—a truly defining moment."

"Yes, sir—I learned from this experience and next..."

"Exactly! Next time is tonight. I want you and Johnny to work on the team covering the protest. I want both of you deep in the heart and capture the feelings, the moods, the stories of these protesters. If... and when things happen, you may roll with the action a lot more than you did today."

"Uuuhhh... yes sir, yes sir. I won't let you down," she

mumbled. She was at a loss for words and fought to control the pulsing excitement in her heart.

Mr. Howell leaned forward in his chair. His tone changed, it was more fatherly and warm. You did a great job today, Ida. You know... I've been watching you for a while now. Keep up the good work."

"Thank you, sir," said Ida. She walked out of the office and saw Johnny waiting down the hall. She gave him a confident smile, and he immediately relaxed. However, as she passed him, she stopped and gave him a mock look of anger. "Next time, no close-ups of Luke Skywalker."

He responded, "my bad" and they both laughed in relief.

CHEW WAS DRIVING HOME AFTER being relieved of his duties for the day. That was after he had most of Luke Skywalker's face and body chewed off by the General Manager of the park. The same person who made the final decision with regard to all promotions. The G.M. told Chew he would have to seriously consider whether Chew would ever be mature enough to handle the responsibilities of a full-time manager. The words of the angry supervisor were devastating.

Chew's thoughts were interrupted by the sound of a blaring horn, directly behind him. He looked in his rear-view mirror and could see steel, bull bars attached to the front end of a big, black truck. He looked down at his speedometer and noticed he was driving the speed limit. He also confirmed he was in the right curb lane. Yet, the driver of the truck behind him kept laying on the horn and driving up his rear end, as if he was doing something wrong.

He continued to drive the speed limit and remained in the right lane, hoping the impatient driver would leave him alone and move on. He wondered if he had done something to irritate the driver of the truck but had been so deep in thought, he wasn't sure. Chew drove for another mile and the driver of the truck kept pressing him. He slowed down below the speed limit, hoping the driver would pass his vehicle. He didn't need any more problems in his life. The driver of the truck continued to ride his rear end for several seconds then suddenly swerved into the left thru lane and started to pass him. Chew looked straight ahead, so as not to incite the driver anymore, slowing down even more.

As the truck approached parallel with his vehicle, Chew caught an object out of the corner of his eye being thrown from the truck at his car and his driver's side window shattered. Chew swerved right, as a maneuver of subconscious survival, while glass fragments sprayed and embedded in the left side of his face. His vehicle jumped the curb, blowing out his right, front tire. His car came to a screeching halt just short of striking a telephone pole. Apparently, he didn't know it, but he pressed the brake pedal and his vehicle was now sitting halfway across a sidewalk, smothering a bush while in front of a local Walgreens pharmacy.

Chew sat in his car for several minutes, trying to calm down his racing heart and consoling himself. He felt the sting of tiny shards of glass in his left cheek and neck but didn't feel like broke any bones. He looked down on the passenger floorboard and viewed a barbell collar, used to secure weights on a bar and usually found in a gym. He picked up the lead collar and examined it.

Who would do something like this? I could have been killed with this thing.

He exited his vehicle and checked for damage, painfully sighing at the sight of the blown tire. He looked around for any passerby's or witnesses that might have stopped to help or provide information on the big, black truck. Nobody... not a single person stopped. He shrugged his shoulders and heaved a deep sigh before popping his trunk and beginning the process of changing the tire.

Chew finished up just in time for the police to arrive and offer their aid. He let them know what happened. They advised no witnesses called in to report the crime. They just happened to be driving by during routine patrol. The concerned officers offered to take a report and put out a B.O.L. for the truck but Chew knew it was pointless. All he saw was a big, black truck with steel bars. He never saw the driver or a license plate. If nobody stepped up and helped, then there was nothing for the officers to investigate. There was no way he could positively identify anything. Not to mention, Chew couldn't help but feel more than a little anxiety and fear at the thought of testifying against the suspect, if he was identified. He must be a nut.

He thanked them for their offer of help and their show of compassion. Chew said he would file a report later, if needed. He re-entered his car and started the slow drive home, once again. As he drove home, he wondered why his foot saved him. He wished he hit the tree. To make matters even worse, his cell phone rang, and it was Ida. For the first time, he felt hesitant to answer her call, too embarrassed to even face her by phone. He would rather run off the road twenty times before he would ever want to disappoint Ida. He let the phone go to voice mail. He wanted to pull over and check it, but he couldn't handle another defeat.

A few minutes later, she called again. He couldn't take it. He had to answer her call. He pulled off the roadway, parking far from the entrance to a local store, across the parking lines. He stared at the phone, indecision rampant. On the fifth ring, he answered. "Uh... hey, Ida." He was a shoo-in for Eeyore.

"Chew, I'm so excited. You are the greatest. My producer loved the story."

"Huh? He... what? I mean... what?"

"I don't know how you were able to plan that, but it was so—

aaammmaaazzzziiinnnggg!!! They kept me on the air for the whole thing. We filmed it live and my producer said I was great! And guess what?"

"That's just incredible, I mean..."

"I know, you're not going to believe this—I was just assigned another live segment, TONIGHT!

"Tonight?"

"All because of YOU!"

As her words sunk in, Chew jumped in his seat so high he hit the ceiling. "Wow... I mean, WOW! Yeah, yeah, I practiced with my lightsaber for hours and hours."

"I know—you were great."

"Well... the... uh... Luke Skywalker thing wasn't really on purpose."

Ida ignored the comment. "I owe you so much... thank you, Chew, thank you, thank you."

"Anytime, Ida," he said. He wiped a tear from the corner of his eye.

"See you tomorrow morning?"

"You know it," said Chew. He hung up and screamed. It felt so good. He popped open the glove compartment and found his favorite CD. He flipped on his favorite Bee Gees song and danced in his seat.

A SHOPPING CART boy viewed the commotion and steered clear of the car, bouncing in the parking lot. You never know about people these days.

 avid the Gambler

MR. HASHBRACK SAT IN David's office, holding his head in his hands and unable to proceed, while David waited, smart enough to know he should remain quiet. Let the courage build, the tension grow to a crescendo. He adjusted his glasses several times, unsure where to put them. This was a whole new situation. Finally, he took them off and placed them on David's desk. Perhaps, he didn't want to see David's reaction.

"I don't even know where to begin with this... can I trust you David? Can I really trust you?"

David looked him square in the eye. "Of course you can, Sir. I'm here for you, whatever you need."

His eyes fell again, staring at nothing, on the floor. "Have you ever noticed anything odd about Bob?"

"No, I don't think so, sir," responded David. He studied Mr. Hashbrack. It was clear he carried a heavy decision in his mind.

David felt like pushing, but a little voice kept telling him to exercise patience.

"Did you know we have back door access to all work computers?" Mr. Hashbrack asked.

David raised his eyebrows and straightened in his chair. "Um, no, I didn't know that. What do you mean by—back door?"

"Well, it's in everybody's contract, in fine print. We don't have to take a computer from somebody to look at their files. I can remotely access each work computer and take control of it," said Mr. Hashbrack.

"Huh... that's interesting. I mean that's good. It should be that way."

Mr. Hashbrack grabbed his glasses, holding them at arm's length, looking through them at David. "Well, I think Bob forgot that part... and a few other very important rules... and laws." He blinked his eyes several times, like he was hoping the images in his head would disappear... but they wouldn't.

"This doesn't sound good," said David.

"It's not. It's horrible." He put the glasses back on his face, one side lower than the other, crooked. "I found an anonymous letter on my desk, accusing Bob of looking at porn while at his desk."

"What?"

"Yeah. At first, I thought it was a joke, but," he paused, looking around the room, making sure they were alone. He lowered his voice. "I pulled up his computer and discovered something worse... much, much worse."

"Like what?"

"He had files going back three months..." Mr. Hashbrack squeezed his hands into fists and then rubbed one balled-up hand with the other, "they contained numerous recordings of our women's locker room... including the bathroom with the small shower." His fingers shot out and widened as he finished, like big, physical exclamation points.

"I don't know what to say, sir," said David.

"What's there to say... I'm ruined. Twenty years of my life with the Old General Store and I'm going from being the next partner to working the shelves. This will cost this company millions." He wiped his brow, accidentally knocking his glasses off his face. They fell to the floor. He reached down and viewed his hand shaking badly. He leaned back up, leaving the glasses on the floor. "Not to mention those poor girls. This sicko violated them. How do I tell them?" Mr. Hashbrack put his face in his hands again.

They both sat there in silence for several minutes before David broke the ice. "If you don't mind me asking... who else knows about this?"

"Me, you... BOB... and... whoever left the anonymous letter. That's it so far... I guess."

David moved around his desk, grabbed a chair against the wall and moved close to his despondent supervisor. "Let's think about this. We can guarantee, we know... and of course, Bob. But, did you say, the anonymous note said Bob was looking at porn?"

"Yes... they saw it."

"Not necessarily. As a matter of fact, if they recognized the women in the videos, don't you think that would have been pointed out in the anonymous note?" David asked.

After a moment, Mr. Hashbrack's hands fell downward from his face. He placed his hands on his knees, creating at least a semi-rigid structure. His head rose, a tinge of hope filling a small part of his brain. "Yeah... I guess that could be true, but there's no way of knowing for sure."

"No, there isn't, but I have a pretty good feeling the anonymous person saw, what they think, was just regular porn on

Bob's computer." David tried to sound gentle and re-assuring. He didn't want Mr. Hashbrack to go over the edge.

"You really think so?"

"Yes... I really do," said David. He paused as he moved even closer to Mr. Hashbrack, inches from his ear. "What if we could get rid of this?"

Mr. Hashbrack's head shot up and turned toward David.

David continued, "if the anonymous person wanted this thing exposed, they would've gone public with it, instead of slipping you a private note... right?"

Mr. Hashbrack felt his face with his fingers for several seconds. He looked on the desk and then down to the floor. He reached down, grabbed his glasses, and put them squarely on his face.

"You see what I mean?" David asked.

Mr. Hashbrack nodded his head in agreement. David made him feel like there was still hope.

"Listen, I know Bob. If we deal with him the right way, we can get rid of him... and you can get rid of the files in his computer... right?"

"Yeah, I mean, is that the right..."

David interrupted him. "Do you think those women want naked videos of them floating around?"

"I... I guess not."

"Then yes. What good would it do anybody to keep them?"

"You have a point, David."

"Right, no Bob, no video files—problem solved."

Mr. Hashbrack stared at David, his words working their way into his brain. His career, his whole life, years of hard work... why did it have to be this way? Why did Bob do this? His shoulders dropped in resignation. "Ok, if we were to do this... how?"

A leader is defined by his actions under adversity, not while the seas are calm and the wind is your friend. David had been waiting for this moment. It was his chance. He was cool, calm and collected. "First, we have to make sure Bob is the only one with the files. You need to ask him if he is the only one who has access or has used his computer. That's the first thing. Then, you need to ask him if he has ever shown anybody the files." David looked at Mr. Hashbrack to make sure he was listening. "My guess would be somebody may have been walking by and saw something. I'm sure they have no idea Bob is spying on his co-workers."

Mr. Hashbrack nodded again.

"If he tells you he is the only one who has used his computer... then you give him the opportunity to quit."

"And if he doesn't quit?"

"Then tell him you'll fire him and he'll face criminal prosecution," said David.

"What do I do if he denies making the files?" Mr. Hashbrack asked.

"That's why you ask him, first, if he's the only one who has access or uses his computer. The only other person is you. We know it wasn't you... right?" David asked.

"Of course not!"

"Then—it has to be Bob," said David.

"What happens if he talks?"

"Convince him, if he ever wants to get another job, or even better... stay out of jail for several years, then it would be in his best interest to quit and keep his mouth shut... forever," replied David.

"What about the cameras, David? What do I do about the cameras?"

"Nobody would suspect anything if I stayed late. I'll find them and get rid of them," said David.

"You would take that risk?"

"I think you deserve at least that much, sir. You've been an inspiration in my career and I'm not going to see you go down for something you didn't do," replied David.

Mr. Hashbrack sat for several more minutes with his head spinning, trying to put it all together. It was all so overwhelming. He rose, feeling like he was ninety-years-old. "Okay... I'm going to go back to my office and call Bob." As he walked away, he muttered, "my God."

AFTER HE LEFT, DAVID sat and thought about the situation. Bob put himself in a bad position. *I shouldn't feel sorry for him. Why do people make these kinds of decisions? This could be the biggest break of my career.* David spent the next hour fighting with conflicting sets of emotions. Did he do the right thing? Is he doing the right thing? *Is it right I benefit from Bob's mistakes?* After no small amount of internal debate, David concluded it was Bob's fault, he alone, put himself in a bad position. Why shouldn't he be the recipient of something good happening to him... for once?

Once he arrived at his moral conclusion, it was like a light switch. David bubbled over the prospects of the fortunate turn of events. Mr.Hashbrack, would see how loyal he was and would most certainly reward him. David felt his luck couldn't be any better than it was at the moment. He went back to his computer screen and opened his Fidelity account. Shouldn't he run with it? Ride the wave?

He checked the stock ticker for BioPharma and couldn't believe his eyes. He did the math and realized the stock was down over 43%. Had Mr. Hashbrack not walked in and interrupted him, he would have bought at a much higher price.

How lucky can I get?

He daydreamed and saw himself opening the front door to his custom home on the lake and walking into the huge master bedroom with the attached office. There she was, Deianira, luxuriating on the king size bed in a lace and mesh corset with her long, dark hair resting softly on the sheets. She called to him. She wanted him. And he would have her. He would have it all.

He awoke from his daydream and figured out potential profit numbers, based on varying scenarios of stock growth. Once the drug reached FDA approval, it would be a financial windfall. Finally, he hovered above the keys in a near paralysis of fear. It had taken his whole life to accumulate his current state of wealth. Somehow, he had talked himself into the position of risking it all on one stock... and the advice of a mysterious woman.

How many times have I wanted to pull the trigger and chickened out? This is my time... isn't it? He thought of what Deianira said to him and suddenly, the decision became crystal clear.

"I'M NOT A CARAMEL MACCHIATO GUY," he boldly announced to the world.

CHAPTER 17

ess's Oatmeal Cookies

"UUUGGGHHH," BESS SAID TO herself as she stepped off the scale.

In one week, Bess had to face Dr. Welborough and as much as she adored him, she knew it would not be a pleasant visit. Ever since she broke her ankle, Bess had gone in the opposite direction, adding—not subtracting weight. This was against the strict advice of the good doctor.

She could feel it now. A sense of impending doom, she couldn't shake it. Was it the aches and pains or something else? Was her mind playing tricks on her? Was Dr. Welborough being overly dramatic about her weight because he cared about her so much? Or was she in real danger because of her food addiction and related problems? Bess tried to focus her thoughts on the chores of the day, but she couldn't escape the feeling, the sixth sense warning her, crawling on her skin. What?

A familiar scent drifted into the room, it effused and dissi-

163

pated the feelings of doom. It was the aroma of hot butter on a hot grill. In particular, the smell of butter and fresh batter, turned golden brown in a waffle pattern. It drifted with confidence into her room. Her mind clouded over and she was soon absent of troubles, drawn out of her room, following the scent into the kitchen.

There, with an irresistible breakfast, stood her most awesome children. They had all stepped in and taken over. Each one played a role, committed to individual chores, in helping their mother recover from her injury. It was almost too much, because literally, Bess's only responsibilities were to eat, sleep and heal her ankle. She hobbled her way to the breakfast table where a fresh pile of hot waffles beckoned her, along with thick-cut, slices of bacon and a large bowl of red, fresh-cut strawberries.

Is there any better smell in the morning than a hot, butter-splattered griddle, steaming waffles, the sound of hot, greasy bacon crackling in the pan and the tart, juicy explosion of strawberry flavor in your mouth? Bess didn't stand a chance. It wasn't long before she lost the battle again and devoured five waffles and almost a pound of bacon. She generously laced the waffles with not just any syrup, in her house, she only used the good stuff. Fresh and rich maple syrup drawn straight from tree to table. The deepness of the flavor penetrated the taste buds and left a lingering caramel, sugary taste—pure joy.

And to top it all off, she liked to add a few drops of the greatest honey in the world, Bobby Steele's very own 3B Wild-flower Honey out of Flovilla, GA. Somehow, the company had waxed the bees into working together to create the deep, multi-layered sensation. Uuummm-uuummm-good!

The last two waffles were the toughest to consume as she had to scarf them down in between children entering and leaving the room. After all, they were still trying to help keep control of her appetite. She wasn't supposed to eat three waffles, let alone five. Their job, according to dad, was to help regulate her food intake. Bess couldn't help it, she soon became the master of child manipulation and psychology. She used her wiles to make them feel sorry for her and her handicapped situation. They bought it and looked the other way as she grabbed a little extra here and there. Bess convinced herself, it was a matter of survival. Food needed and wanted her love. Who was she kidding... nobody could stand between her and food.

When she finished and there was nothing left to eat, she hobbled her way down the hall to see why Emma was a no-show for breakfast. She found her alone, staring into her bedroom mirror. Bess stood in the hallway for a moment, quietly studying her daughter. It was at the moment, Bess noticed for the first time, her daughter looked a little on the heavy side. Bess felt a strong pang of guilt and wondered if Emma was following in her mother's footsteps. She knocked on the door. Emma turned away from the mirror and began making her bed. Bess walked into the room and sat down at the foot of the bed.

"How're you doing, sweetie?"

"I'm okay, mom. How's the ankle?" Emma glanced toward her ankle and looked away, focusing on placement of the pillows at the head of the bed.

"It's getting better every day," she said as she patted the spot next to her. Emma continued to pat and fluff her pillows. "You know, Emma, I love life, I really do... but sometimes, I love life a little too much... if you know what I mean." Bess looked down at her own belly and laughed. It was an honest and true laugh.

"I know, mom."

"I really do want to lose weight, Emma. This is not good for me. And I've made the poor choices that put me here."

"Mom... I'm okay. I'm watching my weight. Trust me on that," said Emma.

"Well, we're definitely not a Denise Austin, kind of family...

that's for sure. But I wasn't raised with a pack of Orca whales either," Bess said, then wailed again with laughter. Usually, her self-deprecation would at least garner a chuckle. Emma wasn't laughing. She looked sad. It bothered Bess. In a rare moment, she drew more serious in her tone, "I guess... what I'm trying to say is... try to use just the good things from... um... from me. Not... all of me."

Emma and Bess sat silent for several seconds, the words and feelings being absorbed. And then Bess, in only the way she could do it, added, "cause that would be one helluva meal."

Emma laughed. Bess grabbed her around the waist and pulled her close. It was time for a good hug.

Bess left her daughters room, satisfied with the interaction. She walked back into her bedroom and looked in her own mirror. She really loved herself inside and because of that, she was never really affected by the whispers or the stares or the rude comments that came her way. She loved her children and her husband so much.

But was that enough? Deep down, she knew she was heading down a one-way path to the end and the wrong finish line was growing ever closer. She could feel it. She felt ill, physically uncomfortable, often in pain. Her knees alone were silent killers. She ignored the signs and symptoms and kept on trucking along.

How do I find the courage to stop eating? Can I do it before it is too late?

Her ever-tired husband interrupted her, trudging into the bedroom after another long and arduous midnight shift. He removed his clothes as he melted toward the bed and dropped in a broken heap. He tilted his head and looked at Bess, flashing a sly grin. "Unbelievable. How is it possible?"

She raised an eyebrow.

"I know you go to bed, beautiful. You must sleep beautiful,

too. How else could you look so good—this early in the morning?"

She smiled back at him and chuckled, "you little charmer."

He kissed her on the cheek before laying his head on the pillow, pulling the covers over him and snoring, within seconds. She looked at him and decided he needed a little extra help to really have a good, restful sleep. Bess locked their bedroom door, moved to the foot of the bed and quietly slid under the covers.

THEY WERE SITTING DOWN for dinner, when Tim emerged from the bedroom. He sat down at the head of the table and looked around at his wonderful family, finishing with a smirk toward Bess.

Bess stated, "boy, you really slept good, honey. What's your secret?"

He turned a satisfying shade of red. "I don't know. I just seemed to be really, really relaxed when I went to sleep this morning."

Bess laughed as they smiled, eyes stuck on the other, an unbreakable bond.

"You people are so weird," said Tyler, referring to his parents as he dug into a mountain of mashed potatoes.

The rest of the kids laughed in agreement and the usual dinner feast began. After dinner, the kids cleaned up the dining room and kitchen while Tim and Bess sat together at the table. It was time to catch up on their schedules and activities. Bess brought out the big activity calendar, and they hashed over all the upcoming events for the next week.

When they finished, Bess thought about the earlier conversation she had with herself. She decided to go for a walk up the hill to the par three seventeenth hole and practice chipping and putting. It may not be much in the way of exercise, but it was a start. Tim stated he was going to stay behind and fix the leaking sink in one bathroom before he had to go back to work.

All the children, except Emma, grabbed their putters and a few golf balls to join their mom. Actually, they ran ahead, while Bess hobbled up the hill in her walking cast, carrying a plastic container, a wedge and a putter. By the time she joined them, they scattered balls all over the green. She dropped half a dozen balls in the thick rough about ten yards from the green and decided she would practice a little flop, release and run to the cup. The greenskeeper set the hole on the top shelf, farthest from the dreaded moat.

She worked on her flop shot for about thirty minutes while the kids played in the bunkers and ran around the fringe. They bounced around playing "you're it" and scattered balls all over the place with an occasional scream of "duck" or "watch out". It wasn't long before Gerald the ranger arrived on his customary, last run around the course, before he closed for the night. He drove up in his golf cart, stepped out and surveyed the scene. A moment later, he was ambushed. Matt, ever the clever one, saw Gerald coming and hid in the bushes, waiting like a hungry panther for his arrival. The moment Gerald stepped out, Matt climbed onto the golf cart and leapt onto Gerald's back.

"I got you, Mr. Gerald," Matt squealed in delight.

Gerald was caught, again. He was so foolish, the kids thought. It seemed like he never saw it coming. But even at 68-years-old, he was still feisty game for the predator. It was a sight to see, kids running around, Bess keeled over laughing and a bald, geriatric old man bouncing around the green. He snorted, huffed and puffed like an aged, wild stallion making one last buck for freedom. He finally bucked Matt off, disposed of him in the grass and took a moment to get his wind back. He thought to himself, he wouldn't do this for anybody other than Bess and her family. Not even his own spoiled grandchildren.

Bess walked up to him as he was recovering from his wild

bronc run and to his delight produced a large, plastic container of fresh oatmeal cookies with extra raisins. "Looks like this horse needs oats," she said and laughed her joyous laugh.

Gerald laughed with her as he grabbed a cookie. He finished the cookie with ease as they leaned against his cart, watching the children play. She held the container in front of his nose, and he grabbed a second one.

"Not bad, uh? Kids made that batch."

"Made with pure love... just like their mama," he replied. He looked at the kids and waved the cookie in the air. "These are SSSSSOOOOOO—AWESOME! Great job, kids." With that, he thanked Bess, shook his fist at Matt and drove off to finish his rounds.

Bess grabbed her putter and decided to drop some putts from about forty feet from the cup. She realized, with the sun setting and her rather poor vision, she couldn't even see the hole. She moved to about six feet and worked at draining a few putts. Out of the seven balls, she missed one.

I can't believe I missed the last one.

She walked up to the ball and set up to tap it in when another golf ball rolled up and smacked her ball, sending it careening away. She looked up and there was Tyler about 20 feet away, with a big grin on his face.

"You little bugger," she proclaimed.

Before she knew it, the shootout began. All the kids grabbed their balls and lined up at varying distances and places on the green. She set up in her best goalie formation and held her putter like a goalie stick, ready to beat away any attempt at an undeserving goal. The kids fired their putts at her in a barrage. She swatted the balls away with her stick and blocked them with her feet.

"Nobody's scoring tonight," she yelled to the kids.

They yelled back with assorted challenges in between their spasms of laughter. Everybody ran around chasing balls and then firing them back at the impenetrable goalie in the growing darkness.

And then... it changed.

Bess blocked a golf ball and, in her enthusiasm, sent it screaming back down the hill toward the front of the green and the tar pit beyond. Cheese, who was at the middle of the green, saw it coming and missed the block. The ball ran between her legs and continued its downward descent toward the muddy pond. Cheese turned and gave chase, running toward the front edge of the green.

NOBODY NOTICED.

SHE WAS TOO FAR for Bess to see in the darkness and the rest of the children were in their own pursuit of balls and firing shots at Bess. Cheese reached the front edge of the green at almost full speed and in the darkness didn't see the severe slope, precariously dropping toward the tar pit. As her front foot struck nothing but air, she fell into a roll and upon reaching the bottom, launched, head first, into the mucky water.

The tar pit welcomed her with open arms, sucking her in... and she disappeared from view.

The sounds of Bess's thunderous laughter and the other children's screams of fun drowned out the splashing sound made by Cheese's little body. Bess continued to divert several shots until Tyler finally snuck one between her legs and past her goalie stick. He jumped up in victory and Bess dropped her goalie stick in mock frustration before retrieving the winning "puck" from the hole. She turned to give it to Tyler and suddenly felt a cold, deeply penetrating fear. The fear only a mother knows, a mother's seventh sense. She squinted her eyes into the darkness, scanning the green and surrounding area. She counted her children. She was short by one.

"CHEESE?" She called out again, this time louder, "CHEESE!"

THE KID'S heads popped up and froze. It was the sound of the mother warning the pack, a predator was amongst them. It was a sound... almost unrecognizable. It was new to them. They always felt so safe. They looked at their mother. Her face terrified them. Bess searched her memory for a moment, trying to recall where she last saw Cheese, before scrambling toward the front of the green, heart pounding out of her chest and sweat forming on her brow. She saw it immediately—Cheese's putter lying on the slope between the green and the tar pit. Something punched her in the gut. Her knees buckled.

"CHEESE!!!"

THERE WAS NO ANSWER. She looked back at her children. "GET YOUR FATHER!!!"

She charged down the slope and ran into the tar pit. It welcomed more company. Within a couple of steps, she sank waist high in the muck and she wasn't stopping.

Tommy, Matt and John took off like rockets, running toward their home, while Tyler and Katherine looked on in horror, watching their mother sink deeply into the thick muck. She dove into the muck, searching, prying and praying.

Within a minute, they could hear a mini-van's engine roaring up the street. Tim didn't waste a second. He jumped the curb, drove onto the golf course and down the hill. He slid to a stop in the middle of the green, the bright lights of their van projecting into the black pit of hell.

THE SIGHT before him brought a shiver of horror to the core of his soul.

BESS STOOD, struggling to wade forward in waist-high muck. She was covered in thick, black mud from head to toe. Lying across her arms, lifeless, was little Cheese. Her little limbs hanging and bouncing off of her mother's thighs as Bess struggled to escape the tar pit. Bess's head was black with muck, except for her eyes and the trail created from the streaks of tears running through the muck and down her cheeks. Her mouth stood open, wailing in agony.

Tim ran forward, jumped in the tar pit and grabbed their precious child. He cradled her in his arm and reached in her throat with his finger, trying to clear her throat of any obstruction. He scrambled up the bank, laid Cheese on the green and told Katherine to get his phone out of the car and call 911. He checked for vital signs and started CPR on Cheese.

Bess struggled to escape the black death, crawled up the bank, heaving for air and collapsed next to Cheese. She stroked her muddy, mottled hair and hummed their favorite bedtime song. She knew nothing else.

It wasn't long before they heard the sirens of the fire paramedics. They crested the hill, moved in and directed them away from their daughter. The paramedics surrounded their tiny, priceless treasure, working to bring her back to life. Tim and Bess stood there, as black and dark as their hearts, gripping each other's hands in vise-like grips.

Gerald heard the paramedics coming and drove his cart to the hole. He stepped out and watched from above the green, one of Bess's cookies still clutched in his hand. He viewed the children, huddled to one side, hugging each other... crying. He saw Tim and Bess, covered in black muck, hands locked tight and standing above the paramedics. *Their faces are so dark,* he thought. He didn't recognize them. They were strangers. And then he saw the little body, so tiny, obscured by shadows and the bright yellow of the firefighter's uniforms. He looked to the sky and prayed, with everything left in his soul.

HE LOOKED DOWN AT CHEESE... and the cookie made from love... fell from his hand.

CHAPTER 18

oberta and Robert

"YOU SAY YOU'RE A nurse, eh Ms. Roberta," inquired Robert. They had slowed down and were making their way through a dense part of swampland. Robert had told her he wanted to show her one of his favorite nesting grounds. He was still sitting in the pilot's seat with Roberta in the lead and just below him.

Robert's legs rested on either side of Roberta. "You know... I got this big toe that's kind of yeller. This old toe tends to keep me up at night, what with it swellin' up and such. I got the hardest time sleeping." He pointed to his toe. "You mind bendin' over and takin' a good ol' look at that there big toe?" With that, he lifted and dropped his foot on her thigh.

She turned her head and looked up at him. "Now you KNOW Mr. Robert, I'm not about to look at your big ugly toe. But you keep it up and you might see MY big toe heading your way, where the sun don't shine."

He chuckled in delight at her sharp tongue but took his time removing his foot. It wasn't for lack of respect, he wanted to tease her a little longer... poke the bear. She looked away from him and the slightest smile crept across her face. Something about Mr. Robert, she couldn't quite figure it out. He slowed to a crawl, and she found herself in awe at the natural colors, sounds and even the feel of the Everglades. She felt very comfortable, even though she'd never been in a swamp before. He came to a complete stop as the sounds of the grunting of several birds could be heard in the near distance.

"From here, we're going to paddle in, ma'am. We don't want to spook em," Robert whispered.

He grabbed the single oar laying down near the front of the boat and stood there, weaving his way thru the partially submerged grasses until a pink-colored mangrove came into view. As they drew closer, she realized the pink spots were moving.

He whispered back to her, "Roseate Spoonbills."

She had seen the bird in nature magazines, but this was her first time viewing them in person. They were breathtaking. It was obvious how they achieved their name. Their bills were long and flattened into a spoon shape with a body shaped like a football. They have a white neck and partially feathered, yellow-ish-green head with red eyes. They are pale pink with brighter pink shoulders and rump.

Robert guided them closer and closer, their grunts and calls indicating he posed no menace to their preservation. She marveled at how deftly he became fluid with the environment. She did her best to remain still and quiet. He pointed to one particularly, majestic bird sitting in the mangrove. The bird sat studying the airboat with feigned interest. The bird had a couple of scars on its bill and some feathers looked missing, bent or broken. She could see a human-made tag on one of his legs.

He moved beside her and whispered in her ear, "that's ol'

Julia. She was tagged with a monitor years ago, for preservation studies by the Audubon people." He became quiet and let her study the bird for a minute. "She's still a fine old lady... over 15-years-old... what a beauty." Robert said it with the admiration of somebody who had just seen the bird for the first time, not somebody who had lived in the Everglades for years and years.

She closed her eyes and listened to the sounds of nature with Robert standing by her side. It was several minutes later when she heard the gentle swoosh of the paddle pushing them away. She didn't even hear him leave her side. Once they were clear, she asked, "wasn't that bird a little weathered and worn compared to the other birds?"

He stopped paddling and turned toward her. "Oh... I tend to cotton toward an old bird, a little more seasoned and some life between the ears. A man can get used to that kind of spirit for living."

She blushed as he turned away and fired the airboat back up.

As he piloted along, he pointed out different plants, trees, birds and animals. And of course, there were the alligators—lots and lots of alligators. It was most notable when they approached a stretch of land in the airboat and a sudden movement would reveal an alligator, scurrying off the shoreline and disappearing under water. Roberta couldn't believe the speed of the reptiles on land. She shuddered at the thought of occupying the same piece of land.

THE SUN WAS GOING down when Robert reached a clearing and turned off the airboat. "There's no better place to watch the sunset," he said.

She felt comfortable with Robert but the thought of being in the swamp after dark did not sit well with her. She protested as Robert opened the cooler near the back of the airboat and produced two, ice cold, Sweetwater Georgia Brown beers. "I gotta sweet tooth for a good craft beer, ma'am. I'm hopin' you ain't one of those Miller Lite type women?"

"What do you think?"

"Alright then," said Robert. He chuckled as he handed her a beer.

She accepted her favorite beer with a nod as Robert returned to his seat, stretched out his legs and dropped them gently to her sides. She couldn't quite understand but as she sat there, layers of pain and anxiety seemed to sink with the rays of the sun. She looked at the soft shadows, the reflections and the harmony in which the ecosystem worked. It seemed so simple. All a person had to do, was be patient and see. Just see. She touched her hand to her chest. Her heart had slowed to unfamiliar territory. She felt like it was barely beating. In that moment of peace, she realized how much she had pushed herself, how much she had absorbed the pain of others. She accepted the moment, the gift... without guilt.

The sun and the beer went down perfectly together and the Everglades grew a dark shade of black. It was all around them, thick and dark. And then she realized, they spoke no words as they viewed the sunset. Yet, Roberta felt like they communicated the whole time. And it was perfect.

Robert turned on the spotlight to direct their path. The mood of the swamp changed and they could hear new sounds emerging in the night, the nocturnal species coming to life. They made it less than half a mile when the engine sputtered, coughed and came to a halt. Robert scratched his head and with a small flashlight checked the tank. Roberta stood close to him, afraid to hang in the shadows.

Robert muttered, "I'll be darned, plumb outta gas."

Roberta's head spun around in alarm, "you... what? You're kidding?"

"Oh, we'll be alright ma'am. I've spent many a night out here. Other than a few skeeter bites, it's awfully peaceful," he teased.

She smacked him on the shoulder. "We will not be spending the night together, Mr. Robert!"

He couldn't help a laugh. She felt a mixture of fear and a strange desire to embrace this new adventure. She realized she didn't want the night to end. He reached into a small trunk and produced a flare gun. He lifted it above his head and fired the flare high into the air.

"Now don't you worry, Jed will see that flare and come a runnin.'"

Roberta looked at him and nearly punched out the teeth on the other side of his mouth. "Jed went home... remember?"

"Aye... eiddy, eiddy, eiddy," he muttered in sudden bewilderment. He grabbed another Sweetwater Georgia beer, took a long swig and sat down.

Roberta looked at him, perplexed. "What're y'all doing? Call Jed and get him here... now!"

"You mean with one of those newfangled phones?"

"You mean a cell phone?" She shot back.

"You know, I been meaning to get one of those things," he said as she looked at him in disbelief. "Half the time they don't work out here... at least that's what I been told anyway," he grumbled, clearly realizing he was in the doghouse.

Roberta couldn't believe it. She was with a backwoods buffoon. She looked around for her purse and couldn't find it. She scoured the boat from bow to stern. And then it struck her, she remembered... it was in her car. The cold hand reached from the shadows and Roberta, the tough ol' nurse, felt the claws of fear. She was out of her element. This was nothing like an emergency room. She had no control over anything. The realization of being stranded in the middle of nowhere with a swamp full of snakes and alligators and such, caused her no small amount of concern. She looked at him and poked a finger into his chest.

"Mr. Robert, you better get me home and get me home now."

He looked at her and knew she meant business. He also knew she was scared and felt terrible about that. "Alright ma'am. We're a long way from my shop but I know a little island, not far from here, that has an old building with some construction equipment inside. We might find an odd can of gas in there."

"We better," she replied and sat back down in her seat. "Now crack open another one of those beers for me. I might as well not go thirsty."

He smiled at the woman's gumption, gave her the beer and paddled. It was a good thirty minutes of paddling before he finally entered a cove with a small opening between the grasses where he brought the boat to shore. Even then, he had to wade several feet in dark and murky water to reach dry land.

He showed her how to use the spotlight on the airboat, grabbed the small flashlight and advised he would be back in a jiffy. She didn't fail to notice how carefully he studied the waters before entering and wasted no time reaching the shore, once he did. The thought of what may lie underneath the water, brought shivers up and down her spine.

While he was gone, she listened to the sounds of the night. Without Robert, they didn't sound as friendly or inviting. She moved to higher ground, using his pilot's seat. While sitting there, she noticed how low the airboat sat to the water. She didn't like it. She turned on the spotlight and stared down the path, anxiously waiting for his return.

THANKFULLY, IT WASN'T TOO long before the grasses parted in the distance and Robert came into view, carrying a large gas can in his good hand. She breathed a sigh of relief... everything was going to be all right.

"Eiddy, Eiddy, Eiddy ma'am." He hailed her like the local hero, returning home with treasure. He wasted no time, wading into the water and moving toward the airboat, shoulders back, chin up.

She couldn't help but break a smile. He reached the airboat and hoisted the large gas can onto the deck.

"We'll get you home right quick, ma'am. Ol' Robert's gonna take care of you."

She was about to say something when she saw something move behind him. She strained to see in the shadows, into the dark and muddy water. The night was so black. She reached for the spotlight as something large and blunt surfaced, just feet from Robert. She pushed the spotlight toward the surface of the water. And it came into view.

THE ALLIGATOR CHARGED.

BEFORE SHE COULD EVEN SCREAM, Robert recognized the look of terror in her face and jumped as fast and high as he could, a desperate attempt to get his body into the boat.

HE ALMOST MADE IT.

THE MASSIVE ALLIGATOR WAS HUNGRY... very, very hungry. And this meal would satisfy him for a good, long while. It rushed out of the water with incredible intensity and precision, chomping down on Robert's left leg and then twisting down, underneath the blackness of the water.

Robert, still attached to his leg, disappeared from view, beneath the water's surface.

The rocking of the boat caused Roberta to lose her grip on the spotlight and fall. She rose, grabbed the spotlight and shone the light on the spot she lost sight of him. She grabbed the wooden oar and raced to the front of the boat. The water churned, like a small hurricane raging just below the surface. She stared, unsure of her next move, hoping the alligator would surface and she could save Robert.

But then, the churning stopped... and there was nothing. Even the sounds of the night disappeared, as if nature was providing a moment of silence, for one of their fallen. One of their children.

Roberta watched, in shock, as the waters returned to their calm state. She thought she had seen everything as a nurse but this pure, in your face, raw terror shook her to her core. Roberta fell, more than sat down in her chair, still clutching the oar. The horror of what she witnessed sinking in, fast and hard. Robert was gone. She was alone, in the dark, a stranger visiting a merciless land.

Out of nowhere, Robert broke the surface of the water and his head bobbed across the glow of the spotlight. He gasped for air as he reached for the boat. He started dragging himself onto the front of the boat again. Roberta dropped the oar, grabbed his arm and pulled.

He was almost in the boat when the alligator came in for the second attack. The alligator thought the death roll had drawn the life from his formidable prey and felt disappointed to return and find his meal had escaped from the dining table. He would not be denied his due reward for the hunt.

Roberta saw the alligator breach the surface and pulled Robert with every ounce of strength in her adrenaline-surged body. Robert fell just far enough into the boat to escape the closing jaws of the crazed alligator. However, it wasn't enough. The alligator, in his haste for another bite, landed on top of the front of the airboat. It must have realized the chase wasn't over, clawing with its hind legs to reach the deck and continue the hunt. It would not give up that easy. He already had a taste, and he wanted more.

Robert lay face down on the deck. He knew the alligator had joined them on the airboat. He looked up at Roberta and yelled at her.

"GET BACK ROBERTA... GET BACK NOW!!!"

Roberta refused. Her grip became even stronger on his shirt and she pulled with all her might as he struggled to stand up. It was just enough. They made it onto the pilot's seat with Robert falling on top of her.

Unfortunately, the alligator successfully scrambled onto the boat. However, as luck would have it, the alligator's massive size hindered its pursuit of Robert. The alligator was too big to wiggle down the aisle past the front seat, support struts and the metal wall of the airboat preventing forward movement. The alligator hissed at Roberta in disgust, not ready to give up. It posted there, on the deck. It was an ominous, impatient hunter, waiting for another opportunity. This was his hunting ground. The sheer size of the beast weighed down the boat so much, the front end dipped down, perilously close to the water.

Roberta stared down at the hissing beast. She realized it had wedged itself in and might be stuck. They might be safe, for the moment. She slid out from under Robert, helped him sit in his seat and stood on the other side of the boat, away from the alligator. It was time for her to go to work. She began her assessment of Robert. He was breathing in rags and going into shock. She visually scanned his upper body and saw no signs of severe trauma. It wasn't the upper body she was most worried about at that moment. Roberta looked down at his legs, expecting some trauma, but what she saw rattled even her experienced nature. He threw her off, showing no outward emotion of pain, stoic in battle.

The alligator had bitten off Robert's leg just below the left knee, shreds of pant leg the only thing left to show a leg was once there. She leaned him back on the seat and stripped him of his leather belt. She prayed the jagged amputation was low enough on his leg, she could apply the tourniquet below the knee.

She struggled to see in the moonlight and couldn't reach the spotlight, so she had to physically feel the stump with her fingers to know exactly where his leg ended. Robert grunted in pain when she hit the spot. She won her first victory and applied the tourniquet below his knee. She felt he had a reasonable chance of saving the knee and the rest of the leg, but first, she had to prevent him from dying.

She calmly spoke to Robert as she worked and told him he was in great hands and would be fine. But she didn't dare confide in the fact that his leg was gone. That news would best be delivered later, when he was stable and receiving additional care in the hospital.

Robert's breath became more ragged, and she worried he incurred some lung damage. She soon found out. While she was looking for anything she could use as a weapon or first aid, Robert slid off his chair and fell toward the huge, cold-blooded animal. The alligator lunged forward, and his jaws snapped shut, inches from Robert's head. The alligator's size saved Robert from certain death, as again, the alligator couldn't move any further forward down the aisle.

She pulled Robert away from the alligator and heaved his sagging body back onto his pilot's seat. She never realized all those core yoga sessions would pay off in such a profound way. Roberta decided, she had to tie Robert to the chair. She took her belt off and it was obvious it would not fit around Robert's waistline. She smacked herself in the head and thought how much fun her friends would have if they knew she made a "mistake." She realized she should have used her belt for his leg and his belt to tie him to the chair.

Luckily, a quick search of the back of the boat uncovered some rope. She was wrapping the rope around the front of Robert when he gasped in pain. He broke out of his semi-conscious state. "The beast swatted me with his tail and broke my ribs."

She replied. "We'll work around those ribs, Robert. You're going to be just fine." She squeezed his hand while looking him in the eye.

"Well, at least I kept my teeth this time," he joked.

She looked at him and deadpanned, "I've seen those teeth. It might've been a good thing."

"Well, lord in tarnation," he crowed and then violently coughed.

She told him to quiet down and the sass would have to stop until they reached the hospital. She didn't tell him, but she was growing more worried he had a punctured lung to go along with the broken ribs.

She found an old, oil-stained blanket in the small, rear bin and wrapped it around Robert. She checked his leg and the tourniquet application. It looked and felt secure. It served its purpose. She then wrapped her arms around him and slid her arms up and down, trying to bring the warmth back into his body. She couldn't afford to have him fall victim to shock.

What now? She wondered.

She didn't have to wait long to find out. As she held him, trying to figure out a plan, she thought she saw something rise above the water just outside of the spotlight, in the shadows. At first, she thought it was the fear, creating hallucinations in her mind. But then, ripples of water shone under the spotlight. And then it surfaced again.

"Oh my God," she cried.

The second alligator swam into the view of the spotlight and paddled toward the front of the boat. She knew Robert had left a scented trail directly to them as the blood loss from his leg soaked the front deck of the airboat and surrounding water. She remained calm on the outside so as not to alert Robert, but her heart raced on the inside. The alligator's head grew as it rose from the darkness of the water. As it leaned its head on the front of the boat, it made a rolling and deep, grumbling sound.

NNNOOO!!! She wailed inside.

The alligator didn't care about Roberta's feelings. The alligator was living by instinct and knew there was wounded, fresh prey within reach. Helplessly, she watched as the alligator gained its footing and placed its two front legs on the front deck of the boat. As the legs drew forward, the claws scraped the bottom of the boat, like a witch's nails on a sadistic chalkboard.

And then the situation went from bad to worse.

The weight of the second alligator dipped the front of the boat under water. Each time one alligator shifted their weight or position, it was just enough to dip the front of the boat under the surface. Roberta stared at the water swirling around the front feet of the alligators.

The boat's sinking!

Her eyes lit up in pure terror and now she couldn't scream even if she wanted to. She left Robert and scrambled to the back of the airboat, attempting to balance the boat out and bring the front of the boat above the water. Unfortunately, the second alligator responded by finishing his ascent and dropping his entire body onto the boat. Roberta watched as the front of the boat dipped under the surface again and the water seeped in like the sands of time in a short hourglass.

THINK ROBERTA THINK! She screamed inside.

She looked at Robert. He was passed out again. *That would be the better way to go, how do I...* It struck her like a lightning bolt.

She looked at him again. He looked like one of her patients. She was in the emergency room. She wasn't in a sanitized, white-walled environment with the convenience of modern machines and medicine, but this was a life or death situation. This is where she shined. This isn't the alligator's lair. This is her place.

Roberta's heart slowed, her thoughts cleared, and her hands stopped shaking. She assessed her theater. And then she saw it... the oar. She had dropped the oar. Somehow, the handle of the oar ended up lying across her seat and the other end of the oar now trapped underneath the belly of the first alligator. Can she do it? Can she use the oar as a lever and lift the massive beast over the side of the boat?

As quickly as she thought of the idea, the second alligator dashed her hopes as it moved forward and stopped with its head just short of the oar's handle. There was no way she could even touch the oar, without being attacked by the second alligator. It didn't matter to her. Just another problem, and she was the problem solver. Again, she went into strategic ER nurse mode and studied the options quickly and efficiently. As was often the case in a crisis, she could always remove herself from the situation and work with unnerving skill toward a solution.

She took mere seconds to formulate a second plan. She found the flare gun in the trunk and loaded another round. For a foolhardy second, she looked at the can of gas sitting next to the second alligator and thought about shooting the gas can and blowing up the alligator. She couldn't believe it but the thought made her laugh. It was absurd. Not only was the idea improbable but also, if they survived the blast, they needed the gas to get home. And would it even blow up?

Instead, she set up in her old track position, choosing to forget she hadn't run on a track in over forty years. She crouched on the side of the boat away from the beast alligator and stared directly at the second alligator, only a few feet away. Luckily, the beast had not moved further forward. Or, did it know by remaining there, it was flooding the boat? Could it know? Is that possible?

"You can do it, Roberta," she said out loud. She needed to hear a voice of confidence.

She rolled back and forth on her feet to loosen up and dropped to get in the downward dog position before catching herself.

What is wrong with you, Roberta? She didn't have time to warm up. She had no idea why she started doing yoga moves. She felt water on her toes. She was out of time!!! It was now or never. *Do I charge first and shoot or do I shoot then charge?*

She took a good look at the second alligator and decided to shoot first. It must have been 50 years since she last was on her uncle's farm and shot his old Smith and Wesson revolver. There were many times she was invited to the range by police officer friends over the years. She was sorry now, she had never followed up on the offers. She aimed the flare gun dead between the eyes of the second alligator and pulled the trigger. She was just off target. The flare struck the alligator in the right eye. The alligator discharged a guttural scream and retreated, scurrying backwards off the front of the boat and into the darkness of the water.

She rushed forward and squatted below the oar, resting it on her shoulder. Just as the monstrous alligator turned toward her, she gave it all she had and completed a full squat to standing position. The oar bent and she heard the splintering of wood as it threatened to snap in half under the weight of the alligator.

However, the beast found itself helplessly lifted into the air and gravity did the rest, as it slid down the shaft of the oar and caught the top edge of the side of the boat. It stopped there, hanging on the edge, for a precarious moment and then fell overboard into the water with a great splash.

Roberta held the oar with both hands while she worked on catching her breath. She felt like bending over and throwing up, the exertion and terror of the moment creating more than a little trauma to her stomach. She refused. She feared the moment she looked away, the beast would find a way back on the boat. She stood guard, watching, until the beast swam away into the darkness. She scanned the area for any other signs of danger. She was about to turn back toward Robert when she heard his voice.

"If that ain't the damnedest thing I ever seen."

Wearily, Roberta looked at him. The adrenaline rush had subsided and now she was suffering from the after-effects. She felt like she could sleep for a month. But, that wasn't possible. At least, not yet. "How about we pilot this thing together, back to the dock?"

"Yes, ma'am," he said. He wasn't about to argue with this hellion. He didn't remember much after that. He knew she tied him to his pilot seat. That was about it.

IT WAS A FULL DAY later when Robert woke up, lying in a hospital bed. With groggy eyes and mind, he looked around, unfamiliar with his surroundings, trying to piece together what happened. He felt something in his hand. He looked. And there she was, sitting bedside with her hand wrapped in his hand. She realized he was awake and withdrew her hand.

"How long I been asleep?" He asked.

"About 23 hours," she replied.

He smiled and chuckled, "and you been here holdin' my hand the whole time?"

"Don't you go gettin' any fancy ideas, Mr. Robert. I've done that for many a patient in my career," Roberta countered and stared him in the eye.

He stared right back, the only difference being the big silly grin on his face. Finally, he broke the ice. "Hhhmmm... well I gotta tell you. That there big ol' gator did me one huge favor. Since he ate that toe, I've never slept better."

She tried to continue the stare down but she couldn't hold out. The man was absurd. She broke and giggled. He chuckled and soon they both erupted in laughter. They had shared something. Yes, it was horrific. In times of considerable trauma, often, the participants are laid bare. Their true character revealed, for good or bad. They settled down, looked at each other, then looked away. The room grew quiet as feelings erupted just below the surface.

"Eiddy, eiddy, eiddy," he exhaled in a whisper.

Roberta looked out the hospital window. It was so bright and sunny, not a cloud in the sky. The world seemed so beautiful. Even though they were in a hospital because an alligator ate his leg, she didn't feel a sense of despair. Instead, she felt hope... and something more. She didn't want to say it, but it was there. And she didn't want it to go away.

"Well, I guess, since I'm up and at em'... you probably gotta get back to that nursin' job uh yours up north."

She turned back to him. He held a look of concern on his face. She smiled. He smiled back. He was a fine mess; missing teeth, uneven-shaved face of stubble, completely odd and unkempt. Not to mention, he lived in the Everglades, where an alligator just ate his leg for dinner. All in all, a complete mess.

"Actually, I let them know, I have a real bad patient down here I need to straighten out." She reached down and grabbed the call light, dangling near the floor. She placed it on his bed, next to his hand. "From what I can tell, he's a real problem."

"Eiddy, eiddy, eiddy," he muttered. He rubbed his jaw in thought. "Hey, I was wonderin'... you didn't happen to save them Sweetwater..."

Roberta cut him off. "That's enough yapping, now put your head down on that pillow and get some sleep." She grabbed the magazine on the table next to her before continuing, "You're interrupting my enjoyment of Country Living magazine."

HE OPENED his mouth to reply, took one look at her, and decided it might be best to get some rest before he tangled again with the prettiest alligator wrangler he had ever seen.

CHAPTER 19

 hew is Spiderman

IDA WOKE UP, TIRED from the long night. She and Johnny spent hours at the protest, collecting footage and interviewing protesters. At times, the protest turned ugly, and it wasn't easy keeping it together, focusing on the camera, and not worrying about a brick or other item knocking her out from behind.

The live segment was a full sixty seconds. She didn't feel as nervous as earlier in the day when she was at the water park. The success of the water park spurred her confidence. She thought about it and probably the constant threat of violence at the protest concerned her more than speaking in front of a live audience. Johnny said she did a great job. She relaxed in bed for a few minutes, reliving the previous day's activities. She thought about Chew. He carried the enthusiasm of a child, innocent in nature and so enthusiastic about life. Everything about life. She tried to remember the last time he had a "bad day". She couldn't think of one. He belonged to the elite few in society who looked at life with sparkly eyes and couldn't see past the good in people. And to her and Percy, he was loyal to a fault.

How many men in her life have come close to being as loyal?

Her thoughts drifted again and settled on Percy's father. He was so strong, so physical, yet... he gave up. He gave up his wife and child. Gave up everything. Was he really that strong? And then she felt shame at thinking of him as weak. He would have hated her if she ever accused him of weakness. He didn't know she could have helped him, that weakness is not a disease but a human condition of life. In all the time she was with him, he never talked about his time over there. Never said a word.

Why did he wait so long to write that letter? And why did it have to be his goodbye?

She got angry with him again, feelings of abandonment and rejection surfacing. She wondered if their love was nothing more than a fantastical dream, created in her head to satisfy her inner needs and subconscious desires. Perhaps, he never loved her. And then she thought of Percy. He wasn't in the room with her, but she could see him clear as day. She could see Demarco in his eyes, his manner and his courage.

NO! Demarco would live on in the way they should remember him. He was a proud United States Marine, and he was a leader among men. The tears formed in the corners of her eyes again and she gently wiped them away. *He loved you, Ida. You deserve love.* She gathered her strength and ordered herself out of bed.

CHEW FOUND THE COSTUME a little tighter than he imagined. He looked in the mirror and the bottom of the Spiderman costume failed to cover his entire mid-section. *Was Peter Parker really that skinny?* The pants were also awkward. The stretch fabric left little to the imagination. He looked down and looked back in the mirror.

"Hi, I'm your friendly neighborhood pervert."

He rummaged through his underwear drawer and found and old jock strap and cup. He took off his Spidey pants and added the accessory to create a more "acceptable" look. He put on the spidey boots. *They fit—YES!* And now, the final piece, the mask. He held the mask in his hands and stared at it. *So cool. This mask is perfect.* He placed the mask on top of his head and tried to roll it down over his face.

"Oh no. Chew, why?"

Like everything else, the mask was too small. He recalled the day he ordered the costume. He "planned" on losing weight, therefore, he purchased the suit at his anticipated new weight and body size. Who was he kidding? He did it again. Of course, he didn't lose any weight. He pulled hard and successfully covered his mouth and drew it down, under his chin. However, the mask was so tight it trapped his mouth in place and he could barely breathe. With no small amount of effort, he removed the mask and took a deep breath. "Man," he muttered.

He looked at his watch and realized he was out of time. Ida was probably at the door, ready to run. For the moment, he kept the mask perched on the top of his head and then, before he surprised Percy, he would put it on for the exciting reveal. He walked through his kitchen and viewed his cell phone sitting on the kitchen counter. He felt around and couldn't find any pockets on his costume. *Spidey doesn't have pockets? Of course not. No, wait, the one with Andrew Garfield did. But where'd it come from? It came out of nowhere.* Just then, he saw Ida exit the back door of her residence and begin her stretch routine. *Oh man, I'm late.* He rushed out the backdoor.

"Good morning, Chew," said Ida.

"Good morning, Ida," he said with a big Chew smile. "You were awesome on t.v."

"Thank you, dear sir." She bowed straight into another stretch. She rose as she stated, "I loved every minute of it." She moved toward the corner of the house. "And I love your Spidey costume." She started into her jog and disappeared around the front corner of the house.

Chew couldn't help but smile, cheek to cheek. He opened the door to her house and entered the kitchen. He didn't see or hear Percy. Perfect. He felt around his body to make sure he had everything. He started toward Percy's bedroom when he froze, staring at his wrists;

My web shooters.

He felt around again. He didn't have them. How could he cover Percy in webbing if he didn't have his web shooters? He paused and decided it would only take him a minute to run back to his house and get them. He looked toward the bedroom again. All quiet. He was sure Percy was still fast asleep. With Spiderman stealth, he slipped out and headed back to his house.

THE LARGE BEAST-LIKE MAN didn't hear the whirring sounds of the locking blade as it spun around. He didn't realize he found a rhythm and the set of handcuffs were creating their own sense of harmony. His focus held firm on the woman ahead, cresting the hill. The children's song he picked as their song, felt perfect. He sang the tune under his breath as he followed the fit and vibrant woman.

Ida started down the hill. She felt more tired than usual. She slowed down to put in her ear buds and choose a selection of upbeat songs to help with motivation. She cranked the music and before long, stepped up her pace. She focused on the path ahead while thoughts of her recent broadcasting success whirled in her head. *Now what, girl? You rocked it last night. Is this the beginning of your new life? Am I on my way? YES! I'm unstoppable!!!* Ida raised her arms in victory.

The shadow in the white van watched the woman raise her hands. It didn't matter. He didn't care. As long as she kept running. That's all that mattered. Run, run... run to the woods. Don't stop. He sang his song while behind her, his voice reached a deep pitch. The song electrified him.

He completed another verse.

Ida never looked back, so intent was her focus to grind through her workout. Nothing would stop her. She crossed the park's entrance, running strong.

He continued driving toward the park and his voice turned feverish.

Another verse. One to go.

Ida reached the woods, feeling re-invigorated. The run was stimulating her senses and she found herself engrossed in grandiose dreams of her exciting future.

He stopped the van on the road, next to the wooded section of the park. He looked at himself in the rear-view mirror, hesitant with nervous energy. A deep grumble grew at the pit of his stomach. It had to get out. It was the final verse. Could he do it? He could taste it now. It coarsed through his veins, grew into a fully-grown beast. It had to escape,

"Hhhmmm? Where is that bluebird?"

Finally, the day he dreamed about for so long. He raced ahead of Ida along the wooded path... the monster was loose.

. . .

CHEW LOOKED IN HIS kitchen and he couldn't find it. He looked in every drawer, in every shelf and in every cupboard, with no luck. "What the heck, Chew!" He scolded himself out loud. He tried to re-trace his steps, looking in the bathroom and bedroom. He couldn't find it, not in the bedroom closet, under the bed, nor in any of his dresser drawers. The search exhausted him, and he worried about leaving Percy alone for so long. He dropped his hands in defeat. *Forget it... dang it, Chew.*

He walked back into the kitchen, heading for the back door when he glanced at the wall peg where he routinely hung his jacket. It wasn't there, in its place hung the plastic bag containing the pair of Spiderman web shooters. "YES!"

He couldn't wait to shoot Percy with the web goo. This time, he was going to win the battle for sure. He took his time, loading the web shooters onto his wrists, assuring a perfect fit. He did a quick test into his kitchen sink. The web shooters were awesome. A silly string of spray covered the kitchen sink. He started to leave when he changed his mind, deciding to clean up the mess first.

He ran the sink, wet a couple of paper towels and quickly cleaned up the mess. As he finished, he looked at the clock and realized it wouldn't be long before Ida would return from her run. He felt a pang of guilt and rushed out the door. As he approached the back door of Ida's house, he went back into Spiderman mode.

Ooohhh, this is going to be so exciting.

He ever so quietly opened Ida's kitchen door and slid across the kitchen floor in his soft Spidey boots. He made his way into the hallway corridor in perfect silence with no sign of Percy. He started down the corridor leading to Percy's room when he froze in complete and utter horror.

. . .

A LARGE, beast-like man stood in the hallway, silent, facing the open door of Percy's bedroom.

THE LIGHT from Ida's bedroom revealed part of his face and shadowed the rest. Chew didn't have to see the man's whole face. What he saw, scared him more than anything else in his entire life. The man looked like a starved jackal, salivating in the joy of a fresh, ready to devour meal. The man stared into Percy's room, unaware of Chew's presence.

Chew couldn't move, his brain unable to comprehend the simplest commands of life. He couldn't see, from his position, the view of the beast. If he could, he would see Percy, innocently playing in his room. Percy sat facing away from the door, playing with an Iron Man figurine, battling Thanos. In his pursuit of Iron Man justice, he never saw the real threat behind him.

Chew shifted his weight. It wasn't a conscious act. He had no plan. He didn't want to move. He wanted to close his eyes and believe it was a dream. A single wooden board, aged and weary, creaked its disapproval.

The man turned his head on a slow swivel and drew his entire focus... his entire existence... onto Chew.

His face sunk and turned into a cascade of twisted anger, frustration and hate. He looked like somebody who just lost his favorite toy in the world and was now looking at the person, responsible, for the excruciating loss. The beastly man growled an inhuman and shuddering growl and it grew in fury under his breath. Chew, without thinking, raised his wrists and fired his web shooters at the monster. The webbing shot forward a few feet before limply falling to the Earth.

As Chew's eyes followed the webbing's path to the floor... the monster charged.

Chew felt his body thrown back into the kitchen like a small and ragged doll. He flew backward, his body slamming hard against the stove. Chew scrambled to rise to his feet, cold fear driving his legs up. Before he could fully rise, the man lifted him with both arms, like Chew was a barbell being pressed into the air. Chew found himself amazed, and at the same time terrified beyond belief at the man's strength. The man slammed Chew's body, again and again, into the upper cabinets above the countertop. The animal roared as the cabinets broke free of their mounts, crashing onto the surrounding floor. Ida's chinaware and glasses spilled out, spreading in broken, abstract patterns across the floor. Chew felt his body thrown over the counter and into the melee of reckless fury. As he landed, he felt the hard corner of a broken cabinet stab his back. He bounced off the cabinet and landed face-first amongst the shattered fragments.

The crazed monster worked his way around the countertop and began throwing the broken cabinets and pieces out of his way. Chew stepped on an unbroken plate as he rose up. The plate slid across the floor under his weight and his leg went out from under him. He could hear the man's heavy grunting as he closed in on him. As Chew scrambled to his feet, a broken cabinet struck him in the side, sending him flying to the ground again. He lifted the cabinet off him and out of nowhere, it fell into view. Ida forgot it...

The Tigerlight.

Chew grabbed it off the floor and rose to face the beast. The beast threw the last of the cabinets between him and Chew, panting in his rage. Chew extended his arm toward the man, ready to depress the pepper spray. The man stopped in his tracks, and for a second, Chew thought he would retreat. But no, he laughed. He laughed at the little fat man's attempt at saving himself. Comic book props don't work with real bad guys. Chew watched as the man reached behind his back and produced a large, shiny knife. Chew gasped. The beast couldn't help but grunt with pleasure at the thought of carving the fat man up into bacon-sized slices. Chew had become an unexpected bonus to his twisted plan of horror. He stepped forward, ignoring the strange object in Chew's hand. And Chew let him have it... a full burst of spray from the Tigerlight.

The reaction was instantaneous. The bloodthirsty killer let out a wounded cry and covered his burning eyes with his hands, in shock at the effectiveness of Spiderman's toy. The pain caused the beast to bend over, covering his face with his hands. He screamed with a mix of fury and pain. He removed his hands and Chew could see the effects of the spray. The man's eyes were red and swollen shut, his nose and mouth spewing a mucous-filled froth. He blinked over and over. As Chew stepped backward, a piece of wood splintered under his weight. The man's head shot toward the sound. He drove forward, swinging and thrusting the knife, seeking flesh. Chew backed into the corner, by the rear kitchen door, as the man worked his way closer. Chew looked at the door. He had a chance. He could run out the door and never come back. But he did not.

He would not leave... no matter what... not today... NOT EVER!!! For somewhere beyond the madman, in danger, was the boy he loved. The boy who needed a hero.

"YOU WILL NOT HURT MY SON!!!"

WITH CHEW'S location given away, the crazed man charged, intent to impale his prey like a raw skewer of meat. He didn't have to... because Chew was coming for him. They clashed like two rhinos in a heated, raging exchange. But there was only one, true alpha male. And his name was Chew.

Chew drove him backwards and rammed the unwanted murderer against the countertop. The man's lower back snapped and bent. Chew reached down and put one arm between the man's legs and one arm over the man's shoulder. Chew did his own lifting. He was Hulk Hogan, and he was going to body slam the man into oblivion. With a primordial roar, Chew lifted the monster high in the air, above his head. And then... the pain.

It felt like a hot poker as it drove deep into him. It slid between his shoulder blades and sunk deep into his back. The pain took his breath away, he froze in place except for his arms, shaking under the weight of the man's body. A foot staggered and his body almost gave out. He felt an urgent need to drop the man, reach back and get the hot blade out of his back.

AND THEN HE SAW HIM. Percy.

THE LITTLE BOY stood in the hallway's corner, silent, engulfed in fear. Chew forgot his pain. He needed to get to his boy. Chew heaved the beast high up and slammed the man to the ground with splintering authority. Unfortunately, the power with which he threw the man caused Chew to hurtle forward. He tripped over the man's body and his head came slamming down against the edge of the marble countertop.

CHEW FELL TO THE GROUND... unconscious.

IDA FINISHED HER RUN, in near record time. *It's funny how*

that works, she thought. Earlier, she almost talked herself out of training and now she was bursting with energy. She slowed from a jog to a walk as she closed in on her house. She stopped on the front lawn and did a few warm-down stretches. It felt good. She finished, walked around the front corner of her house, and nearly walked into the back of a white van, parked deep in her driveway.

The euphoria she felt from the run, drained and replaced by a palpable, pulsating fear. Something is wrong. This is wrong. She ducked low and worked her way to the front of the van. She peeked her head in the driver's side window. There was nobody in the van. She scanned the inside. It startled her—a small, hideous looking mask that sent immediate chills up her neck and spine. It sat on the passenger seat.

She felt scared, a deep penetrating fear for herself. It only lasted a moment as her thoughts turned to Percy. She moved past the van, into her backyard. She looked at her wrist. It sunk in, she forgot to take her Tigerlight. She saw a brick, lying against the house. She never noticed it before. She picked it up in her strong hand and quietly grabbed the door knob of the back door. She twisted and the sound felt deafening. She pushed the door open, slow like a steady wind. The door reached the halfway point and stopped. She pushed harder. It didn't budge. For some reason, the face of Jack Nicholson poking his head through the door lit up her mind. She peered inside but the brightness of the morning caused a darkening effect of the kitchen. She struggled to breathe. An invisible force choked her. She couldn't swallow.

She brought her body against the door and pushed. Nothing. She squinted her eyes, straining to find something familiar. Something to re-assure her that everything was fine, her mind creating unnecessary forbidden thoughts. She didn't know. Ida knew what she had to do. She stuck her head between the door and the frame. It felt like she was putting her head in a guillotine. Her head pushed past the light and into the shadows. The white of her eyes broke the interior.

The first thing she viewed was the clear view into the kitchen. It didn't register why. Her mind couldn't figure it out. She looked to the right and viewed a mangled kitchen cabinet, perched on her small kitchen table. She heard the faintest sound of a whisper. She looked past the table, into the hallway.

She saw Percy.

Now, nothing else mattered. She slammed her shoulder against the door. It opened a few inches. She drew back and slammed it again. This time, the door gave way, the cabinet obstruction spitting free. She wasn't prepared for the sight before her.

A man, a massive-sized man lay face up on her kitchen floor. She looked closer and realized his neck was bent around a piece of one of her cabinets. His eyes were swollen and red. One eye stood open and dust had settled over it. He was dead. She looked past him at another body in a Spiderman suit, face down in the rubble. She knew it had to be Chew.

She rushed to his side, failing to see the blood drenching his shirt as the color blended with his Spiderman costume. She looked at Percy. He walked to her and stood next to her. As she kneeled there, she put one arm around Percy. They stared at Chew. His chest rose and fell. He was alive. She placed her hand on his back and felt the blood-soaked shirt. It made a squishing sound. She looked at her palm... it was red.

She felt afraid to move him. She wasn't sure what to do. She grabbed her cell phone and called the police, never letting go of Percy. The police were there within a couple of minutes, assessed the scene and called for an ambulance. She thought an officer said Chew was struggling to breathe but hanging in there. She watched him apply a pressure bandage to Chew's back. She thought the officer said he was ex-military. The ambulance arrived, she lost sight of him or she couldn't recall how they got him to the ambulance. She kept hugging Percy, burying her head into him. He squeezed his mother. He didn't cry.

Chew was being lifted into the ambulance on the gurney when he woke up. He reached out and grabbed the door, preventing the paramedics from pushing the gurney into the back of the ambulance.

"PERCY... PERCY!!!" He yelled out Percy's name like a mother calling for her cub.

The paramedics gave another good push. Chew held on tighter. He wasn't going anywhere until he saw Percy. He yelled for Percy again. Ida heard his cry. She let go of her son. Percy ran and jumped onto the rear bumper of the truck. He scrambled onto the gurney. Chew wrapped him up in his arms. They cried, together.

"What happened?" Chew asked.

"Spiderman saved me."

Ida stood in silence as the tears ran down her cheeks. She watched the two of them together. She realized she was not only crying in joy for her son's safety... she was also crying for Chew. Feelings began to surface and threaten to overwhelm her. What would she have done without him? What would their life be like without him?

The paramedic finally persuaded Chew he had to go to the hospital. Percy gave Chew one more good hug and let him go. A paramedic led Percy off the gurney, and he jumped the last step to the ground. As the door closed, Chew yelled out to Percy.

"I love you, Iron Man."

"I love you too, Spidey."

Percy and Ida held hands and watched the ambulance speed away. Percy turned to Ida.

"I told you he was my superhero."

Ida looked at her son and kissed him on the forehead. She turned back and watched the ambulance drive away. She stared at the ambulance as it raced from sight, lights and siren blaring. She didn't see the lights. She didn't hear the siren. She could only see Chew.

HE WAS IN THE hospital for almost three weeks. During that time, he rose from a floundering assistant manager to a local and national hero. As it turned out, Chew stopped the monster that left a trail of broken families across five states over a span of twenty years. And he did it with singular courage and fearlessness. The news media loved the story, and the public loved Chew even more.

In the time he was in the hospital, they interviewed him no less than twenty times, by everyone from the local news network to CNN to Good Morning America. They labeled him as an American hero. And, the fact he did it in a Spiderman costume made it even more intriguing and news worthy.

The owner of the water park even came to see him and offered Chew the new position of Guest Relations Manager. They would give him the freedom to choose his own hours and the ability to interact with park guests as he pleased. Chew loved the idea and the generous raise wasn't bad either.

Chew appreciated the attention but all he really wanted was to be home with Ida and Percy. It's not that he didn't see them. Ida brought Percy to the hospital every day. Percy was a ball of fire each time he saw Chew, the hospital environment unable to contain his excitement and enthusiasm when he visited his own, personal superhero.

However, Ida was always quiet. She was not her talkative self. At times, Chew felt like she was studying him and when he looked toward her, she would look away as if she didn't want to interact with him. Her behavior baffled chew, and it worried him. He questioned all the things he did that momentous day and came up with a thousand and one ways he felt he screwed up. Any, of which, could turn Ida against him.

IT WAS PROBABLY A month after they released him from the hospital when Ida gave him the answer, he wasn't sure he wanted to receive. By that time, the media requests had died off as they moved forward to the next big thing. Life had settled back into a normal and comfortable routine. It was a sunny Monday morning. Unexpectedly, Percy had told Chew he could play the hero for their make-believe games and asked him to dress up as Han Solo.

Chew crossed the yard and quietly snuck into the kitchen with his DL44 blaster, drawn and ready to fire. He worked his way through the kitchen and living room with no sign of Percy. Chew didn't find this unusual as the battle often played out in Percy's room. Chew quietly worked his way down the hallway and with a bold leap, framed the open doorway of Percy's room, with blaster ready for fire. But, there was no Percy to be found. Chew looked under the covers, under the bed and in the closet. Percy was not there.

Chew exited the room and scratched his forehead with the blaster. He was going to search in the kitchen when he heard the voice of Ida, softly flowing from behind the closed door of her bedroom.

"He's gone for the day, Chew... can you come in here for a moment?"

Chew was now even more perplexed, as he had never set foot in Ida's bedroom. His heart quickened and as he reached for the door handle, he noticed his fingers trembled. He wasn't sure what was going on, but he couldn't wait to find out. He opened the bedroom door and his eyes nearly bulged out of their sockets.

Ida lay sprawled across her bed, in full Princess Leia regalia from the slave scene with Jabba the Hut. The outfit and scene that led to millions of young men dreaming of a romantic interlude with the captivating princess.

Chew stood, stunned to silence, awkwardly framing the doorway, not sure whether to enter or exit, heart pulsating through his shirt.

Ida gazed at him, from head to toe. "I didn't know Han Solo had a light saber."

He looked down. He dropped his hands in front of him while turning fifty shades of red.

"Well, don't just stand there, Han... get over here... and save me." She stood up as he crossed to the bed and wrapped her arms around his neck. "You're my superhero."

CHEW CLOSED her mouth with his lips, wrapped his arms around her and softly lowered her to the bed.

CHAPTER 20

$\mathcal{D}$avid's Stock Payoff

HE SAT THERE IN the corner, buzzed and jittery, sipping his fourth Caramel Macchiato of the day. He outlasted the retired couple next to him. For two hours, he listened to them talk about their plans for a round of pickle ball and how different foods affect the overall quality of their bowel movements. David wondered how they could have anything left in them as they must have visited the bathroom at least five times.

Then there was the young college student, fixated on her laptop and sipping away, repeatedly interrupted by her cell phone, studying with full intent to learn nothing. She wore ear buds and spoke into her Bluetooth speaker in hushed tones, as if anybody cared what a 19-year-old college student had to say. What life-changing advice could somebody with so little life wisdom have to give?

And then there was your typical oddball, buried in his computer, but at the same time, looking around and scrutinizing every single person. As if they were a government agent ready to pounce on him for whatever acrimonious message he was sending into cyberspace.

Through it all, David would not give up. He had called Mr. Hashbrack who granted time to deal with his personal issue. So many things had changed over the last three months. Mr. Hashbrack had given him a substantial raise and moved David to a better office. David had the sense, at least unofficially, he had become Mr. Hashbrack's right-hand man.

The only real problem he had at work came in the form of Mr. Hashbrack's secretary, Constance. Around mid-morning, every day, he would get his cup of coffee from the executive kitchen and often run into her. For some unknown reason, she seemed cold to David. He would say hello and she would often ignore him. Several times, he even had a cup of fresh hot coffee in her favorite Starbuck travel mug waiting for her with her favorite Hazelnut creamer. David wondered how many people would go to that length to get along.

At one point, he even flirted with her and thought about granting her wish and sleeping with her. But, to his surprise, she didn't seem enthused by his attention. Either way, the awkwardness and discomfort David felt during the daily inter-actions ended, quite unexpectedly.

It came out of nowhere, her illness. It was rumored she didn't even know the extent of her health issues. Either way, one day she didn't show up for work and later discovered in the hospital, kidneys failing and suspected damage to the brain. It was a very sad state of affairs as she was loved and respected by most everyone at the company. They started a fund on her behalf to help cover medical costs and David was the first one to donate with a generous check. He felt it was the least he could do.

It was close to two in the afternoon when Deianira pulled into the Starbucks lot. He couldn't believe his eyes. After three months, countless hours and a few hundred dollars spent sitting at Starbucks, she finally came back. She would have to face him. He would not leave without some answers.

She strolled in and he couldn't help but find himself awestruck again at how beautiful she was. Deianira's long, dark hair bounced as she walked, and her Mediterranean features were unmistakable. He looked at her like a living goddess. He couldn't help it. Hesitation crept through his stomach, rooting him in his seat. She placed her order and stood waiting, back to him, oblivious of his presence. He watched her stroke the keys on her cell phone and scroll through her messages... or maybe review stock symbols... he didn't know. She picked up her coffee and never looked his way. She walked toward the exit, his opportunity fading, voice lost. As she reached for the door, he pushed her name out of his mouth.

"Deianira."

She stopped with one hand on the door and turned to look at him. She stared at him for a moment as if she didn't recognize him and then a smile emerged. "David, how are you?" She walked to him and sat down at his table. He felt better but nervous.

"I... I'm good Deianira. How're you?"

"Couldn't be better," she said and smiled with a demeanor, normally reserved for big shots in fancy suits. "Back to the Caramel Macchiato's, huh?"

How does she know that?

"Yeah, I've been thinking, it's not bad to focus on one good thing and skip all the different flavors." The statement was made with an intended, subtle undertone of flirtation.

She inspected him for a moment and then handed him her cell phone. He looked at her, perplexed.

"Put your name and number in there... in case I need it one day," she said.

He turned flush as his heart sped up. The move took him by

surprise. He felt like his fingers were shaking when he punched in his numbers. Hopefully, she didn't see it.

"David, what do you do where you have the time to hang out at cafes all day?"

He laughed before responding, "I actually do work. I'm in the leadership program for a General Manager position at the Old General Store."

"Hey... I know those stores, some great prices. I wish they would go public," she stated.

"Yeah, I think we're pretty competitive in the market. I don't see why they would go public."

Deianira ignored his comment and continued, "you know what? I think—yes, a good friend of mine used to work at one."

"Oh, really, what is her name?" David asked.

"Even if you worked with her, you probably wouldn't remember her. She's the real quiet, innocent type."

"I have a pretty good memory for people," said David.

"Her name is Diana."

David lowered his head and appeared deep in thought for a moment. "No, no... I can't say as I remember a Diana working at my store."

"I didn't think so," said Deianira. "Well, I have to run... business you know."

She rose to leave, and David nearly forgot why he had sat in the Starbucks for three months. As she turned away, he stopped her.

"Excuse me, Deianira. Speaking of business... do you have another moment to talk about BioPharma?" He lowered his voice as he finished.

She turned back and moved closer to him. He could smell her perfume. His head grew dizzy. "Isn't it crazy... the stock market, exciting yet draining," she said with a renewed sense of excitement.

"The stock is down over..."

Deianira cut him off, "I know... as of this morning over sixty percent. Which is bad news and great news at the same time."

David didn't see it as good news. He saw nothing good about it. In fact, it scared the hell out of him. She had no idea he invested his entire life savings into one volatile stock

"What do you mean? How can it be both?"

She lowered her voice to a whisper again, "When they were twenty-eight percent down, I invested 2.5 million dollars. Now, they are over sixty percent down. The profit from 2.5 would have looked a lot better had I waited."

"What're you going to do now?" David asked. Even though it should have elicited some level of guilt, the news she was in it for way more than him made David feel better.

"I sure as hell am not selling, I can tell you that," she stated and laughed. She returned her focus to David and looked at him with a diligent look of seriousness. "They are still a few months from completing the trial... the trial that will fly through the FDA. Unless I get a call from my source telling me the whole thing fell apart, I plan on dropping another two to five million into the stock."

David looked at her in shock and at the same time felt a lot better about his position. He couldn't stop himself from giving off a look of smug satisfaction. He started dreaming again of the stuff he was going to buy with his windfall.

She picked up her coffee and "clinked" his coffee cup. "I've got your number. I'll be calling you. Don't worry, David. You can be a Caramel Macchiato and still get a taste of the good life."

He watched her walk out the door and leave, deciding to hang around and finish his coffee. He wanted a few moments to surf the Internet and look at a few new Audi's, maybe some shiny black ones.

. . .

A MONTH WENT BY and David didn't hear from her. The stock slowed its descent, which he lacked the knowledge to understand if it was a good or bad sign. He felt so out of his league and the thought of studying the inner-workings of the stock market... at least at this point, seemed, well... pointless. He had to trust her. Why not? They were in it together. He tried not to think about it too often. Let the stock market do the work for him. Besides, Mr. Hashbrack announced he would open the next Old General Store. He also announced David would be the General Manager. It was a busy time for everybody as the holidays were approaching and he ended up celebrating the promotion alone with a good glass of wine and a perfect cut and seared filet.

The grand opening of his own Old General Store was something he would never forget. There were crowds of people, all there to buy from his store. He couldn't have been prouder. One of the first things he did for himself, was order the old-fashioned office door with the smoked glass insert. He accented the smoked glass in gold leaf with his name in bold and his title underneath;

DAVID SWEENEY
GENERAL MANAGER

HE COULD HAVE STARED at his door for days. And he often stood, outside of his office, for several minutes at a time. He found that funny. Maybe he should have put his desk outside the door. It felt that good. The months went by and David found he was too busy in his role as General Manager to spend a lot of time at Starbucks. He cursed himself for not getting Deianira's phone number. She never called him. Not one time. He couldn't understand it.

The one thing he did was check on the stock ticker at least once a day, more often than not, several times a day. The stock continued to plummet as the news of FDA approval did not materialize. Why? He couldn't figure it out. He searched the Internet for information about the company, he studied the role of the FDA. He tried to check all the boxes. He knew she warned him the approval was several months away, but that didn't help his nerves or his stomach. Not one bit. With the pressure of the job and the constant worry over his financial future, he lived on prescribed antacid medication and assorted herbal remedies. Nothing seemed to work. He was even hospitalized for several days with a disease called Diverticulitis. He felt like if he didn't hear from Deianira soon, he would probably have a complete breakdown.

IT WAS MONTHS LATER when she finally contacted him. By that time, he was a complete mess. Nobody seemed to do their job right, he couldn't get a handle on all the responsibilities and worst of all, the BioPharma stock had tumbled over 87% since he invested his entire life savings into it.

It was out of the blue and when he felt like he couldn't survive another day, the mysterious vixen contacted him. The text read;

I HAVE news about our stock. Meet me for coffee at noon.

HE READ the text and dropped the phone in front of him on his desk. A minute later, he picked up the phone and read it again. Another minute later, he repeated the process. No matter how many times he looked at the message, it did not provide enough clues to reach a conclusion about the position of their stock. Is that good news or bad news? Who would leave somebody hang like that? Why not call and talk to me? What is wrong with people?

He couldn't wait another three or more hours. He texted her back and demanded to know whether the FDA cleared the drug.

No reply.

He waited fifteen minutes and texted the same message again.

Nothing.

He spent the next two hours, texting her every thirty minutes, pacing his office and staring at his phone. She did not reply to a single text.

He drove to the Starbucks on auto-drive. He felt numb, his mind unable to process anything other than the anxiety of the stock issue. He arrived and backed into a parking space. He was early. David watched every single car enter the lot. He strained to see inside of every vehicle. He needed to see her, needed to know. Finally, the scheduled meet time arrived. For some reason, he thought of an old Western he watched the other day. Two gunslingers met on a dusty street in a small town... at high noon. He popped another 10-15 antacids in his mouth and walked into the Starbucks. He wasn't cut out to be a gunslinger.

He ordered his usual and Sydney the Barista didn't remember him or his favorite coffee. He snapped at her, unable to understand how she could forget him. She apologized for not remembering, offering him a free coffee. He accepted. He sat down at looked at the time;

High noon

He looked at the parking lot. He didn't see her vehicle. He looked around the room. Nothing. He stared at the woman's bathroom while he sipped his coffee. He looked at the time;

12:15 p.m.

David texted her again. *What is going on?* He screamed inside. He stopped drinking the coffee. He walked up and knocked on the door of the woman's bathroom. There was no answer. He opened the door and checked the stall. She wasn't there. He sat back down, wiping the sweat from his hands. He texted her again; Nothing. He had to distract his mind. He watched one of his favorite YouTube videos where people fall while doing stupid things and invariably injure themselves. He felt no guilt, amused at the people in the videos, clear they did it to themselves. The time ticked on;

2:00 p.m.

He had already emptied his bowels at least four times and his stomach felt twisted into a pretzel. He alternated between calling her and texting her every fifteen minutes. Neither one producing any results. The manager of Starbucks approached him and asked if he needed medical help. David was so frustrated, he nearly threw him into the stand of coffee merchandise.

5:00 p.m.

She texted; CNN Business News. I am sorry.

"WHAT... WHAT DOES THAT MEAN?" He shouted into the phone. He tried to type in CNN Business News on his phone, but his hands were shaking, and he kept hitting the wrong keys. He got angrier and made more errors. It was a vicious cycle. Finally, he reached the Internet site and scrolled their top stories. About halfway down he found the press release:

BioPharma has announced they are seeking bankruptcy protection as a result of losses stemming from their failed miracle drug; rejected by the F.D.A.

BioPharma, a small drug development company, was under investigation for several months for falsifying research and testing results. Authorities have seized numerous medical records and charges are expected to be filed as early as next week against company representatives. To some insiders, it was no surprise as medical experts had warned their results were unexplainable. BioPharma lost in their gamble to push an unsafe and unproven drug into an unsuspecting market.

•

DAVID FINISHED the last line and his legs gave out. Unfortunately, he missed his seat and landed in a crumbled mess on the floor. He sat there, on the cement floor, reading and re-reading the CNN story. His stomach turned to knots. He felt like he was going to throw up.

WHY... *why would somebody do this to me?*

THE FRUSTRATION and misery boiled into anger. He screamed at the top of his lungs as he rose, challenging anyone and everyone with penetrating stares of insanity. Sydney the Barista hid behind the wall, dialing the police. The manager of the Starbucks started toward him. It was his duty, his restaurant. But, as he approached David, he changed his mind. He shrunk back, with arms held in a non-aggressive manner, just like he was taught. David felt tears run down his cheeks. He felt weak, helpless. He couldn't let people see him like that. He wiped his face as he charged out the door.

David took refuge in his vehicle, feeling a level of anger he had never experienced before. For a moment, he imagined seeing Deianira inside the Starbucks, waiting for her coffee. He floored the gas pedal, flying right through the glass, into the building and mowing her over. It was just a flash, an angry distorted image. He dismissed it. The thought of going to jail scared him and he realized his prized vehicle was the only thing he had left in the world.

It was all gone. Everything. He invested his life savings... on a sure thing. He had the winning number. He had Deianira. She belonged to him. They were going to live in a million-dollar house on a lake. He had it all planned out.

But... he didn't even own a house, a condominium or even a trailer. He was still making payments on his ride. And she didn't belong to him. That was a fantasy. It wasn't real. All that time; the thoughts, the dreams... nothing more. He grew angry again. He studied his face in the mirror.

"WHAT DO I DO?" He heard the sound of a police siren. He had to go. He had to do something.

IT WAS THREE HOURS LATER, when Mr. Hashbrack received a call from one of David's managers.

"I'm sorry to bother you at home, Mr. Hashbrack," said Tony.

"It's no problem, what can I do for you?"

"It's David sir, there's been an accident," Tony said.

"What do you mean... an accident?"

"Umm... he's dead sir. I don't know what happened. The police want you to call them. They said right away."

Mr. Hashbrack clutched his chest. He couldn't reply.

"Mr. Hashbrack... sir?"

"David's dead? How can that be?"

"I don't know, sir. I just know the police want to talk to you. I have the officer's name and number. His name is Investigator Stefani, sir," said Tony.

Mr. Hashbrack took the information down and called the detective, reaching him on the first try. Investigator Stefani didn't waste any time. He was straightforward and clear in his explanation of the known details of David's death. He finished and stated he had a few questions. Mr. Hashbrack answered the detective's questions and listened to details of the expected, follow-up investigation. As he listened, Mr. Hashbrack felt the anxiety grow with each exchange. Finally, and not a moment too soon, Investigator Stefani advised he had enough information for the time being. Mr. Hashbrack thanked him for his service and hung up the phone. It was in the nick of time.

"May God have mercy on my soul."

He laid down on the couch, fearing he was in the early stages of a heart attack. He called for his wife of thirty-five years from the other room. She walked in, took one look at her husband and knew something was wrong. He looked at his loyal and loving wife. She deserved the best of him. He dropped his head in shame.

"I HAVE to tell you something... I've made a terrible mistake," he said.

 ess and Lil' Cheese

SHE WAS STILL IN BLACK, from head to toe. This time, covered in the silk of a long sleeve dress. She felt so, so alone. She saw nothing but darkness around her. There were voices around her. They were unintelligible, garbled sounds that had no meaning and made no sense. Everything was so black. She just wanted to curl into a ball and escape. But how could she escape? The pain was everywhere... eating her soul... searing her heart, coal black. Pain that was so large and consuming, it turned the world into an infinite darkness around her.

Tim sat next to his wife, Bess. His hand covered hers. He couldn't help but feel like he was holding the hand of a stranger. Her hand stood limp and cold. It felt more like one of those life-size rubber hands, one you might find at a Halloween store. He fought the urge to remove his hand. It couldn't be this way. It isn't real. He couldn't let go because he would never let go. Somewhere, she was there. Hidden. Since the accident, he tried to talk to Bess several times but each time he tried; she was not there. Bess was gone. By the day of the funeral, he could not look at Bess at all, in fear he would cry again and this time never stop.

Emma, on the other hand, was such a big help. She kept the family spirit up. She cared for the people who offered well wishes and the multitudes of people who rang their door. She arranged the funeral service at their church. She arranged the burial service. She even arranged the wake and the catering. Tim felt like she stepped up and took care of things where nobody else would or even could. He couldn't help it but Tim shied away from Bess and leaned to Emma for support. He looked across the aisle at his rock of a daughter and she gave him a re-assuring smile.

What would we have done without her?

When Emma smiled, Bess lifted her head toward her daughter and then returned to her cave of darkness.

They conducted the funeral in muted tones and soft words, the sermon delicate and well-spoken. The pastor tried to bring understanding to such a great loss, but deep down, he knew there were no words. Could any words lessen the burden in a parent's heart over the loss of one of their children? Especially one as young and inspiring as Cheese?

They held the wake at Tim and Bess's home. Friends, family and neighbors brought enough food and accessories to feed a football stadium. Which was probably necessary, as a steady stream of people came to pay their respects. It seemed like the train of people was endless. A testament to the profound effect the family had on the community.

Bess sat in her chair in the living room and never moved. Her head down and mind absent. At the beginning, several mourners approached Bess and attempted to pay their respects. The encounter left them empty and haunted. Bess would not talk or respond to their words or gestures. It was so unlike her that it traumatized her friends. They left, bursting with tears and a sorrow hard to put into words. It was as if Bess's soul had been taken and replaced by a slate of blackness, an impenetrable wall of pain. Tim found the whole thing unbearable. He stood in the living room and as each new guest arrived, if necessary, he ushered them past Bess. He accepted their condolences, pushed them through the living room and returned to his post. He had to be close to Bess. But he couldn't bring himself to get too close.

Tim noticed Bess didn't cry. The last time she cried was in the swamp. There were no tears when they announced their daughter was dead. That she wouldn't be coming back. There were no tears when they went home. There were no tears the next day... or the next. There were no tears at the funeral. It was as if she were a broken robot, scrubbed of its memory. She was a cold shell of hardened steel. Tim couldn't understand it. He couldn't stop crying and he needed Bess, and she wasn't there. He needed her strength. He couldn't do it alone and he felt resentful at her lack of compassion. He didn't want to... he dearly loved his wife... but he did. The children cried on his shoulder; they cried in his arms and they cried in their bed. They didn't understand either. They desperately needed her, and she wasn't there.

Except for Emma. She didn't cry either. She never shed a single tear. But she was there for the family. Not only that, but Emma seemed to be unusually perky and helpful since Cheese's death.

Tim looked at Emma as she was greeting guests at the door. Again, he felt she was doing a great job helping the guests deal with the loss of Cheese. He knew, he should be the one handling things, but he found himself grateful Emma stepped up and took the job from him.

He heard Emma laughing and noticed how much better she made the mourners feel. He never noticed it before but at that moment, Emma seemed a lot like her mother. Even with Emma's help, Tim felt like it was a long day, the longest day of their lives. By the time it ended, he was more than ready for bed. Tim found himself in and out of consciousness. No matter how tired he felt, he didn't sleep well. And, at least one child would lie on or around him, nestle, grasp or seek comfort in their bed. It used to be, Bess would hug and hold a child in need. She would serve as a wonderful pillow of comfort. The greatest kind. But now, Bess slept in the chair. Night after night.

It stayed that way. Tim continued the restless nights with one or more children seeking his comfort, Bess absent. It wasn't for lack of effort; he tried to get Bess to come to bed. But she just sat in her chair., staring into the corner. She never said a word to anybody, her eyes hollow and vacant.

The weeks went by and Tim had to go back to his jobs. He was out of time and at risk of losing at least one. He knew Gertie's wouldn't fire him. To his surprise, the first check he received while exercising funeral leave had a note attached from Mr. and Mrs. Abernathy, signed and all. The note almost demanded he take as much time as needed to heal and they would support him and his family. He cried when he read it. And they held to their word. The checks kept coming well after he exhausted his leave time. It was an act of true kindness and typical of the way the Abernathy's ran their business. Tim didn't want to admit it, but he found he looked forward to going back to work. It's hard to believe he would ever think that way when he used to yearn so deeply for time at home. But, the emptiness of their house was sucking the life out of him. He couldn't take the drastic change of atmosphere. It felt catastrophic to him and spiraled him into depression.

He tried to talk to Bess. He tried to hug his wife. He fought, hoped and prayed for even a morsel of her former self. Nothing. She just wandered around the house, stared at the refrigerator or sat in her chair for hours on end. Tim would come home and the curtains, which, prior to the incident, he didn't even remember the color as they were never closed, were now always closed. The once, bright and cheery house now a dark and foreboding cemetery. One month went by, then two months and counting. Tim prayed before he went to work, while at work and while driving home. Even the tiniest sign of life, anything. But there was nothing.

The kids tried to help. Emma was a workforce in her mother's absence. On a daily basis, she planned meals, made school lunches, organized chores and brought emotional healing to suffering siblings. The children did their best to stay out of the way, remain quiet and go about their business. They still needed the love of their mother. The first few weeks, they constantly begged their mother for attention. To be held, re-assured and comforted. A child's heart is a simple mechanism. With no love in return, slowly... they withdrew. They couldn't feed their souls from an empty trough. They all put a shield around their hearts while around their mother. In a sense, she became the enemy. The enemy of love.

IT WAS ALMOST THREE months later, when neighbors suggested Tim host a small barbecue party and they would work together, an intervention for Bess. Everybody knew how much Bess loved a party. Perhaps, a little get together could start the road to recovery. Tim was against the idea but finally relented out of desperation. His heart was in shards as he grieved the loss of Cheese, without Bess for comfort. He felt hopeless as he watched his beautiful wife dying of a broken heart, before his eyes.

The day of the party arrived and Tim couldn't help but feel a little glimmer of hope. He was up early, smoking his famous ribs and the smell was luxurious and intoxicating. He couldn't wait for Bess to come outside. There was no way she would be able to resist at least one heaping plate of his lip-smacking ribs.

Cannonball Ralph arrived and immediately made his way to the smoker where he took a long, gratifying sniff of the dripping, succulent ribs. Tim wondered if Ralph was going to hug the large smoker and his body would have to be peeled off the hot shell. Needless to say, with the look in Ralph's eyes, there was no stopping his position at the front of the line. Tim smiled and looked past him, hoping he would see Bess with the same type of reaction. Maybe those two would even get into it and another famous duel would surface, to the delight of the tentative crowd.

Unfortunately, he didn't see her. There were probably thirty people milling about the backyard. Other than Ralph, it was all so completely different. It was hard at first to put a finger on it, but then he realized... Bess's laughter. Bess and her glorious, booming, laugh of life. It was the energy, the driving force, the Pied Piper of the neighborhood. Without it, there was no real laughter, no joy... and no real family. Tim knew everybody missed Cheese but nobody could have anticipated the effect of losing Bess. Not just the family's loss but to the entire neighborhood.

Tim walked into the house and found Bess in her usual spot, seated in the living room chair. She was dressed in her usual colors, black on black. He started to approach her and then retreated. He just couldn't do it. He walked to the corner and stood like a little child in time-out, fighting the tear forming in the corner of his eye. He couldn't let it fall, the river would follow. He silently watched her. He forgot about his ribs, forgot about his guests. He assumed sentry duty; watching his wife, hopeful someone, something or anything at all would provoke her to emotion. He would take any emotion at this point. He just wanted to see... something.

Emma greeted the guests at the door. Again, she had taken

the lead and greeted each guest with a smile, a hug and encouraging words. Each guest would make their way past Emma and immediately approach Bess. They were also hoping for some sign of life. But nobody made it inside. Bess sat silent, cast in stone.

Please... somebody. Please Lord... help us get to her... please! Tim begged in his head.

And so it went, for at least the next hour. Tim watched and with each new guest came new hope. He waited for a face Bess might acknowledge, a comment that would draw open even a sliver of her heart, a soft touch that would melt away at the surface.

BUT NOBODY REACHED HER... that is... almost nobody.

THERE WERE PROBABLY ten people seated in the living room around Bess, Tim still in the corner, when it happened. Frances, the dear old lady who lived down the street, sat on the couch near Bess and Emma stood nearby. Frances reached up and patted Emma's hand, capturing her attention. "Dearie... how are you feeling?"

"I feel great, Ms. Frances. I'm doing really well in school and things are going great," Emma said with an emphasis on the word great. She followed with a refreshing smile.

"That's good... you're such a sweetheart. And how's the rest of the family doing, dear?" Frances asked.

"Ohh, everybody is doing great, Ms. Frances," said Emma.

Suddenly, there was a noticeable shift of weight as Bess leaned forward to the front edge of her chair. She shifted her body toward Emma. At any other time, it would hardly be worthy of the slightest glance or notice. But in this case, it felt similar to the awakening of the fire-breathing dragon in the

Lord of the Rings movie. Everyone felt it... and everyone froze, including Tim. Bess's head rose until it reached the level of Emma. Her eyes shifted across her face, set like poisoned darts, directly at Emma. Her body heaved with sudden emotion.

"Did you just say..." Her throat grumbled... "GREAT?"

Emma looked at her mother and for the first time in her life, she felt deathly afraid. "Uh... um... yes mom... I... that's not..."

Bess's mind unwound. "So... life is GREAT you say. You run around here... like nothing is wrong... JUMPING FOR JOY. What's so joyful, young lady? ANSWER ME!"

Emma looked down, shame and pain mixed together in violent swirls of darkness.

Bess whispered through clenched teeth. "I asked you," and then raised her voice, "WHAT'S SO JOYFUL?"

Emma continued to look down, the act crumbling. The attempt to fill her mother's shoes, too big. The pain she had successfully buried, now surging and overtaking her. "I... I... what, I mean is... I'm doing okay, mom."

"Cheese is DEAD. Cheese is DEAD I SAID!!! And you are just Miss Happy Face around here... AREN'T YOU?"

Emma's face drained. Her mother broke through the facade. It was all crumbling, the pain washing over her in a relentless torrent of despair. "I... I... was just..."

Bess cut her off, "just what, Emma? Eat another whole chicken and a box of Pringles. Look at you... you're so busy having a good time you're getting fat. You might want to do a little less opening of your mouth... for talking... AND EATING!!!" Bess stared at her daughter in complete contempt.

Emma looked at her mother and then looked at the stunned guests. She tried hard to force a smile, she really did... to do what she had to do... to be the heart of the family. But it was too big a role, even for one so fervent in desire and filled with so much love for her family. Her face contorted as she tried to smile. "It's okay... I... I..." her face sagged with the weight of her pain. She couldn't finish.

Tim felt glued to the wall, chained to a room of torture. He didn't know what to do, he didn't know if he could do anything. He wanted to rush in and force the two together, hold them... make them feel. But something stopped him. Bess sat up in her seat and continued to pierce her daughter with her cold-blooded eyes. The room became agonizingly quiet.

Emma lifted her head. She had to look at her mother. She had to tell her mother the truth. "I miss..."

"YOU SURE DON'T ACT LIKE IT!!!" Bess pierced Emma's heart with the poisoned darts.

Emma felt her face begin to give out, she started to bring her hands up, as if to catch her face... from falling. She didn't want to break down in front of her beloved mother. She wanted so badly to be strong for the mother she loved and the family that needed her. But, the crack in the great wall had begun and as her face contorted, the pain surfaced like a throbbing, unstoppable force. It was too much for anybody to bear, let alone a young lady barely entering adulthood.

She viewed her mother put both of her hands on the arms of the chair and clamp down on them like a huge python, squeezing the life out of a helpless victim. She felt like her mother was squeezing the life out of her... and relished it. Emma couldn't hold it in any longer and released a long, slow quivering sob. The sobs grew into a broken crescendo and then the words came out like the raging turbulence of a broken dam,

"I'M PREGNANT MOM!"

EMMA'S HANDS successfully caught her face as her head fell into them. She stood there and sobbed. It was the type of cry where the release is so great it is hard to even breathe.

Tim broke out of his shock at the exchange and started to move toward Emma. He felt like everything was in slow motion. He couldn't get to her fast enough. Yet, he wasn't even sure he was moving, his mind unable to process the world. Bess released her grip on the chair. Her face contorted and slowly changed shape. Her eyes came to life as she stared at Emma. They grew with knowledge as she recognized her oldest daughter. Memories of her former self raced through her veins and charged to her heart. Her face softened and warmed like freshly stoked wood in a backyard fire.

"My sweet angel, Emma," she cried out.

The gates of emotion released and flooded the room. She opened her arms wide for Emma as the well broke and the tears flowed freely down her cheeks. Emma sunk in her mother's arms and curled up in a fetal position. The chair held them, mother and daughter, releasing their pain together as one.

Tim sobbed in the corner. When the time was right, he would join them. The most important thing, for now, was the fact he knew Bess's heart had started beating again. He wiped the tears of silent joy from his face. It was of no use; the rivulets of renewed hope would not be stopping anytime soon. He felt the other children around him. He hadn't realized they were in the room. They were all there. He wrapped them up in his arms. They were a family again.

IT WAS EARLY MORNING, a few days later, when Bess woke up and found herself staring in the mirror. Yes, she had lost weight, quite a bit of weight. But she didn't look or feel healthy. It was all related to grief.

She decided, it would be okay to indulge in a rather handsome portion of blueberry pancakes, bacon and hash browns. It was one of her morning favorites. She strode into the kitchen and carefully brought out the ingredients and tools necessary to bring some morning happiness. She whistled as she made breakfast for everyone and watched as they piled in and devoured pancakes like they hadn't seen a real meal in months.

She found herself looking closely at each child and would swear they all looked like they had aged at an inconsiderate rate. Each one looked a little bigger, a little more mature and perhaps a little wiser in their approach to life. She finished feeding and taking care of their needs and soon found herself alone, ready to enjoy a palatial stack of hot and buttery goodness. She sat down in front of the steaming pancakes and found herself unable to eat a single bite. She couldn't quite understand what was happening. She sat for a long time, staring, as the steam from the stack of pancakes slowly dissipated. She twisted the hash browns apart with her fork; they were golden-crusted, soft and buttery. She picked up a slice of bacon and twisted it in her fingers. It was thick and burned down to the perfect shades of browns.

After considerable thought, Bess picked up the plate and disposed of the contents in the refuse. She toasted a slice of multi-grain bread, peeled a fresh orange and boiled, two hard-boiled eggs from the refrigerator. As she spread a small dab of raspberry preserves on her toast, she looked up at the top of the fridge and smiled.

I'M GOING to be okay. I love you, Cheese. I will love you forever.

SEVERAL MONTHS LATER, THE day finally arrived. Bess received word Tim was en route to the hospital with Emma. A new baby was ready to start a new and exciting journey with a family committed to love, forgiveness and compassion. Bess was hanging upside down and chalking, when Lou yelled she needed to get off the rock and get to the hospital. He didn't need to say another word. She immediately let go and the auto belay system gently dropped her to the ground. She laughed at the irony, now, she really wanted it to go fast. She was so excited, she was willing to risk another injury.

Lou helped her unhook, and she gave him a big wet kiss on the cheek. He blushed in surprise and she laughed with joy. She started to swagger away and then looked back at Lou, as if to say, how dare you look at my butt. He blushed again, and she really laughed. *She sure is something,* Lou thought.

Bess entered the hospital room and couldn't help but notice how much Emma lit up the room. The last few months were not easy. The process of pain and healing, long from over. But, during the same time, Bess and Emma reached a whole new level of bonding. A friendship that would prove to serve them well for the rest of their lives.

Tim and Bess were by her side for the whole delivery process. It was a blessed journey for everyone in the family. The only hiccup occurring when Bess challenged Doctor Leslie to a fight, because she wanted to be in the "catcher" position and receive the baby when it emerged from the birth canal. Tim stood at the head of the bed, not sure whether to call his buddy, start a wager pool in the hospital waiting room or stand between the two combatants as they hashed out their differences. In the end, he made the smart play by staying out of it. His job was to hold his daughter's hand and caress her hair. Emma knew the sex of the baby but refused to tell her parents. She wanted it to be a surprise. Her mother pled and begged her for weeks and Emma remained steadfast in her silence. Luckily for everyone, the doctor emerged as the victor in the battle for position rights for the delivery. Tim was glad he didn't make the call and bet as his money would have been on Bess.

Emma had a flawless delivery. The baby emerged from the

birth canal as Bess stood next to the doctor. Tim watched as Bess's hands began to tremble and cover her mouth in joy. Dr. Leslie handed the baby to the nurse and the baby's vital stats were checked. She was healthy. The nurse turned to Bess and placed the newborn girl in her arms. Bess wrapped the baby in her bosom, tears dropping onto the blanket. She walked the baby to Emma who held a tiny knit ball in her hand. Tim, filled with emotion, stood next to the bed, hand on the rail for support. Emma unrolled the ball. It was a baby's cap.

And stitched to the cap were the words, "Lil' Cheese."

Emma studied Bess's face. She had a feeling but wasn't sure how her mother would react to the idea. Bess touched the stitching, using her fingers to trace the letters. She stopped for a moment then placed her fingers on top of the words, like a hand on a heart. Bess nodded her approval and bent Lil' Cheese's head toward Emma. She put the cap on her child's warm head and Bess placed Lil' Cheese in her mother's arms. Emma wrapped her baby in her arms, just like Bess.

IT WAS TWO DAYS LATER, when Emma and Daphne "Lil' Cheese" Wolo were cleared for release. Tim was at work, so Bess picked them up alone, in her minivan. She had a brand-new car seat waiting that was checked and installed by the local police department. For a second, she thought she wasn't going to make it because she couldn't help but smack the rear end of the young, good-looking police officer as he finished installing the seat. Luckily for her, he couldn't get past the "buns of steel" comment before he broke up and joined her laughter. The other delay was due to the stop to purchase a huge bag of chewy, candy sours. The sours were a mouth-watering treat loved by both her and Emma but forbidden in the house for the last several months.

As Bess pulled into the roundabout in the parking area of

the hospital, she viewed Emma seated in a wheelchair with Daphne in her arms and a nurse by her side. Such a wonderful sight. She apologized to the nurse for the delay by telling her the story of the handsome cop while Emma sat in the back seat with little Daphne. As Bess entered the main roadway, she passed the bag of candy sours back to Emma. Even though she didn't feel hungry, she wasn't about to turn down a candy sour. She grabbed a few and passed the bag back to her waiting mother.

They were only on the road for a few minutes when the new, anxious mom couldn't help but notice a truck, traveling perilously close behind their vehicle.

"Mom, what is that truck doing?"

"I don't know... he's been up my butt for a mile now," said Bess. She looked in her rear-view mirror, the steel bull bars attached to the front of the truck seemed inches from shattering her rear, window glass.

"Can you get over mom and let this guy through?" Emma pleaded.

"I can't, I'm stuck here, honey. I will as soon as I can. Don't you worry," Bess said. She tried to sound calm, but the driver riding the rear end of her vehicle made her feel anxious as well. She couldn't help but keep looking back. *What is this guy doing... is he nuts?*

Bess continued to drive in the left-thru lane of the two-lane highway. She was stuck in the lane. She even sped up, attempting to find a hole between two cars and drop into the right lane.

She didn't slow down, fearing it would anger the impatient driver even more. And she heard the stories like everyone else... road rage tragedies... they could happen anywhere.

As she drove, looking for a way out, the black truck continued riding her rear, closer and closer. Bess felt panicked. She tried to hide it from Emma, trying not to overreact as

Emma kept swiveling her head back and front as her own panic grew in weight. Bess saw the intersection in the near distance and wasn't sure whether to continue speeding or try to slow down and see if one of the vehicles would let her merge into the right lane. She was getting confused due to the pressure of the driver behind her.

She looked again in her rear-view mirror and the truck was so close, she felt like if she slowed down even a mile per hour, it would come crashing through the back of her van. When she looked back to the front, it was too late. She realized the light had already turned yellow, but no idea for how long. She panicked and hit the brakes... then just as quickly remembered the truck behind her... and put the pedal to the metal.

They made it through the intersection, unharmed, to the relief of Bess. Somehow, the truck did not strike her vehicle when she slowed down. How... she didn't know. But, everything was okay now. Even better, she looked behind her and realized the truck didn't make the light. The relief was immediate. She laughed at her good fortune and told Emma the truck was gone, as it disappeared from view.

"Now enjoy some chewy sours, you worry-wart," Bess said and laughed her famous laugh. If Bess knew the thoughts of the other driver, she would not have been as quick to laughter.

The driver of the truck didn't feel the same sense of relief. Not by a long shot. As he watched the mini-van crest the rise ahead, his fury also rose to a fever pitch.

"I'M GOING TO RAM YOU TO HELL!"

He screamed at the top of his lungs into his windshield. He revved his engine over and over again, seething in anticipation of his revenge. When the light turned green, he shot from the crosswalk line like a rocket.

Up ahead, Emma shoved a mouthful of candy sours in her mouth. Bess laughed, making Emma laugh and spit up some candy. She garbled, "I wuv you soooo muuuccch, mom."

She reached forward and leaned the bag over Bess's front shoulder so her mom could grab it. The timing was off, and Bess mishandled the exchange. The open bag of chew sours started sliding down Bess's chest, heading towards the floor. Bess found herself, unwittingly, slamming on the brakes as she looked down into her lap in search of lost candy. She leaned down and miraculously snatched the bag out of the air before a single chewy sour spilled from the bag.

At the exact same moment, the big, black truck bore down on Bess's mini-van, screaming for revenge at close to 100 miles per hour. The driver was no more than a few feet from Bess's rear end when he saw the brakes light up. The driver of the truck slammed on his own brakes and swerved to the right in a frantic attempt to avoid a collision.

Bess laughed with delight at her circus act. Emma poked her mom in the shoulder, warning she would get out and walk home with her baby if she cared more about losing a chew sour in the seats.

"I'm sorry dear," Bess said and laughed again before stuffing an unruly amount of candy sours in her own mouth. "I wuv you soooo muuuccchhh too."

Bess didn't see the black truck behind her, sliding sideways, out of control. The driver turned back hard the other way, accidentally over correcting and making matters worse. The truck lost its traction and went into a spin, crossing back across the left lane and out of control. It careened off the roadway and disappeared into an abyss of trees far below the surface of the roadway.

"And I love these chewy sours," said Bess. She looked in her rear-view mirror. Emma leaned to the right, fast asleep, an arm across the car seat. She looked so peaceful.

BESS FELT HAPPY.

. . .

OFFICER "STEEL BUNS" WAS the first one to find the truck. He didn't have to get very close to see it was going to be his first fatal investigation. The driver's lifeless body hung, halfway, out of the driver's side window. There was no bringing this guy back. It was obvious. The officer called for the Fatal Investigator and started taping off the scene.

About an hour later, the Fatal Investigator arrived. The rookie officer looked at Investigator Stefani and couldn't help but notice that he looked a lot like Mickey Mouse's friend—the one called Goofy. He'd never met Investigator Stefani in person but heard plenty of stories about the eccentric detective. One of the more popular stories making the rounds, were the fact, Investigator Stefani allegedly wore women's silk underwear and pantyhose.

Investigator Stefani had no problem telling anyone that would listen he wore women's pantyhose to increase blood flow, thus providing greater circulation to his brain. Ultimately, he believed this helped him think better and solve more crimes. The rookie officer couldn't stop himself. While the detective bent over to look inside the dead man's truck, the rookie found himself looking at Investigator Stefani's backside. The curiosity trumped the shame of looking at an aging detective's hind end.

It was several hours before they were back at the precinct and going over the contents of the truck. The rookie watched as Investigator Stefani zeroed in on a few items of interest. Surprisingly, one was a Starbucks travel mug. "Did you notice this, kid?" He asked the rookie officer.

"Uh... no sir," said the officer.

He handed the mug to his young apprentice. "Look inside."

The officer looked and there was a green, liquid substance inside... definitely not coffee. The officer did not know what it was. It didn't look like something edible.

"What do you think it is?" Investigator Stefani asked.

"I... I really don't know."

"Antifreeze," said Investigator Stefani.

"What? Why?"

"I don't know why, kid. That's something you might have to figure out. I do know, if you drink antifreeze, you're probably going to end up with bad beans and a pretty long-lasting headache," said Investigator Stefani.

"Do you mean brain damage and... um... I don't know what you mean by bad beans?" The rookie tried to decipher the Investigator's words.

"Yes, brain damage... and kidney damage. What else would I mean?" The Investigator seemed puzzled the kid cop didn't understand his lingo.

"Ok, I can see why you brought that up then, sir. But, why did you have me haul up all this computer stuff?"

"Look at it. Did the license plate come back to a business or a person?" Investigator Stefani asked.

"A person."

"On the back of the computer screen, there is a stamp that says the computer is the private property of the Old General Store, with the address of the store. We need to find out if this guy was supposed to have this, or he stole it," said Investigator Stefani as he attempted to start up the computer.

The rookie started to sway as he thought this was a waste of time. He felt he could understand why the Investigator was labeled as quite odd. Investigator Stefani smiled as the computer lit up with activity. The young officer watched as the tall and bony detective skimmed through the files to nowhere. The rookie lost interest quickly. He sat down in a seat for what he believed would be a long, boring night. However, it wasn't longer than five minutes when Investigator Stefani motioned him over.

He looked at the screen and was immediately flummoxed. It

appeared to be a recording of a small bathroom with a shower and there was a relatively attractive woman taking her shirt and bra off.

Investigator Stefani stopped the recording and looked the kid in the eye. "From what I have found so far, there are recordings going back at least five years." He paused, reached inside the top of his casual pants and adjusted his pantyhose. The silk fabric wrapped around the waist of the Investigator, above the pant line. Investigator Stefani drew his Kmart polo shirt down and accidentally tucked part of the shirt into his pantyhose. "We have some follow up work to do. Call the blonde and cancel your date tonight, hot shot."

The rookie looked at him in surprise. "Ok... wait... what? How did you know?"

Investigator Stefani ignored the question while looking down through his crooked readers. "This guy... what's his name?"

The young officer removed the dead man's driver's license from the evidence bag.

"David Sweeney."

Investigator Stefani sighed, "a piece of work, this Sweeney character... a real piece of work."

CHAPTER 22

*B*ert's Surprise

HE PUSHED THE NUTONE button again. "Gertie... answer me... please," said Bert. No answer. He pushed the button again... and again. "Gertie... it's me Bert... Gertie?" Bert let go of the button but not his focus. She had to answer. She had to be there.

Where are you, Gertie? Please.

It was the morning of the picnic. Sure, everybody was off today, but not them. They worked every day. She said she was leaving, but she couldn't mean it. It wasn't possible.

How could she be gone?

His palm brushed against the note, sitting on the desk, in front of the Nutone. He picked it up and read it for the one-hundredth time. It was simple, to the point and in Gertie's fractured handwriting;

. . .

You. Yes you, will give the company speech today. Be ready, Bert.

BERT DROPPED the note and pressed the button on the Nutone again. "I can't do it, Gertie." Nobody answered. Bert looked at the door of his office. He imagined Gertie walking in, telling him it was all a mistake, she would not leave him. He looked at the door for several minutes, seeing his imaginary moment, over and over again. But that's all it was... his imagination.

He picked up the note again, this time securing it in his desk drawer, careful not to bend or tear it and staggered to his feet. He felt like he was in a haze. His brain, muddied by over-whelming thoughts and emotions, too weak to handle this new responsibility. He ran his fingers through his hair, reached down to press the Nutone again... and retreated. He looked at his office door, he could charge through it and go to Gertie's office. See for himself. Not only could he do it, but he had to, even though he felt terrified of what he might find at her office. He strode to his door and held the handle for several minutes before he summoned up the courage and strode down the hall-way, oblivious to the surrounding activity. He entered Gertie's office to find her long-time secretary, Barbara, busy packing Gertie's belongings in several boxes strewn about the floor.

"Barbara... what are you doing?" Bert cried.

Barbara turned and looked at Bert, the sadness in his eyes almost unbearable. "She... she..." Her voice lowered to a whis-per. She stared at the boxes filled with memories. She didn't want to look at Bert again. It was too much. "Bert, she wants some of her stuff at the other place."

"But... but... this is her office stuff. It belongs here, Barbara," pleaded Bert. He wanted to yell. He wanted to scream in protest. But, his voice seemed meaningless, silent. The pain and sadness in the room was suffocating. Barbara stood, filled with emotion, unable to find the right words to console Bert. He stood with his head down, staring at the cold and brown squares on the ground, swallowing his life. She moved to him and put her arms around him. For a moment, his head sank into her shoulder. It was the first time she ever touched him. He felt like a small, lost boy.

Bert smelled her fragrance and realized it wasn't Gertie. He stepped backward and broke from her embrace. "She will be here today, Barbara. I know she..." Bert's voice trailed off, and he dropped to his knees next to the cardboard boxes. He reached for a picture frame with the face down. He had memorized the picture on the other side, long ago. "Will she be here today, Barbara?"

Barbara dropped on her knees, next to him. She placed a hand on top of Bert's hand, holding the picture. "She is gone, Bert. She said she won't be here anymore." As the words left her mouth like a soft current of mist, they reached the ears of Bert like pelts of ice-hardened sleet.

Bert's shoulders fell and if not for the hands of Barbara, he would have collapsed to the ground. He placed the picture frame back in the box, without looking at the photograph. He gathered himself and rose from the ground. "It's all right." He turned and left Gertie's office.

OUTSIDE GERTIE'S OFFICE, THE mood was in sharp contrast to Bert' feelings. The annual company picnic had begun, and it was off to another great start. Smoked pulled pork fought for scented air space with cotton candy, boiling corn on the cob and the undeniable sweet aroma of gobs and gobs of cupcakes, pies, cookies and other sweet delicacies. All of which provided the perfect companion to barrels of fresh churned ice cream. Kids arrived in their parent's mini-vans, heads hanging out the windows with children jumping from the restraints in their excitement to join the fun. And one of those kids, was Percy.

He turned toward his mother, riding in the passenger seat of Chew's car. "This is amazing, mom. Oh man, oh man, oh man."

Chew felt dually impressed, hiding nothing with the grin of a five-year-old. "I've heard about this thing for years. I can't believe I'm here. Oh-oh, look at that Percy." He pointed out the window at the mega inflatable obstacle course. He looked at Ida. "Are you sure I can be here?"

Ida put her arm around his neck. "I told you, the Abernathy's said I could bring my family when I covered their picnic." She leaned over and kissed him on the cheek.

Chew's grin grew wider. He parked and started to jump out of the car when Ida grabbed his hand. "Hey, remember, once I'm done covering the opening speech, you owe me a dance."

"I wouldn't miss it..."

"C'mon Chew. Let's go," said Percy as he pulled on Chew's arm.

"I'll..." Percy pulled so hard, Chew fell out of the driver's seat and onto the ground. Percy erupted in laughter.

Ida bent over to get a view of her fallen hero. "Go ahead. I'll see you guys by the stage... have fun."

And Chew was up and running with Percy.

Laughter, oh the laughter... strong and harmonious, a symphony of happiness worth its weight in gold. Is there a better sound in all the world than a child's laugh?

They ran from the haunted bounce house, to the super bounce slide, the football bounce house and, of course, the behemoth obstacle course bounce house. Heads bobbing up and down in delight and bodies flying back and forth. It was always amazing how many parents joined their children in the bounce houses and the light of their youth, rekindled with fervor. The Charlie Tucker Band was in full swing, playing songs of the

South. The furious twang of the banjo punctuating the air as folks two-stepped around the dance floor.

Over on the other side, they lined kids up side-by-side so they could use their water guns to spray the mouth of their clown. First one to ring the bell wins a prize. The strike of the vintage Midway Milk Bottles stacked high and crashing down could be heard above the foot stomping. Guests surrounded a 1920s Penny Pitch game, looking forward to the next winner and their eventual turn.

And sitting in a corner, all by itself, the famed Antique Iron Painted Wheel of Chance. Each year, every employee could spin the wheel one time and guaranteed a prize. This year, they meant the prizes to elicit screams of joy and disbelief. From the smallest prize; a $500.00 gift card, to the biggest prize; a new vehicle, they designed the gifts to improve an employee's life. It did not matter how many employees spun and landed on the number with the new car. Bert and Gertie decided they would cover the cost for each one. As they planned, The Wheel of Chance did not start until two hours after the start of the picnic. Bert liked to make sure a big crowd was there to cheer each other on and enjoy each other's good fortune.

The 1930s High Striker was already seeing heavy action. It wasn't long before the first "victim" fell to the iron bell. When Lumberjack Bill arrived and saw the High Striker, he could not wait to show off his muscles and perform for the crowd. He would send that bell into orbit. The Carny running the High Striker had other ideas.

Lumberjack Bill watched the Carny demonstrate the High Striker and appear to strike the bell with adequate ease. So much so, that Lumberjack Bill announced to the crowd he would knock the bell using one arm. He gave it a mighty heave, worthy of felling a tree with one sure strike. If not for the High Striker being rigged, it would have been an impressive display of strength. Instead, the puck fell short and so did Lumberjack

Bill. He had to step aside with head hanging low and allow the next person in line to take a swing at it. The next person in line was none other than Dewey Winkleman. A wiry looking, red-headed 13 yr. old with a feisty attitude.

Dewey liked to put on a show, as well. He spit a dab into his hands, rubbed them together and grabbed the mallet like he meant business. He knew he had cute 14-year-old Lulu watching around the corner, and one way or another, he was going to ring that bell. She was bright, she was funny, and she had the most beautiful blond hair he had ever seen. He never even noticed Lumberjack Bill's missed attempt, his focus diverted by Lulu. The Carney delighted in the series being played out and knew Bert must be somewhere nearby enjoying the spectacle.

Dewey took one mighty swing at the lever and to everyone's surprise... completely missed. The Carney laughed at the turn of events but did not let the situation deter his secret motive. He told the crowd it was the kids warm up swing and now he was ready. Dewey gave the Carney a look of thanks, brought the mallet high above his head and slammed down on the lever. The puck rose and struck the bell with authority. Dewey walked away with a stuffed animal the size of Texas and delivered it into the unexpected but enamored arms of Lulu...and off they went, love blooming.

Lumberjack Bill stared at the scrawny kid and then stared at the high striker. He pushed aside the next contestant and shoved a ten spot into the Carny's hand. He grabbed the mallet with both hands and with one mighty swing struck down on the lever so hard, the entire High Striker shook in place. But, as fate would have it, he was no match for the love-struck tenacity of one Dewey Winkleman. The puck ambled upward and reached the tip of its upward flight just short of the bell. It came back to Earth, bouncing to rest. Lumberjack Bill scratched his head in disbelief as the Carny removed the mallet from his fingers. He was last seen mumbling to himself as he headed towards the food tent, perhaps to drown himself in a trough of pulled pork sliders.

BERT, PERCHED IN HIS hidden lookout spot, saw the action unfold. His mischievous and fun plan working out just as he envisioned. But there was no smile, no chuckle, and no laughter from Bert... because there was no Gertie. He looked and looked from his position over the grounds and she was nowhere to be found. She warned him she might not be there, but he did not believe her.

She can't leave before the picnic, please God, he thought.

He looked at his watch. It was time. The opening ceremony was upon them. It was time to give the annual company speech. He knew Gertie told him to do it. She had been adamant, even forceful.

But, how can I?

It was Reginald again who stirred him from his perch. "Sir," Reginald whispered. He put his hand on Bert's shoulder. He squeezed his shoulder. It was affectionate, kind. "Whatever you say will be just fine."

Bert put his hand on top of Reginald's and continued staring at the crowd below. He held Reginald's hand for several seconds. He knew it was time. He had to follow Gertie's wishes.

Bert exited the plant with Reginald by his side, arm in arm for support. As Bert made his way through the crowd, he kept his head up. He walked slowly, head up, looking at every face in front of him. He shook every hand extended toward him, patted countless shoulders and offered numerous return well-wishes. He appeared relaxed and easy-going. It was a side of Bert few knew.

An unspoken signal made its way throughout the entire picnic area. The games stopped playing, the two-steppers stopped stepping and even the children found themselves corralled by elders and placed in rows on the dance floor. The band stopped and the sounds of nature, only moments ago drowned out, filled the ears of the guests.

Bert kept going. It would have been too much for him to pick up on the change. He focused on taking one step at a time. He focused on the path ahead. He saw and heard nothing else. He wasn't thinking about his speech, or the surprised looks on many of his co-workers. No, he had to get to the stage, even though, his Gertie wasn't there. He waited at the corner of the stage while the last few guests found a position to sit or stand. Once everyone was ready, Reginald led him to the podium.

Bert grabbed the microphone and his gaze shifted into the crowd. He lifted his head and looked at the faces and into the eyes of everyone. He went from person to person, almost as if he was having a silent conversation with each one. They could never explain it but each person felt the connection, felt... a sense of love. It took Bert a good minute to make it through the entire, silent crowd.

"In my office, there is a picture. I look at that picture every day," he said. His tone and manner felt like a coversation between friends sitting in rocking chairs, watching the children playing against a golden sunset, warm and loving. "Gertie and I are in the picture, standing in our tiny kitchen, making our first batches of ice cream." He reflected as he held his empty hand out, "seeing" the photograph.

"We... we had... a dream," said Bert. He stopped to take a deep breath. "We wanted to share our love. Our love for each other, for family and for life." He looked at their workers, their family. They looked back. He drew strength from the bond. "We could show our love through ice cream. The Lord has blessed us with this gift," he said and paused. He looked into the crowd and around him. This time, he was looking for Gertie. He didn't see her. He gripped the microphone stand like a crutch, fearful of falling on his face.

"We also wanted children to feel our love," he said, and his lips quivered. "We always wanted to share our... love... of each other with..." and he stopped. He had to stifle back a sob. He removed a handkerchief from his pocket and wiped his eyes of tears. He looked out into the crowd. He wanted to tell them all how much he loved them and how important they were to him and Gertie.

"Everybody... here... today..." his words cracked with emotion. "You are... our..." Bert couldn't finish and buried his head in his hands. He cried. He didn't want to... but he did. Just then, murmurs and quiet gasps swept through the crowd. A once familiar and dearly loved woman rose from the steps behind the stage.

IT WAS GERTIE.

SHE WAS STILL TALLER than Bert. However, she did not stand with the prominence she once held. Two escorts stood at each side, holding her up. Her face was ashen and grey. Her once soft and elegant hair no more... replaced by the baldness and burn scars of chemotherapy and ill-fated treatments. She looked frail; her strong bearing beaten down over time until she stood with bones protruding through her damaged skin.

However, her eyes, they were still alive... burning with determination.

She made her way to Bert and put her arm around him, just as she had so many years before in their tiny kitchen. Just like his favorite picture. Bert felt her touch and cried her name. She held onto him like a mother would cling to her sick child, protective and absorbing his pain.

She waited with glassy, tear-filled eyes as their employees, their children, their family... dealt with the shock of seeing her. She hadn't been around much the last few months. It was a moment they all needed. When she finally spoke, the world turned quiet.

"I could not give my dear Bert a child. I wanted to... I prayed... we prayed, for the chance to love a child." She paused and looked out into the crowd.

Her voice grew more resonant in sharp contrast to her brittle frame. "What Bert was trying to say to y'all was..." Just like Bert, she didn't look at the "crowd" in front of her. She looked at each one, looked in their faces, saw their stories, felt their joy or pain. "You are our children. All of you... we have loved and treated all of you as our own since the day the Lord blessed us with you." She paused to catch her breath, leaning into Bert.

"We..." She started and stopped when she saw Tim and Bess. She pointed to them. "Tim and Bess, it was Bert's love that found out how bad you wanted your dream house. Tim, he felt so thankful for the care you showed, working on his truck. He was so excited for you, he walked by your house every day for a month."

She then spotted Jenny. "We love you so much, Jenny. It was Bert who took the time to notice a picture and realized Lulu needed help. It was Bert who found the medical trials and made sure we paid for the treatments to cure her." Jenny looked at Bert and for the first time saw him as the father figure he deserved to be in her life. She cried as Lulu emerged, holding hands with Dewey and smiling in the corner.

"Bert has been looking out for y'all and your families since the moment we hired you," she said. Bert stood next to Gertie, her arm wrapped around his shoulder.

. . .

247

Gertie needed Bert close to her... Bert needed Gertie close to him.

She spoke again and her voice cracked, "I'm going to be gone soon..." she paused, and the tears streamed down her face. "I'm going to need y'all to take care of my dear, sweet Bert. He is the love of my life... and now he needs your love. He deserves your love."

She turned away from the crowd and faced Bert. Her head dropped, and she collapsed in his strong arms. Bert led her to the stairs when men appeared off to the side of the stage. They were carrying Bert and Gertie's special swing. The workers set up their swing of memories and Barbara appeared with two giant cones of Gertie's Scrumptious Chunk ice cream. Gertie had her own surprise for Bert and no cancer was going to stop her from seeing it through. They sat down to enjoy their ice cream, their journey, their wonderful life... together.

Gertie motioned to bring the microphone to her as she sat against Bert. "Well, this here's a celebration. So let's hear some music, Charlie." With that she made a signal, the hoedown came alive and people started dancing, singing and playing.

Robert and Roberta sat at the edge of the stage, a cane resting against Robert's leg. "Darlin', now I understand why it was so important we make the drive." He rose from his seat and offered his hand, "how bout a little one-step?"

Roberta rose in her white summer dress with colorful yellow flowers, beaming. She grabbed his hand, and he drew her in. "I love you, Robert."

The sounds of laughter and delight could be heard from miles away. Nothing was going to stop the family of Iris Valley from celebrating life.

Ida spotted Chew and Percy, dancing their own special two-step, called the Star Wars two-step. She made sure to have

Johnny catch a little of the action, it would make for an entertaining moment on television.

The High Striker sounded its bell to the delight of the young and old. Bert heard the bell and smiled at the thought of the Carny playing tricks on the strong men. There was a steady stream of wild, joyous screams, a result of the life changing effects of the Painted Wheel of Chance. Children danced with their awkward-moving parents.

Tim watched Bess as she raced through the mega obstacle course. She body-slammed Tyler before shoving aside Matt and plain running over John. She was a force before, but now with the weight loss, near unstoppable.

BERT AND GERTIE SAT in their swing... soaking it all in, one last time. Gertie sunk her body into the man she had loved since first sight. She rested her weary head on his shoulder and squeezed his arm. She would hold on for one more special moment in a lifetime of happy and blessed memories.

Before they knew it, Bert's special moment arrived. The hot-air balloon drifted overhead. Just in time, as the sun set against a majestic sky. They could see a large net attached to the bottom of the balloon. On cue, Charlie Tucker stepped aside as a special friend of his walked up and grabbed the microphone. He was there to sing Gertie's favorite song. A song by Nat King Cole called, "The Very Thought of You."

The song played and with perfect timing, the contents of the net were released. They fluttered toward the Earth, each petal filled with deep and vibrant colors of purple, yellow, blue and other exquisite colors of nature. There must have been a thousand flowering Iris's floating, descending and filling the sky. Gertie looked up and Bert could see the look in her eyes. He would remember it forever.

The flowers fell softly to the Earth, embracing the husbands and wives, lovers, friends and family members—dancing in each other's arms. The flowers touched the hearts of the young lovers and dreams of happiness together, cascaded within them. Children picked up the flowers and could not explain the way they felt at that moment or why they felt the way they did. It was a simple feeling of un-conflicted happiness.

For all, it was a feeling of warmth, a feeling of compassion, a feeling of love. And best of all, the most beautiful Iris flower Bert had ever seen, fell from the sky into Gertie's lap. It would always be the most beautiful flower of all. Gertie picked up the flower, held it to her chest and sighed. Bert knew that sigh. She was at peace. Gertie and Bert held each other in their arms and absorbed the special moments, displaying like bright fireworks around them. They were the deep roots, out of which grew, the trunk and branches of life, love and family.

GERTIE LOOKED into Bert's soft, warm eyes. "I will never leave you, my dearest Bert. My love will always be with you." She put that most beautiful flower in his hand and squeezed him even tighter. And he knew she was telling him the truth.

The End

AFTERWORD

A few years ago, I published this novel under the name, "A Fragile Path." By launch standards, I did pretty well and felt pleased with the trajectory. However, within a few weeks, I pulled it from the market and shelved the manuscript. Why?

Have you ever dined at a fancy Italian restaurant and relished their homemade pasta and sauce? Then you go home and try to duplicate the recipe, but always come up short? You are missing some secret herb or spice?

Well, that's the way I felt with A Fragile Path. I really enjoyed writing and reading the novel. In fact, I hadn't read it in a couple of years and when I did, I became emotional several times.

But... I was missing the secret ingredient. Again, I sat down, read and re-read the manuscript, making changes, etc. It didn't work. I couldn't find it, whatever "it" was. Guess what? I shelved the manuscript again, possibly forever.

One day, like any other day, I happened to meet a wonderful lady who used to be a librarian for many years and was an avid lover of books. On a bold whim, I asked her if she would be willing to read my manuscript. She agreed and I gave her a copy. From there, I left it to the cosmos. Honestly, I never thought I would hear from her again.

To my surprise, a couple of months later, I received an email from her. She read my novel and provided a detailed review. I read her notes and the reaction was immediate. I found "it". Her notes triggered my brain into action, and I couldn't wait to dust off the manuscript and finally "finish" the novel. It is now complete, and I love how it came out. I hope you enjoyed my novel as well.

Now, here's the crazy part. Guess what my sweet librarian's name is?

SALLY ABERNATHY

Yes, she has the same last name as my two main characters, Bert and Gertie Abernathy. I couldn't believe it. "It" was meant to be.

Finally, I would like to offer my profound thanks to Alex over at SQUIDPIXELS.COM. I love the cover she created and her eternal patience in dealing with me. Thanks to my tribe members who offered great advice and a special thank you to my wonderful librarian friend, Sally Abernathy.

Best wishes,

Chad W Richardson

Made in the
USA
Columbia, SC